The Widow

Also by Nicolas Freeling

The Widow

by Nicolas Freeling

Pantheon Books, New York

Library of Congress Cataloging in Publication Data

Freeling, Nicolas.
    The widow.

    I.   Title.
PZ4.F854Wi   1979   [PR6056.R4]   823'.9'14   79-1873
ISBN   0-394-50336-8

Manufactured in the United States of America

FIRST AMERICAN EDITION

'Argentoratum, cuius ob antiquitem Prolemeus d' Hieronij-
mus, . . . et alii miminere, Alsatiae Metropolis, apud prater-
fluentem Rhenum, aliis, Argentina, aut, si quis ex re, nomen
commutare velit, Aurentina, Sed vulgo Strasburgum dicta;
urbs virtute, magistratuum prudentia, ac integritate, honestis
Studiis, ac nobili schola inclyta.'

Very roughly translated:

'Argentoratum, the town by the silver river, celebrated
from earliest times by a lot of classical authors, the metropolis
of Alsace, near the close-by-flowing Rhine; by others spoken
of as Argentina the Silvery or even by a play on words
Aurentina the Golden, but in the vulgar tongue Strasbourg:
city renowned for courage, the watchfulness of its rulers, for
integrity, for intellectual worth and a noble University.'

Legend to a sixteenth-century engraving of the city, by
Abraham Hogenberg, 1572.
From the original in the Cabinet des Estampes, Strasbourg,
Palais des Rohan.

1. 'Arthur Davidson's lurid imagination'

'It was about eleven o'clock in the morning, mid October, with the sun not shining and a look of hard wet rain in the clearness of the foothills.'

That much was accurate – Arthur knew the opening paragraph of *The Big Sleep* by heart. The rest of it – no. His wife, even if dressed up in the good powder-blue suit, the dark blue shirt, etcetera, would not look like Humphrey Bogart: hell, she didn't even look like Lauren Bacall. Still, the parallel went on amusing him: Arlette was neat, clean, shaved, sober, and didn't care who knew it – everything the well-dressed private detective ought to be. Arlette would have agreed with the word 'private' . . .

She was not calling on four million dollars either. She would have been indignant at all the misplaced humour. She had a literal mind: it was Arthur who had these lurid fantasies. Arthur, like many Englishmen, concealed (thinks he's Tolkien or something) a powerful and eccentric imagination beneath a harmless academic exterior, mild, given to pipes, occasionally rather dirty. Really it took Arthur. And private eyes were forty years out of date: when was *The Big Sleep* published? Nineteen thirty-nine, said Arthur whose memory was phenomenal. Besides being English, Doctor Davidson was fifty, and a sociologist. Made, claimed Arlette, for fanaticism about minor details in greatly beloved antique thrillers. She was wearing black trousers, a blousy top with a

1

belt. No gun. Because of the sharp nearness of the foothills –
one could reach out and touch the Vosges, which were thirty
kilometres off – her raincoat and one of her shapeless Garbo
hats lay next to her, on the front seat of the little almond-
green Lancia that had been Arthur's wedding present.

She was driving down the Avenue des Vosges in Strasbourg.
The traffic lights here have been left uncoordinated deliberately,
to discourage speeding drivers: the boulevard is broad and
straight but when you get a green you have barely time to
shift up into third and accelerate before the next one goes red
under your nose. The Avenue des Vosges is the main east–west
axis of the city. East is the Rhine, and Germany. Strasbourg
does not lie on the Rhine, but seven kilometres inland, a
medieval precaution against flooding when the snows melt.
Nowadays of course it reaches that far. West are the Vosges
and France, and the modern city lurches out about seven
kilometres that far too.

A medium-sized town, a good size; around three hundred
thousand people. In between the Rhine and the Vosges lies
Alsace. Neither French nor German, but since it is on the
French bank the province is French: this was quarrelled over
a good deal in the old days. From 1870 till 1918 it was German.
Nowadays it has again the open flavour of medieval times. The
European Parliament sits here, and the Council of Europe,
and the Court of Human Rights; all in several languages.
Arlette Sauve from the department of the Var, more recently
the Widow van der Valk from Holland, now most legally
Madame, Frau or Mrs Arthur Davidson, fitted in com-
fortably.

She was driving west, towards France. She came out on the
big U of the Place de Haguenau. Ahead lay Schiltigheim,
where they make beer. Large blue notices announced the
autoroute to the north, to Metz; to Paris. Keep on turning to
the left and one works into the southbound traffic, on its way
down to Switzerland. This she did. The first turn-off is
marked Cronenbourg/Hautepierre. Cronenbourg is just
another suburb, where they make more beer. Hautepierre is

2

more interesting and here she was headed; not alas for General Sternwood. Even Arthur's imagination would not find Laurel Canyon Boulevard hereabouts.

2. 'Retrospect of the Widow'

Arlette Sauve was born of petit-bourgeois parents fifty years ago in the South of France. Her father was an antiquarian bookseller in a lazy way, with a mild interest in Mediterranean languages. They lived in a flat over the shop. Out near Cassis they had a small cottage, extremely primitive, with a few fruit trees and a patch of fairly mediocre vines. The shop, which had disappeared long ago, had never made any money, but her elder brother still had the cottage. It was now rather grand: she preferred her childhood memories.

She was tall, blonde, and considered plain. Not tall by Dutch standards; in Holland her looks had been thought striking, while she stayed That French Cow. Some accident of ancestry had given her the Phoenician looks: bony high-bridged nose, large brilliant eyes that were brown in light and a sickly green in shade, a fine upright carriage and a splendid walk. The hair was the fairness called 'cendré': now that it was as much grey as blonde, ashes was the word. It was poker-straight and tiresomely fine. No hairdresser had ever been able to do anything with it. Let it hang, it hung like a corpse. Pin it up, where it looked sculptural, it fell instantly down again. For some years she'd had most of it cut off. Gamine with a fringe; never really a success either.

Toulon in the thirties was very dull, all anticlerical civilians and clerical naval officers. In the forties, still dull, despite or because of the war. One was Darlaniste or Pétainiste, Gaullist or Giraudiste, they were all right-thinking and very noisy and boring about it. The French, the Germans and the Americans,

3

roughly in that order, were destructive. One was both Catholic and Communist, not always at the same time. The noise rose to a paroxysm and finally everyone was Gaullist. When the novelty of this wore off, the poor went back to being Communist and the bourgeois were still Catholic. The port filled up again with other people's cast-off warships.

There had been several Arlettes. They hadn't really melted into one another except at the edges. There were still several, superimposed as it were. Kept well under control as a rule. Now and then one of the old ones would pop its head out, and squeak.

But the sum was greater than the component parts: too bad about logic.

There had been the goody schoolgirl, terribly well brought up and top of the catechism class, blouse always clean, toys always tidied.

And a big revolution from all that as a student; the anarchist stage and not washing much; which hadn't lasted long, mercifully. One didn't blush about it; pretty normal. One did blush, and had regrets lasting up to this day, at being atrocious towards one's parents.

Once that nasty student began again to wash it remained fanatic, and obstinately virgin till marriage: well almost, until the deplorable evening when Piet, in the interests of experimental science, filled it to the brim with Pernod, and was extremely gallant about the consequences (she'd eaten lots of lobster, and between that, the virginity and the Pernod, been sicker than a dog all night). But how quietly, how kindly, Piet had brought – and emptied – buckets, been good with towels wrung out in cold water, eau de cologne, handling angry tears and harsh words. Nobody had forced her to drink pastis or take her clothes off. And had there ever been such a fuss about doing so?

Arlette, Catholic in her schooldays, went Communist at the university, attracted the odium of the right-thinking and went to Paris, where she even more unsuitably made the acquaintance of a Dutch policeman, married him, worse still, and

4

worst of all made a success of it. Piet van der Valk, too intelligent to be a good policeman and with too much character to be a successful one, did make a good husband.

For more than twenty years they lived together, fighting furiously and on the whole happy. Most of that time in Amsterdam. Piet got shot by a neurotic and spoiled Belgian woman Arlette took a great dislike to. It smashed him up enough that he limped, and was put out to pasture in a provincial town, getting promoted in return for being demoted. He managed to draw attention to himself in spectacular fashion once or twice, and finally to everyone's surprise was promoted again and given a bureaucratic job in the Hague, obscurely concerned with reforming criminal law. Just as one could have a quiet existence at last he got curious again. And shot again, this time for good: he died there on the street. Stendhal, a writer she admired, did the same, after saying there was no disgrace in dying on the street: one must not, though, do it on purpose.

She had borne him two children, both boys. They had been a turbulent handful. Both students by this time, out of the house and nearly off her hands. They had a younger adopted daughter, called Ruth.

As the years had gone on Arlette had become steadily less French, without ever any temptation towards becoming Dutch. Piet van der Valk had become a great deal less Dutch, while loathing the French or so he said. They both kept very strong – well, call it regional characteristics. Both behaved in a very xenophobic way when at all vexed.

Piet, while still well under fifty, found his bad leg a bore. And the less said about ninety-nine per cent of police work the better. He had always a fear of finding himself retired prematurely, on political grounds probably while using the medical pretext. He was anxious himself to retire prematurely: it seemed to him that he was still at his best. The cottage had been borne of this. As a child he'd never been in the country. He came out of a poor district in Amsterdam; his father had

5

repaired furniture there. Arlette's childhood cottage had great importance in her personal folklore.

They'd both had windfalls of money; nothing much, not enough for anything grand. There had been a great deal of quarrelling about where the cottage should be. She didn't want to be anywhere in the south, a point easily enough won, Piet being a disliker of sweaty climates. But she did want to be by the sea. He was infuriating about this. As though one ever saw any sea in Amsterdam. What was this Dutch passion for hills and forests? A silly, romantic side he had. Aquitaine? No, far too hot and full of ghastly Dutch as well as English: it would be a ghetto. Touraine then? Arlette liked the Loire country: so did he. It was alarmingly expensive – Holland then was very cheap in comparison to France and he would only have his pension. But it went on tempting until the dreadful day he discovered that Maigret had retired to the banks of the Loire. If there was one thing he hated it was jokes about Maigret. An utterly frivolous pretext, she said extremely cross.

He'd always had a soft spot for Alsace; been there once and fallen in love with it, silly emotional thing to do. He liked it being neither French nor German, he loved the 'blue line of the Vosges'. He liked the local white wine, a lot too much she said. She wasn't keen. Frontier people are savages, she said with Mediterranean snobbery. Wotan Mit Uns. They talk a vile and incomprehensible patois and I'm sure they all sleep with their mothers. Collaborators to a man. And so on at some length.

He'd overborne her. And she had to admit she'd been very taken with the little house. A bit too primitive for now. Blow all this pump lark he said, putting in sanitation and spending their last penny. Two happy summer holidays they'd spent there together, and a marvellous snowy Christmas. He began to build furniture, and talk with zest about retiring.

He was buried there now, the nearest thing there was to being home. Arlette stayed on there, buried with him. What's a widow more or less, in a village?

But it's no place for an adolescent girl, and Ruth was

growing up, and the country schools more and more insufficient. Ruth saved her. She thought of living in Strasbourg with no very great joy. But the schools and the university are among the best there are.

They found a little three-room flat: Arlette was experienced with flats, and it was cheap, warm, and easy to keep clean. In the Krutenau, between the centre and the university. Handy for everything, and for the Hospices Civiles, the huge central hospital that has grown from medieval Hotel-Dieu origins to a formidable patchwork of every succeeding century. She worked for, and got a physiotherapy diploma. This, with her pension, earned her a reasonable, even a comfortable living.

About Strasbourg she had mixed feelings. It is much better than a provincial city: even as a regional capital it has unusual riches and resonance. The Roman frontier post of Argentoratum, the town by the silver river, became the Town of the Streets, the Crossroads City attracting all that was best in both France and Germany, a byword for seven centuries for intellectual brilliance and religious tolerance. The cathedral is the happiest blend of early and late Gothic, the Renaissance and eighteenth-century buildings beautifully proportioned. The opera is good, the Philharmonic outstanding, and Arlette had always been a devoted concert-goer.

It has acquired too much suburb, and is far too big now, but the old town, long girdled in its fortifications, has not changed as much as one would fear. The new town, built by the Germans after 1870, is notable for the best town-planning and the ugliest architecture to be seen anywhere. Strasbourg lives in a happy dichotomy of the extremely beautiful and the absolutely hideous. The people have the same two extremes of character.

Contrary to carefully fostered legend one eats badly. Too much tough fresh pork and greasy sausage, and too little of anything else. Enough to convert one to orthodox Judaism, said Arlette snappishly.

Ruth grew up, became a student, went through awful stages.

7

At times insupportable. She lived in a studio now, and probably in sin and squalor too. She had become herself; it was normal, inevitable. They no longer saw very much of one another.

Life began to get very boring for the widow.

3. 'Hautepierre with a Manchester accent'

Hautepierre in bureaucrats' jargon is a Zup. A Priority Urbanization Zone, but a French zup sounds more sympathetic than an English puz.

The road began to wind. Unhelpful noticeboards were saying 'Maille Cathérine', 'Maille Karine', and 'Pedestrian Shopping Precinct' without saying which was where. The mailles or links were hexagons of housing blocks, bound into a tangled chain by one-way streets. Get into all this, and unless you are a native you'll never get out again.

Arlette parked her car. She wanted 'Maille Eléonore' of which there was no mention. She might have a long way to walk. She walked; she liked walking.

Arlette strode along; nothing to notice about her. She hadn't bothered buttoning her raincoat. Her bag hung on her shoulder by a sling with her arm through it and her hands in her pockets. Not just here – you can get your bag snatched anywhere in Strasbourg. The usual technique is two boys, or it can just as well be girls, on a moped. The first steers in close alongside, the second combines a snatch with a shove while the first accelerates away and round a corner. Nothing to it. She didn't believe the incidence of petty crime was any higher here. It probably wasn't a place to loiter in alone after dark. Nowhere is.

The sky was fine; big and open, massive heaps of cloud in every shade of grey down to the horizon where it got bluish-black. The rain was losing no time, but would be another half-hour.

Place looked nice; cheerful, even welcoming. None of those terrible rectangular blocks scattered haphazardly on bulldozed subsoil with nothing between but draughts: each of the 'links' is designed to be a village in itself; distributed in an irregular pattern; loosely tacked together by approach roads. The effort has been honourable. The roadways are lined with grassed banks, and a great many trees have been planted. Quite a lot have been broken, but a good deal remain. They are still immature: trees, alas, are slower than concrete.

Arlette could put a name to the first link because of a large notice over an arcade saying 'Shopping Centre Maille Cathérine'. The housing blocks were not bad at all, cheerfully irregular, not more than six or seven stories; plenty of the small balconies were gay with geraniums. One could do a lot worse, she thought. The interior of the hexagon was landscaped too with hillocks of soil, little paths winding about, large lumps of stone, a playground for little ones with logs to climb on and a sandpit. A cluster of rather shoddy huts was plainly kindergarten and bits of primary school.

Not many people about. Men would all be at work of course but she would have expected more women doing their shopping.

'Whereabouts is Eléonore?'

'No idea,' said a man in a hurry, curt.

'Sorry,' said a woman. 'This is Cathérine's all I know.' A more leisurely woman, with a basket on wheels.

'Through that way. No, wait now, that's Jacqueline, or is it? I'm a bit vague.' Arlette walked on; she'd plenty of time.

'Over there,' said an elderly man with a dog. 'Just keep on straight.'

The buildings were different in character. One judges, in France, not so much by the exteriors as the entrances. A few green plants grouped around an artistic arrangement of large smooth pebbles set in roughcast – 'standing'. This last replaced by a small fountain in a goldfish pond – 'grand standing'. The letterboxes are great giveaways too. Some blocks here had a surprising amount of standing, others none at all: grim traps of yellowish tiles with the foot of the fire stairs sticking out, like landings in a prison. She understood: in order not to create ghettos the municipal planners had mingled 'HLM', that coy acronym for Moderate-Rent-Habitation which means a council house, with private-sector blocks that can be bought and sold, and owned.

Arlette, who had lost her way already despite a usually good bump of location, came out in an angle where trees had been grouped round a sort of courtyard, half asphalted and half just ground stamped hard. Dusty in dry weather and undrained puddles after rain. She thought she understood. The municipal architect, worthy man, had done his best. The idea of little villages had been all right as far as it went. But there was no centre to them. No corner grocery or even a pub. No joyfully tatty dirty-shop selling sweets and newspapers and all the gossip. The big money had taken over. An entire 'link' separate from the others to allow cars to come, and park, had been built around a gigantic supermarket, with a covered gallery of speciality shops all around. Here was the warmth and the light, the animation and the colour. Here, and nowhere else. Apart from the little arcade in 'Cathérine' where the mums went if they had forgotten something or were in a tearing hurry, there was no activity. The huge Pedestrian Precinct thing was a cancer, sucking all life from the other links, through the fine grey threads of path and underpass and little footbridge. The insides of all the other hexagons were drained and languid, joyous only when the voices of the children at recreation times echoed shrilly between the blocks.

Three small boys were languidly trapping, kicking, heading a football on the dim play space. Why weren't they at school?

'Hoy,' she called to the nearest, a lanky overgrown child with a mop of fair hair. He stopped and turned politely after executing a 'corner'. A sudden grin of unexpected vivacity.

'No speak the language, Missis,' the child said in English.

10

Norma's child! Well, she'd found her way. But she hadn't been ready to talk English yet; had to gather her wits.

'I'm looking for your mother but where does she live?'

'Me mum?' in so broad an accent that she had to keep her face straight. The boy considered, studying her shrewdly. Not a bailiff! Maybe one of those social-assistant women, or likely a schoolmarm. 'None too sure. Gone out, likely enough.' A child accustomed already to helping fend off unwanted visitors.

'I said I'd come this morning. She'll be expecting me.' The English even in an accent as strong as his own reassured him.

'Ey, Ian,' he bawled across the playground. 'Our mum gone out?' The answer was incomprehensible but not to him. He grinned again broadly.

'Can always try, Missis. End block over there. Door at the left. Three up on the corner.'

'Thanks very much,' said Arlette politely. One of the HLM blocks. She studied the row of names on the bellpushes. She didn't even know Robert's name, and it was just 'sociological' curiosity. A loose net, that had gathered all sorts of fish. French names, and the heavy Teutonic names of Alsace; Spanish and Portuguese, a couple of blacks, a couple of Arabs: but all in the proportions you would expect for the whole city. Not a dumping ground for underprivileged immigrant labour.

The hallway smelt, the stairs smelt, the lift smelt worst, being a shut-in box, slightly but unmistakably. Smell not so much of poverty – these people certainly weren't 'poor' – as of backwardness, neglect, a low and uneducated mentality, apathetic, with no energy for much more than bare survival. Piss, cabbage, stale sweat, general unwashedness hung faint but certain on the air. But efforts had been made to scrub off the graffiti and keep the stairs swept. There were the usual notices about fire and how to call the cops or an ambulance, an elaborate roster of people's turns at cleaning the landings and tidying the garbage chute, and a few brave ones done in

11

colour with fancy lettering and roneo'd, from outside, about
the cinema club and the pathetic neighbourhood activities, as
well as rules about dogs and not playing ball-games. Arlette
was borne upwards depressed. Depression gathered when she
rang the bell on the landing and the door snapped open on the
other side. She did not turn but she could feel the curious, and
somehow malicious stare, like a draught on the back of her
neck. Norma's door opened finally, after a loud noise of
lavatory being flushed, just as Arlette was going to turn and
stare back. Norma's look was suspicious too, but her face
cleared at once. "S you. Great. Come on in.' She shut the door
firmly, put her tongue out at the landing beyond, winked at
Arlette and gave her a friendly clap on the arm. 'Real nice of
you to come. Don't mind the kitchen, do you love? – that ol'
sitting-room's in a mess again. Kids! Not to worry – have it
straight before Robert can start moaning. Make some tea,
shall I? Not like yours I'm afraid. Lipton teabags! But in
France you know it's either that or the really classy stuff what
I can't afford.'

'I don't mind a bit.' Depression had vanished instantly.
What right had she to feel sorry for herself? Norma might
well break down into a violent cry, as she had yesterday, but
it would go over like the rain, now right above their heads and
due to break any second, and be again good tough resilient
Norma. And untidy it might be, but there was no smell. She
probably put the children's socks to soak in the bidet, but she
was scrubbed, and so was the flat.

'Going to pee down,' said Norma slapping the kettle on and
looking out of the window. 'Them brats are all right but the
little one's out doing the shopping.'

'All the way over to the supermarket?'

'Naw – don't go there much. A few things that's cheaper
but it's you know, that tender trap. Karen went to the Suma
over in Cathérine. That big one's too far anyhow. Have a beer
or a cup of coffee and you've lost all you'd won. Nev'mind.
Lemme get this pot warm. Spend most of me time here, t'tell
th'truth.' Norma made efforts sometimes to speak less broad,

12

but you could see her heart wasn't in it. What was the use
speaking posh? Arlette spoke posh, having had it explain
that it meant port-out and starboard-home, an English cc
ception of class structure she found typically subtle. Could one
speak both posh and with a French accent?

Ting-ting at the door. 'That's Karen.' The little one, with a
big basket pathetically freighted with fish-fingers and instant
mashed potato. Small and dark like the mother, with a fringe
and brilliant eyes. 'Hallo,' she said, friendly. 'I'm Karen.'

'And I'm Arlette.'

'That's a nice name,' approvingly.

Arlette knew she'd been right to come. It built confidence.
There was very little she could do for Norma. Technically
nothing at all. But the half-hour yesterday, and again today.
of moral support – that was enough. It broke the isolation.
Norma didn't even want help much. Her cry of anguish was
borne of being all alone; but her toughness and her startling
self-respect would see her a long way. She'd always be in
trouble, spend her whole life falling down stairs, but would
always pick herself up.

'Geta train ticket out of that Consulate,' she was saying
reflectively, picking a tealeaf off her lip. ''n even if I can't, can
always hitch-hike. Not the first time, is it duck?'

'No,' agreed the little girl sturdily, not knowing quite what
she was talking about, but backing Mum up instinctively.
Rain clattered suddenly on the windows and they all looked
out. The smaller boy, carrying the football, came racing across
the open space. The bigger one came walking rather slowly,
nonchalant, hands in pockets. What's a bit of rain? They both
came in with that tough delinquent shamble, more or less
sideways, eyes downcast. Both said the same thing.

'C'n a have a biscuit then, Mum?'

'No way,' said Norma. 'And let's have you smartened up a
bit and say howdyedo to Mrs Davidson then.' They held their
hands out in the French way they had learned to copy: these
two children's hands, unexpectedly warm, dry and small,

touched Arlette oddly. The small girl had switched on a transistor radio, and was listening raptly to a German announcer giving the waterlevels on the Rhine.

'Bingen. Zwei. Neun. Siebenundzwan –'

'Let's have some fucking music then.'

'Hey,' said Norma, not in the least pretending to be shocked; just restoring discipline. The boy grinned, winked at the fifty-year-old Arlette in so comic a way that she could hardly keep her face straight. Not exactly innocent, being indeed blatantly sexy, but the forthright childish openness was so attractive. She had never seen less self-conscious children. They moved in this hostile, suspicious French world with the ease and dignity of young wolves.

'I'll be buzzing then,' when the rain slackened.

'All right love,' said Norma. 'I'll remember you.' She stood on tiptoe to give her a kiss. 'Won't give no trouble. Slip out quietish, while Robert's at the pub.'

'If you manage to send one of the children – I'll come and drive you.'

'Nice of you – but won't have time. Got to choose the moment, like.'

Arlette knew she would not take money.

'Come on,' she said to Karen, 'you come with me, show me the way through back to Cathérine.' As she left she saw the door on the landing open again a crack.

Pretending to scrabble in her bag for the car keys she fished up a fifty-franc note. But even the tiny one showed strict upbringing: it pursed its mouth and shook its head.

'Don't be daft,' said Arlette. 'You have the right. Packet of crisps all round.' The child looked, made up its mind, grinned like Norma, crumpled the note in its paw, tongue-tied. She bent to give it a kiss but it was already racing away. She drove off soberly. She had to put the fan on a minute, to get the condensation off the windscreen. That tedious Robert would stand there gibbering and waving his shotgun, but Norma would see to a tactful quiet exit. And would bring up the baby like all the others. Abortion? No way.

14

She would be late for lunch anyhow. She had left a word in the electronic notebook on the kitchen table, and Arthur would cope. It was a long way round to the Meinau, and the midday rush was beginning. Quicker to go through the town centre now than round by the quays. Fortune with her turned on green lights all the way to the Hospital Gate, out of the old town and across the bridge to South Strasbourg; the Colmar road out as far as Suchard Chocolate, and turn left after the football stadium.

The Meinau. Rue du Général Offenstein. Large quiet bourgeois villas with trees in the walled gardens, sombre with closed shutters and locked gates. Nothing distinguished Siegel-the-Dentist's house from the others, but she had looked up the number in the phone book. Unostentatious, well-bred . . . Arlette parked down and across the road, where she could observe. The Lancia was not a conspicuous car, and certainly not around here.

Not that there was anything to observe. Just 'the lie of the land'. Get a glimpse, if possible, of the protagonists. Everybody came home to lunch in this part of the world. Twelve-fifteen.

A small, shiny, dark blue Fiat with pale beige leather. Nice little car. Much like her own. Not as nice! But cleaner – very highly polished indeed, as though the cops that stood loitering all day by the side gate of the Préfecture had been rubbing it up. For this surely was step-ma Cathy. Small, neat blonde woman of that lean, hard, rather standard prettiness, in boots and a leopard-skin that might be nylon but wasn't. As highly polished as the car. She left it on the pavement, locked it, not looking anywhere, disdainfully, unlocked the gate, locked it again after her. Whisked into the house. Not about to snatch up the kitchen apron and go to work – be servants there, and lunch on the table at twelve-thirty on the dot. Career woman, Cathy Pelletier: the Prefect couldn't get on without her. But we work to a tight timetable here: twelve sharp he has an official 'apéritif' known as a wine-of-honour with some chamber of commerce or other, and Cathy's off, to be in the

15

bosom of her family for two hours precisely. Twelve twenty-two.

A six-cylinder Jaguar stole silently down the street; lean, hard, elegant in a standard way like Cathy. Siegel's good taste. Dark burgundy colour like a ripe plum, very nice. Turned haughtily, stopped across the pavement in line with the gates; he wasn't leaving his car on the street, not even for lunch hour. His office building, on the river by the Pont Royal, has an interior courtyard.

Siegel got out to unlock the gates – they were very careful with their gates. There wasn't much to be seen of him; a dumpy man with a full padded profile and a slightly tip-tilted insolent nose – it was this that gave him away as Marie-Line's father: not much resemblance otherwise that she could see. Dark tight-fitting overcoat and Anthony Eden hat. He arranged the gates meticulously, got back into the Jaguar, which quivered slightly, like Cathy when he got on top of her in bed. Drove in, parked exactly in front of the door on the circle of gravel, came back to lock the gates. She got him full face then. Shrewd discreet eyes, full small mouth in the full face. Not, certainly, a man to take lightly. Held himself upright: no sign of the characteristic dentist's deformation.

Arlette went on waiting, for Marie-Line, anxiously at first, till she remembered that lycée classes finish at a quarter past the hour. And the Gymnase Jean Sturm, where the scions of Protestant good families are still sent, is right in the centre of the old town.

Twelve thirty-four. A Peugeot moped, Marie-Line's face closed and indifferent between the wind-tossed corn blonde hair and a navy-blue double-breasted pilot jacket. Hopped athletically off the bike, felt in her pocket for keys, wheeled the bike just inside the gate and left it leaning against the wall. Strolled slowly across the gravel. Not bothered at being a little late for lunch. Would they have waited for her? Cathy might have taken a drink. Siegel didn't look like a drinking man, and a dentist doesn't allow his stomach to rumble. Unfold the napkin and head down at once, eating slowly and chewing

16

thoroughly: proper digestion is more important than waiting five minutes for an eighteen-year-old daughter. A slight nod – mrh. Back to the leading article in *Monde* – no! A *Figaro* reader more like it. Solidly right-wing!

Nothing left to see; she drove home at leisure, grinning, remembering one of her son's disreputable but engaging girls. Flat-hunting in Paris; one has to buy *Figaro* for its classic 'To Let' page. Tear the page out indignantly: give the rest to the clochard at Saint André des Arts – keep his feet warm maybe; that was all the beastly thing was good for. The girl had made a comic anecdote, miming her ashamed look sneaked quickly round, even though all Paris knows why a left-wing student is buying a *Figaro* . . . Yoh – schrecklich, as they say in Alsace.

4. 'The widow's observatory'

Arlette lived in the Rue de l'Observatoire, morning sun at the back and evening in front, no southerly aspect but worth it for the trees of the Botanic Garden. And the little Observatory, pleasing like all things with domes. What on earth did it observe, in the middle of smoggy ol' Strasbourg – but it didn't, she suspected. Measured earthquake waves or something. The Director, quite plainly, had one of those ideal jobs. Spent much time on his carrots-and-leeks there – the Observatory Garden is not strictly Botanic, but he borrowed their gardeners happily.

If one wanted to be Whimsical, which Arthur occasionally was, this was her observatory.

She found Arthur at the kitchen table, surrounded by crumbs, eating a Dutch sandwich she had taught him. Rye bread, bacon that has been cooked in pea-soup, slightly underdone celery-root ditto, plenty of Alsace mustard (which is mild). He was reading *Newsweek*, getting, by God, greasy

17

thumbprints all over it which was revolting – piggy English habits Arthur did have. Pipe, and all the mess going with pipe, also on the table. Like a canary, Arthur couldn't live without a circle of scatter of about a metre's radius. He looked up, waved cheerfully, mumbled something through the mastication: it seemed to be a hospitable invitation to join in the piggery.

She'd only been married a month – scarcely – but had been fending Arthur off for two years.

'Marry? – never. Think of it. Mrs Davidson, Madame son-et-lumière. Frau Davidson – I'm Jewish enough as it is from sheer refusal to eat pig all day – yoh, schrecklich – horreeble.'

'Can't understand,' agreed Arthur placidly, 'what all these Davidsons are doing in Scotland. There's even a tartan, singularly hideous – sort of mustard.'

'Who were the ancestors?'

'Generals, thousands of them, in obscure things like the Royal Engineers. I don't believe one of them ever heard a shot fired in anger, but let it pass.' She couldn't even remember where she'd met Arthur first. For someone supposedly with total recall this was bad. But equally typical of Arthur . . .

He drank some milk, put his pipe in his mouth, and buzzed off.

'Sorry, lots of work. You can manage dinner, tonight? Oh good. I'm not in a properly cooking frame of mind.' Nor was she, but no matter. She saw him out of the window, bicycling. Pipe, clips on trousers, in no hurry. The University quarter was two minutes off. He was not in the Faculty – on loan in mysterious ways; commissioned for sociological studies by the Council of Europe, financed by them, or the European Cultural Foundation – or somebody: he was vague on the subject.

The bicycle made recall total. Arthur had fallen off it, distended ligaments in the knee, come to her for physiotherapy.

'How d'you come to do that?' making a polite remark.

18

'Not wearing clips, caught my trousers in the chain. Classic when you think of it; like catching one's tit in the wringer.' She'd laughed, at the correct, polite French, the English accent and the sudden colloquialism. Life was boring.

Four years she'd been in the Krutenau. A small three-room flat in a quiet solid house of the Art Déco period, with lianas and stylized flowers. Five stories high, which meant sun and air. The plumbing was 1900, but worked. Window boxes. The Rue de Zürich was wide at this point, and had plane trees. It was noisy and dreary, and unpicturesque. The Krutenau is picturesque – it is one of Strasbourg's oldest quarters, largely a tumbledown medieval slum due for demolition. Arlette was not romantic, and did not yearn for the Street of the Preaching Fox or the Bridge of the Cats. Preferred rooms you could clean and plumbing that worked.

Four years, pestered by that boring menopause, with a tendency to sudden heatwaves and finding herself too fat for her skirts.

All over now. Ruth grown up. Fifty. The widow had fined down and become again handsome. Big streaks in the lion-coloured hair; heavily lined around the large fine eyes, but the upright walk and the high-bridged Phoenician features were unchanged. She had not been to bed with anyone. She had no man. She was amused by the appearance of Arthur in the role of beau, and even shteady. Ruth's crude phrase: Ma's got a shteady.

'*What* kind of sociologist? Behavioural – I knew it. Thick as fleas around here, or is it thieves?' He was funny, thought Arlette, but a fake. She felt touched, and grateful, but emotionally bankrupt. A man who appears on the doorstep, invites you out, makes exaggerated compliments, brings flowers . . . They'd gone round the corner to the *Preaching Fox*. Food in Strasbourg is just grub, but the white wine is dry and good. It was nice to find they had the same tastes. She drank a lot, enough to say unnecessarily she hadn't any intention of going to bed with him.

'Do you think this Calvados will be real, or just so-called?'

Arthur had sense, or sensibility, or just sociological experience enough to leave her alone.

'Why bother at all?' gratefully. 'The local marc is good enough: why go in for folklore?'

'I don't want to go to bed with you,' he said next time they met, 'I do of course, very badly, but I want to marry you first.' This went on for a longish time.

He did say that this Harriet Vane lark was very tiresome. She asked who this was, and got Lord Peter Wimsey books by return of post. She replied mildly that she hadn't been saved from hanging and wasn't afraid of being thought grateful.

'If I didn't think you had better arguments than that . . . as a prospective mistress, you're about a thousand per cent frustration. None the less; Harriet has excellent arguments and is rather nice.'

'Mm,' said Arlette. 'Nineteen-thirties intellectual females . . . bluestocking. Bobbed hair, shapeless skirts. You got them into bed and instantly they began worrying about the Spanish Civil War. Harriet with children . . . Incidentally I'm too old for childbearing.'

'He neither considers himself, nor wishes to be considered, in that agricultural aspect.'

'I've had enough of children. And teaching paraplegics to swim . . . A lot are teenagers you know: motorbikes . . .'

'Heartbreaking.'

'A professional doesn't see it that way. I was in a swimsuit and a boy gripped me insolently by the tit. Rather encouraging – both ways.'

'And what did you do?' asked Arthur a little sourly.

'Oh, held him under water a while.'

These two years were preposterous, Arthur was to say later. And hideous. Work had been difficult too; scrabbling about, lot of politics to have his grant renewed and Get Published. He'd tried to make things up with an estranged wife, who'd married again, divorced again. Fiendish woman.

'You must have been out of your mind. And that was my fault?' asked Arlette.

20

'My doing entirely, where you're concerned. Responsibility.'

'That's what it all boils down to, doesn't it? Taking one's responsibilities.'

'Sociology is largely about people who fail to.'

The woman killed herself in the end. Arthur told her at last, spitting blood and mumbling, looking as if he'd just had all four wisdom teeth pulled.

'*Not* your responsibility,' said Arlette, very firmly.

They were in the village of Illhausern, thirty kilometres outside Strasbourg, but the food has three stars.

'You must be filthily rich,' said Arlette. 'Or is there something special?'

'Strasbourg is quite a good town, isn't it? You know it fairly well by now.'

'I've thought of moving, often enough. The food's awful, and they've little sense of humour, poor dears. But where's better?'

'I've been offered quite a well-paid job here. I'm in two minds.'

'What stops you taking it?'

'You do, imbecile.'

'If that's all there is to it, I'll accept. Or is it the well-paid job that's an inducement?'

'Stop that. You'll agree?'

'I'll agree.'

'Waiter, bring me the wine list please.'

'Do by all means commit follies,' said Arlette. 'We have so few left.'

'How nice to see you looking so happy,' said the owner courteously, bringing a fantastic bottle and a waiter to open it.

'Tell me all about it, then,' she said, tasting.

'Oh, the Council moves in mysterious ways you know, and several are sociological. Great deal of nonsense about pecking order. Bureaucrats are horribly touchy about their standing. Mine,' said Arthur happily, 'will be rather high. Too high, no doubt, for the Krutenau.'

21

'My dear boy, there wouldn't be room. And will there be room anywhere, for you and me together with all this standing?'
'I've thought about this problem,' said Arthur. 'You don't want to go to cocktail parties.'

'Nor play bridge wearing a hat. Nor live in a Council-of-Europe flat. That rhymes. Must be the wine.'

'Stop your nonsense. Get our own flat. You choose it. Used to getting your own way, huh? A Bull, of course.'

'Indeed I am, alas. What are you?'

'A Fish.'

'Oh dear,' said Arlette. 'The combination is appalling. The very worst there is.'

'Stop being superstitious and French.'

'Stop your nonsense, stop being French, how much more of this is there going to be? Pull your pants down woman and put a pillow over your head.'

'I'm being serious. A couple should be a real couple.'

'Certainly. Axiom of the new sociology. None of this now, Wife, serve us the apéritif and run to your casserole.'

'Absolutely. I can cook and wash dishes with anyone. You must have, indeed, a professional area of privacy and activity,' said Arthur.

'I do have a job.'

'You're not satisfied with it and neither am I. We should be able to find something better.'

'Agreed,' meekly. 'I think I'd like some cheese.'

'I ask that thought should be spent,' said Arthur austerely.

5. Chez Mauricette

She had to write a letter.
'Marie-Line,
      I took a look at your house at lunchtime; caught a glimpse

22

of your parents and of you – you didn't notice me; neither did they. That was – of necessity – very superficial.

'I haven't had time for much; enough to confirm that legally there's not a lot to be done: the law, and judges, give a great deal of weight to the father of the family. And very little to women in any circumstances. We both want to change that, but stuff about equal rights, employing a woman lawyer, wouldn't do us any good in my opinion. Just put everyone's back further up, and that's not in my view the way to handle things. I don't myself want to do anything behind your parents' back: it puts us in the wrong, and gives them that much more leverage against you. I'd like to go up against them openly, and see whether I can get anywhere by tact. I won't do this, nor approach them indeed in any way, without your consent and approval. I'd like you, if possible, to come and see me again. I'd like too, to meet Michel. Perhaps we could have a drink *Chez Mauricette* – what about it?

Yours
Arlette.'

It might sound rather ponderous and the elderly aunt, but that was too bad. She had no experience in this job – as yet, thought Arlette, as yet – but a few common sense principles applied. One was never to play a part, and especially not with young girls like Marie-Line, all strung up and nervous, and given to dramatics, greatly given themselves to playing parts. Her account of herself and her family circumstances might be accurate – at least the observations of lunchtime didn't seem too contradictory. Nothing too fundamentally improbable about the girl's tale, but it was almost certainly exaggerated, and perhaps wildly so. She had heard nothing from the other side as yet . . .

Once in a quieter frame of mind, in a climate of confidence, she hoped to find Marie-Line able to speak of her parents with a bit more detachment if not sympathy. They were hardly as bad as all that! Some terrain of entente between the father – or the stepma; she recalled that 'Cathy's not too bad' – and the unruly daughter should be findable, if each were ready to give a bit.

So get the girl first to give a bit ... You can be a mum-substitute if that's what the child wants. You won't get any-where by pretending to be all youthful and playing comrade. A drink in *Mauricette* is as far as you go. She'd never been in the place: it was just an ordinary pub, always full of students. You don't have to bring them home to tea! – which they'd hate anyhow.

Have to go to the butcher, and there's a lot more rain in the air – take the car. Get this job over first. Is there anything on the tape?

There was. A message from Albert – come while she was out this morning.

'Ah, good morning, Madame. Just called to say that the details you enquired about, I'm not in a position yet to give you the information you wanted, the price-structures, yes. So we'll just put off the discussion of that for a day or so, until I'm able to furnish you with the uh, figures. So I'll ring you again, shall I? – yes, Madame, yes, we'll guarantee immediate delivery – of course, of course – au revoir Madame.' Now what the hell? – what was this ass Albert playing at now? Trying again to make himself interesting by playing hard to get, with his act of knowing deep secrets that he could not divulge? Why the pretence? Did he genuinely think there was someone listening to him in the office or tapping his telephone? Well, he was only due at six; there was nothing to rearrange. Not going to worry about him now. A mythomaniac, grunted Arthur, and he was almost certainly right. Go and find somebody else to mystify, Albert.

Don't bother changing – the slightly dishevelled look is all right for *Mauricette*, not to speak of that pig of a butcher. She slapped on a bit of lipstick and whipped out. The phone went as she closed the flat door, the way it always did. She wasn't going to turn back – the recorder would register it.

Chez Mauricette, a few hundred metres up the Boulevard de la Victoire, past that gloomy dungeon of the Zoology

Institute full of coelacanths and suchlike cattle – forbidding it all did sound – was exactly as she expected, an old-fashioned, small pub, rather pleasant. Crowded in the front, narrowing to a bottleneck between the bar and a big stove that over-heated the atmosphere, it broadened out at the back, and, as expected, was full of students. Character was given by a huge number of climbing plants going up a trellis, swinging in baskets, in a brass pot on chains – everywhere there was space. The brasswork and the big old stove gave a comfortable Belgian feel.

And there was Mauricette herself, presiding at the bar, making loud jokes and forcing the accent a good deal: it is thought funny, and creates popularity – a small dark woman with an unnaturally black shiny fringe and harsh lined skin, and a smile full of gold teeth.

'I only want to leave a line for one of the girls – Marie-Line; big tall blonde girl, perhaps you know her?'

'Sure, no problem. Not seen her today – they drop in after class as a rule.' Mauricette turned to stick the envelope in the corner of the big mirror. 'Hey,' facing round again, 'you're not called Arlette by any chance? Note for you too then, from her I dare say.'

She ripped it open. A big scrawl with a felt pen.

'Arlette I can't get out and I'm desperate – unless you find a way to help me I see nothing else for it – I'll cut my veins. I'm getting Françoise to post this – you can rely on her –

Marie-Line.'

Oh, curse the silly girl.

'Sorry, I'll have to ask for the other one back – the date's fallen through.'

'No problem,' indifferently.

Merde – how to word this? Damn, wasn't a table free? Have to push a few armfuls of tropical foliage out of the way and do it on the corner of the bar.

'I will have a drink after all – got any jenever?' In this post-office lark, no harm in letting Mauricette see one was of the right blood!

25

'You bet. Straight as she comes?' The tiny tulip glass brimming with the colourless schnapps – there was the smell she had missed. Wrapped lump of sugar on the saucer from Beghin-Say – one might almost be back in Holland! She tore a page from her notebook and scribbled.

'Marie-Line, for heaven's sake calm down and do nothing that only plays into the hands of whoever thinks you behave irresponsibly –' She got an idea, sipped from the brimming glass; Mauricette was hanging about with curiosity. 'The girl who left this – it must have been just a short time ago?'

'Françoise!' in a screech. 'Here a sec.' This was all getting too public as well as too dramatic . . .

'Marie-Line gave you this note for me? – wait, would you like a drink or something, I'd like to sit down a minute, just to know what all this is about.' A small girl with an urchin face and an urchin-cut, behind those enormous silly glasses the girls affected. Big pretty forget-me-not eyes, asparkle with interest and excitement.

'You're Arlette? She told me about you last night. Got into trouble staying out. I should be going to class really – oh rats, I'll cut it. I'll have a beer, and thanks. Come and sit down then. No, the others are going, class at three but it's only physiology, digestive tube or some crap.' The table was littered with coffee cups but a grubby sort of boy brought the beer and her schnapps and whisked them away.

'She seems to be in a terrific uproar,' in a chilly voice. The girl calmed down, sipped her beer and became sensible.

'Well, I live nearby. We're friends too. I'm not at that crappy Gymnase, thank God – the other sucker-machine across here.' Miles too hot here near the stove; she undid her raincoat and took a taste of schnapps, wished she hadn't ordered it.

'Dropped in after lunch; we generally go that far together on the bike. Seems there was a blow-up at lunch. You know about it, I gather.'

'She asked my advice on a family problem.'

'Yes, I know. I found the advert, I suggested it. She phoned

26

from here. And she went to see you – well, she cut a class. The Brutus – that's that old sneak of an overseer they have there – marked her absent and being more or less in the pay of her father phoned him to say Marie-Line's cut an hour and I thought you should know. Well then, the Pater who's absolutely out of Zola was frothing, and he has her under a sort of curfew: she's not allowed out after supper. She was telling me what you said, and was back late, so two big terrible black marks see, and I guess there was a post-mortem at lunch today. Anyhow I rang for her on my way in, and the old bag of a housekeeper made faces but let me in, and Marie-Line had been crying and wouldn't speak, but she shoved that note in my hand.'

'She said nothing?'

'Only that she wouldn't be going to school because she wasn't allowed out, and I could come and see her, but no more.'

'What about you – will you be marked absent?'

'Oh, I don't care. An hour – I'll say I was at the dentist. No problem,' in Mauricette's accent. 'I mean, my old man's fussy about the exam, but I'm fairly up-to-date on the work. As long as I'm not out late too often . . . That old prick of a dentist, he really belongs in the time when girls got sent to the convent for dancing with the wrong man.'

'All right, I get it. Well, I was writing her a note. I'll finish it – will you take it to her?'

'Of course. Her old man knows mine so I'm tolerated if looked on sourly. I'll be let in.'

'I don't like this hole and corner passing of missives, but there's not much choice right now. There's nothing private in it. I ask you to add your voice to mine. Tell her to cool it. I don't expect her to apologize if she's unable to, but to show herself amenable and not openly hostile, create a chink of light and I can perhaps wedge my foot in it. This nonsense of cutting her wrists – she's not that much of a fool? I'm taking it that's just to jolt me.'

'Did she say that? – lordy: no, and she's not a fool, but she's

27

a very emotional girl and she got tremendously worked up. Ten minutes after she'll have forgotten that.'

'Good. Do you know Michel?'

'Of course, he's a lamb. Very quiet and well balanced. His trouble is he hasn't a penny.'

'Would he come and see me?'

'Course he would. Love it.' Sufficiently spontaneous to hearten her.

6. 'Stocktaking'

She got home to find Arthur stumping about in peculiar underclothes, English and shapeless.

'It really is too bad. A brand one knew and wore as a child, bought in Jermyn Street, very dear indeed and Look at it.'

'It's just the same here,' sympathized Arlette, who crossed the border to buy underclothes.

'Sea Island cotton . . .' working himself up, 'my Führer's Face. Shaved off a big black wrestler . . .'

'How did they get it white?' enquired the woman of literal mind.

He stopped and put on the prosecutor face.

'You've been washing these. With detergents.' She wasn't having any of this.

'You kiss mi bum, mi general.'

'Where did you learn this vulgar expression?'

'Norma.'

'How is ol' Norma?'

'All right. She agrees there's nothing to be gained by staying. Going to bugger off when ol' Robert's sort of not looking. Only sorry to exchange Strasbourg for Salford.'

'Is there really much difference?'

'According to her, Hautepierre's the island of Tahiti by comparison.'

'Plainly,' said Arthur sociologically, 'neither of you has been to Tahiti.'

'Have you? What's there?'

'A Préfecture, more or less that of Les Deux Sèvres, and the French Navy's washing hung out in interminable lines. And not a naked tit in sight. Where are my trousers! I've got to go to a reception for some Belgians.' She put on her apron and went to the kitchen, which was much the same thing.

Arlette who had a wish for consommé put beef bones in the oven to roast and set onions to brown; to make stock. Have to take stock too, of the Situation. It didn't seem as though she were making much money on the job. Norma didn't have a penny. Albert Demazis, who had, seemed to have got cold feet. Marie-Line's parents, who were simply dripping with it, weren't going to scatter largesse. Shouldn't have married Arthur, huh? Then you'd still have your widow's pension!

The Job had been born the day after Illhausern. A Saturday. Unsatisfactory weather, rainy and blowy, then still and bright again after misty beginnings. They had done the weekend shopping together, come back to the little flat in the Krutenau: she made coffee.

'I don't understand this,' she said. 'I'm an average person from a dull narrow background. I've never done anything interesting. I'm now tolerably faded. What is there to run after?'

'Quantifying things is dull,' said Arthur. 'Sociologists are forever collecting figures about Russians whose breath smell and drawing conclusions about toothpaste in the Soviet Union. Misleading, and dull. Now was it Luther who said that if the world were to come to an end tomorrow he would go out and plant an apple tree?'

'Good for him.'

'Yes, exactly. People of your sort are intensely tiresome and one needs them. Now what I want explaining – you keep up

29

this sainte n'y touche act all these years and then suddenly collapse utterly.'

'You looked so vulnerable and pathetic there with your pipe.'

'Two babes in the wood, my God. Why do you stay in this poky place? – you aren't poor.'

'I'm beastly rich. I have my widow's pension, in lovely Dutch guldens worth such a lot in francs. And I have a resounding diploma in Movement Therapy, so the hospital pays me. Won't it be nice to be rich?'

'Yes, I'm grossly overpaid. Now tell me; what's your opinion of the flat in the Rue de l'Observatoire?'

'Quite good. A nice sense of compromise there, between the Esplanade and the Saint-Maurice. That awful wallpaper must be swept out. But quite good. Mm, I've some pretty old Dutch furniture. And a Breitner snowscape.'

'Yes. I hate Dutch furniture; its curves are all wrong. Never did get accustomed to the bowls of the teaspoons being wrong way round. And the other – the one on the quay?'

'Much better, despite the Ill smelling bad. But far too dear. Nicer. Sunnier. Less wasteful. Easier to keep clean. But out of the question.'

'One takes a mortgage.'

'One does no such thing. You marry me because I don't compromise with my beliefs. A refusal to make banks rich by borrowing money is among them.'

'Good. But isn't paying rent capitalism, then?'

'The old woman depends on renting that house: it's her one resource.'

'Mm,' said Arthur. 'I'm sure she's a slum landlord, sweating Turkish immigrants all over Strasbourg. Very well, we agree. I like the Observatoire too. I can bike to work.'

'I bike too. And it's not much farther than here. Now we have to cook.' Arthur got a potato-peeler pushed in his hand. Arlette said, 'I should like an eye-level oven. Oh dear, all this is going to be very expensive.'

There was silence. The dinner was good: the salad, made by

Arthur, outstanding, or so she said. They did the washing-up.

'I'll get you a machine.'

'I don't want a machine; they're a con.'

'I see,' said Arthur, thinking gloomily that he was destined for a career of washing-up.

'It's blown clear,' said Arlette watering her plants. 'We can go for a walk.' Almost as eccentric in Strasbourg as in Los Angeles, but Arthur loved walking, bless him.

He gathered for a spring at this frightful woman.

'I've something important to discuss. It can become peripatetic later. It's about a job.'

'I'm not going to give up my hospital work. Yes it is monotonous, repetitive and frequently useless, but I'm not going to potter round the Rue de l'Observatoire polishing floors.'

'Listen carefully, dearest girl. Apart from a lack of enthusiasm for a wife bustling about in her white overall and her clinical vocabulary, smelling disgustingly of ether, I have an ambition to see you share in my work.'

'Preposterous. No training or experience. What should I be? – a typist.'

'Kindly let me speak. I don't want you in the office. I do want you to have your own interests and responsibilities. I have people in the office. With the training, and mentality, and speaking the pitifully illiterate jargon. Now I have huge areas of work that are necessary but bitterly dull. Others I don't approve of a bit, imposed by political pressure. We are subjected of course to lobbying. I am a mammon of iniquity. To gain some slight freedom, for work I consider valuable, I accept roughly seventy per cent of tripe. Par for the course, about. I should like to enlarge my freedom, in fields that interest me. Now suppose – I have not thought this out but that is my present purpose – you were to do freelance work as a kind of advice bureau. Don't frown; hear me out. A small experimental laboratory.'

'A plaything of yours.'

31

'By no means. Let me put the arguments: I've done that much thought.

'Plaything in no sense. You have your expertise and I have mine. What's a marriage for? Rhetorical question. You're an amateur? I need only say that professionals including me, are narrowed dulled and desiccated by their own professionalism.

'Expertise? There are very few dogmas worth mentioning. One is that the only way to acquire it is to do experimental field work. I believe you to be unusually well qualified. The other sort is the book sort. We possess a vast library. Most textbooks are in any case out-of-date as soon as written. Virtually all the good stuff comes to my desk.

'There exist already innumerable advice bureaux? Two sorts; those that are free and those that ain't. Public ones? – social assistants; admirable women, overworked and under-paid. Choked with regulations, ministerial or municipal. Hamstrung by bureaucracy. The defeat-your-own-end syndrome of all governmental instances.

'Private ones? Have their own axe to grind, alcoholics, battered wives and so forth. Doctors or priests? – all right as far as they go. They give of course valuable and disinterested advice, when they find the time. Like cops, they're all bodies of fine upstanding men, devoted to upholding the Ten Commandments and wondering why it doesn't work. Wrong-footed at the start. All this talk about Justice . . . They're like the fire brigade, they put out fires. But they've no more time for helping people than they have for catching bicycle thieves.'

It all sounded like Piet talking. Arlette took a cigarette and held her peace.

'The ones where you pay – anything from psychiatry to tax-dodging. Most founded upon fear, greed and chicanery: squalid. And far too dear. Even when good obscured by cant, humbug and self-interest.

'I can see difficulties of course. We need patience and some skill. One puts up a board saying Expert? – anyone can, and what does it mean? How to avoid the money snag? I say; the sun's come out – let's go out too.'

32

They crossed the Rue de Jura and walked along the canal where the barges tie up. Under the Churchill bridge past the Citadel park. Past the *Drakkar* which pretends to be a Viking ship, and sells beer. Past the mother-barge, piled with butane cylinders; surrounded by rusty junk and guarded by numerous dogs. The pleasure-steamers of the Cologne-Dusseldorf Line; ten days on the Rhine with nothing to do but overeat. The Pont d'Anvers and the coal harbour, painterly in the autumn sunshine: the nineteenth-century barracks where you can still, if minded, join the Foreign Legion, and the row of Belgian barges with enchanting names like *Praise God Barebones*. They walked down to the corner where the ship-lock joins the inner and outer harbours, Arthur arguing quietly and Arlette being obstinate.

'I don't really grasp,' she said, 'what could one do that isn't – I agree very badly – done already?'

Arthur felt in his pockets, where he collected torn scraps of newspaper, raw material of sociology.

'These are random samples. Newspapers tell one nothing – the scrabble for perpetual novelty. Assize-court reports . . .

'First is an engineer of thirty, highly qualified. He left work one day; said nothing at home. Went on simulating work rhythms, leaving the house at the right time. Spent the day walking about, sitting in cafés, doing crosswords, brooding. After more than a year, think of it, he went home, assassinated his mistress and her daughter, who was not his. He washed and neatly dressed the two bodies; that's quite common. He made then six different suicide attempts. Five days after, he walked into the cop shop, arguably just before they laid hands on him.' Arlette made no comment. Familiar with these things; Piet used to 'bring them back from the office'.

'Second is a teacher of thirty-five. Good teacher; model husband of a devoted wife, who was a childhood comrade. Excellent father of three little girls, thirteen, eleven and ten. Happy childhood in comfortable circumstances. Strangled a shopgirl in a perfumery who surprised him robbing the till. Mystery; he had already robbed the same till twice and knew there was now no money kept in it.'

'No clue at all?' asked Arlette startled.

'Oh yes: compulsive gambler. Tried several times to stop; was put on the casino blacklist at his own request. It is, as you know, one of the most tenacious of intoxications.'

'But these are classics for the shrink. The first is neuropath depressive and the second's like alcoholism; he tries to compensate for a huge hole somewhere in the personality.'

'Sociopath if you accept the feeble-minded jargon. Quite correct – go on.'

'The police don't bother with the definitions, but recognize the states. The instructing judge calls for shrinks, who say greatly diminished responsibility but no legal insanity. Assize court ponders it all, pronounces, rather obviously, a suspended sentence, and these poor people are committed to the shrink-shop, where we sincerely hope, etcetera.'

'Quite so. Some advice and help might have avoided all this, don't you think? Paid advice, quite often. First man was in a good job, and the father of the second in easy circs.'

'You mean the mistress and the wife were highly devoted but something was missing? Intelligence or education or just strength of character?'

'They were too closely involved, generally a good reason for not being able to cope. They may have just lacked detachment.'

They had turned the corner and were walking along the Rhine-Marne canal past the 'Conseil des Quinze' quarter. She did not know what the Council of Fifteen had been; it sounded Venetian and vaguely sinister, but the district is neither. Small bourgeois villas pressed too closely together, with rosebushes and clumps of dahlias in the minute gardens.

'Very well,' said Arthur, 'we agree; a commonplace. People unable to face their responsibilities, or inhibited from doing so. Here's one that's worse, so shocking that it was front-paged. A deliberate avoidance of responsibility, to such a

34

degree that the witnesses, amounting to a dozen, are being prosecuted for failure to assist a person in danger.

'A mining district in Lorraine. Pre-war workmen's cottages in a clump. These are of poor quality; the point is important. Thin-walled wretched things: you hear the neighbours' light-switch snap on. An old woman known to everybody – she'd lived there forty years – was battered to death by ruffians, presumably for her moneybox. What is not banal is that the battering took over an hour and was extremely noisy. The old woman fought. There were screams, crashes, shouts for help. After darkness fell – and upon her – loud noise continued; the furniture was all smashed.

'Now allowing for exaggeration, for a perfunctory, confused and superficial report possibly cut, and clumsily, by some sub-editor, this is a little bit much. Wouldn't you say?'

'Not all that exaggerated, alas, or the bystanders wouldn't have been charged with non-assistance.'

'That's quite an ironic touch: these people are most indignant. They've been charged, while the local gendarmerie haven't yet caught up with the actual authors.'

'Appalling,' said Arlette, 'but only too frequent. A hundred cars will hurtle past an obviously hurt person, covered with blood at a road verge. Each saying "Catch me getting involved – not on your nelly!"'

'These people were the neighbours. Loitering around the block. Who, says the reporter sarcastically, one and all hurried off saying they had to go and see about the soup.'

'Frightened of the ruffians.'

'What – a dozen able-bodied men? Miners! An old woman they all knew, whose screams are setting the whole quarter ablaze.'

'There's something undisclosed, not brought forward,' she decided. 'The old woman was a violent drunk, who often screamed and threw things. Or a moneylender, as in Dostoyevsky. Whom everybody hated and nobody would regret. Or perhaps a witch with an evil eye. Who looked at the cow

35

and the cow died. Nothing's too far-fetched for a Central-European country dorp.'

'Who are you telling! And you must have put your finger somewhere near the truth. But it's beside the point. I was illustrating a flagrant phenomenon, by your own comment as common as a drunk shooting a red light. Individual and collective avoidance of responsibility.'

They had got as far as the Orangery, a pretty urban park in the romantic style of the early nineteenth century. They sat by the lake-side. Canada geese waddled about. A swan looked evilly at Arlette. Go away, she said, hateful beast.

'"There was a young man from St John's,"' said Arthur lazily. 'Irish poet at Cambridge University. "Who wanted to roger the swans. No no, said the porter, Make free with my daughter, But the swans are reserved for the dons."'

'Being rogered by the swans is how I see it. I always did sympathize deeply with Leda.'

'You've a point there,' said Arthur.

There is a pretty pavilion in eighteenth-century style, supposedly built for the Empress Josephine. Orange trees are ranged along its terrace. Behind, a splendid lawn flows to a perspective of trees now ruined by the ugly silhouette of the new building for the European Parliament.

'Cars are absolutely forbidden in the park,' said Arlette crossly, 'and in they sail. I asked a cop once to intervene. He just grinned.'

'The bourgeois,' said Arthur sententiously, 'Are constitutionally incapable of getting out of a car to walk a hundred paces. It might, you see, diminish their self-importance. Responsibilities are evaded by the administration, in this case the Municipality of Strasbourg, which characteristically fails to enforce its own rule, for the convenience of a few parasites.'

'There's the heart of the matter,' angrily. 'How can you blame the people, wretchedly educated and brought up to depend on the whims of their government for avoiding responsibility? Right up to the rather ugly Palace of the so-

36

called Elysée, that same appalling government lies, cheats, and thieves. As do all the others.'

'So we try,' said Arthur tranquilly, 'to rebuild. In a small, humble, individual, personal fashion. This is what we've been talking about for two hours.'

'A telephone number? It's really of very little use. Alcoholics Anonymous, SOS, the Battered Wives, the Sally Army. All more or less soup kitchens.'

'Yes. Anonymous and paternalistic. Old-fashioned. Reformed drunks who got religion. But a name? – followed up by a tiny office – perhaps in the Rue de l'Observatoire? A small advertisement in the local paper? It needs thought. Arlette van der Valk, the Policeman's Widow? Might be more fetching than your own maiden name. Bear it in mind; turn it round now and again.'

'Still sounds very old-fashioned,' complained Arlette. 'Philip Marlowe, the Warm-Hearted private eye.'

'There's something,' quite seriously, 'in that notion too.'

7. 'Redefinition of the private eye'

Arlette did not know, often, why she did things. Followed profoundly rooted instincts, and worked it out later. She had been quite certain – most decided about it – that she would not marry again. Now she'd changed her mind.

Oh well, logic ... Arthur was logical, with that neat Barbara-Celarent-Darii way of thinking. She wouldn't be much of a sociologist.

One decides suddenly to remarry, on Tuesday fortnight. That's a long way away, practically never. But one inescapable piece of logic, even for her, is that suddenly it is tomorrow. At this moment she would have liked to run away. This was all very wearisome. But one didn't bunk rather than face the consequences of frivolous and probably drunken decisions.

There's been the wife of Policeman van der Valk, a long apprenticeship. Making things hard for herself as usual. Storming off, declaring that France is and always has been the bitterest most obstinate enemy of tolerance, liberty and progress: who repealed the Edict of Nantes, hey? And where had Descartes gone, and all the Huguenots? Holland of course. She'd fallen topplingly in love with Holland, much more than with Piet. This was the dawn of the revolution, when to-be-alive-was-very-bliss.

Wore off quick, to be sure. Amsterdam is just another narrow-minded provincial town. Some silly things she said, and some she did, caused catty comment, damaged, said Piet sorrowingly, his career. There'd been the episode with the Political Police, which she'd called a Gestapo; never altogether shaken off. Holland is a family, said the Political Police reprovingly, and you're an Outsider.

Piet was a just and a good man for twenty years and what did you ever do? You bore the children, and brought them up, but what did you do?

So then we'd had Arlette-the-Widow. Who lived a life of bourgeois comfort; well, relatively. Worked herself into a well-greased rut, quite certainly: both a body and a mind trundling along the same tramline. Selfishly cultivating that most delicious of all relationships, so comforting, so consoling, an amitié amoureuse. With Arthur Davidson, a gentle and considerate person whose mild eccentricities were an amusing antidote against boredom.

And now Tuesday fortnight had almost arrived, and poor old Arthur didn't know what he was getting into.

Nonsense: he knew very well. So did she. They had discussed it.

'Does the bedroom window,' asked Arthur 'get left closed or open at night?'

'Open. Because I am not French any more.'

'Yes, the main trouble with the French has always been

38

finding everywhere else, outside the dear old Hexagon, such a bore. Canada say, or India: huge boring meaningless places, not worth the trouble. Napoleon flogged Louisiana, for a shatteringly trivial sum, simply because it was too much of a bore.'

'Quite right. But so has France become a bore.'

'Agreed,' said Arthur. 'Nothing could be more of a bore, or deader, or more of a menace, than the Nation-State, and the French so-called, cannot possibly be more tiresome than the so-called British.'

Tuesday fortnight arrived. She had managed to lose a good deal of weight but threw it all away drinking too much champagne.

'Do you still feel rather French?' enquired Arthur.

'Do you still feel rather English?'

'There's a sound Turkish proverb to the effect that the Fatherland is where the grub is.'

'My dear boy . . .'

The painters in the new flat were very dilatory, as they always are. Arlette spent much time being sweaty on a stepladder. Both the living-room and Arthur's workroom were a horrible brothel. She wanted a workroom of her own: Arthur's Detective Agency, despite being a bore, was in fact occupying her mind a good deal. They went to Venice for a belated honeymoon. Arthur asked about the Detective Agency a couple of times and she said she was thinking about it.

She found a pleasantly large amount in her bank account: that lovely Dutch gulden got higher and higher. She found too a large and beautiful plank of hardwood, and a country carpenter who put legs on it for her. She got an extra telephone, and after some thought a tape recorder. She didn't know quite what she wanted, except that it wasn't a lot of female junk like ironing boards and sewing-machines.

Arthur paid small attention to her doings, being greatly preoccupied with his own workroom. There were far too many books: there always are. Nor was he allowed in 'her room'. This he found quite normal: she had to have some-where to be perfectly private. But there came a moment when she had to take him into confidence.

'Come on in my room ... Don't be a fool; of course you can smoke the pipe. Sit down ... Look, I've decided that on the whole I do like the Detective Agency, but I haven't the least idea how to go about it and you must help me.'

'Advise and consent.'

'Not quite right. But something like that.' Arthur was not yet broken in to her elliptical thinking. 'A little notice in the paper,' she explained. 'Not an advertisement. Kind of a lapidary phrase, that is understood instantly. Like Our Business is Business, meaning don't ever think we're in this for anything but money.'

'Now I see,' solemnly, teasing her. 'Advice and consolation. Tea and sympathy.'

'Stop it. Like counsel sounds oh, fiscal and financial and all things I decidedly am not.'

'Aid.'

'Old clothes and canned milk for earthquake victims.'

'Personal and family problems.'

'And a lot of people are afraid of the expense. Must put that consultation costs nothing. Not that word though – sounds like fortune-tellers.'

'Let me work on this.'

'And when you get people in – how, incidentally, do you get them in? Where do you put them? And if one uses the house for professional consultancy, isn't there some special tax, and won't the rent double?'

'Leave these problems to me; they're technical. Suitably vague definitions are my bread and butter. My esteemed colleague Monsieur de Montlibert who is Professor at the Faculty, doesn't in the least do the same work as myself, but we're both called sociologists. Now I can get you cover for your activities. As for the house – will you allow me to help, on this sort of thing?'

'Of course: I couldn't by myself.'

40

'Right; I fixed the landlady: she's quite agreeable to people coming here. A professional colouring is provided by me. Never mind ologies, but my work is crimino and peno and generally sociopatho in nature. From the official viewpoint, you are a kind of radiologist: you screen people. You build up files: they're a valuable research tool.'

'But isn't this most immoral? To tempt people's confidence, and use the information?'

'I'm delighted to hear you say it,' said Arthur dryly. 'Best possible guarantee. Your files will be confidential, of course. All files are immoral when used to menace individual privacy. The Council of Europe has twice recently exhorted its members to adopt standardized legislation against abuse of computerized information. My statistically-minded colleagues, who just love computerized information, carry a heavy load of responsibility. No, you're a watchdog. In a filthy jargon phrase, you launder the files. I'll show you how; the technique is simple. Identity stuff doesn't appear.

'Now the flat uses another simple technique. We've no elevator to pay for, can afford a few electronic whatnots. That wide corridor at the entrance: we partition that, with a solid inner door to the apartment. Between the two doors is a filter, an airlock – a little waiting-room really.

'Your street door opens to a ring,' explained Arthur, seeing she looked puzzled. 'Sets off a buzzer. That's for people who press your bell simply to have access to the house. The door on the landing, the present apartment door, can be made to open to a push, changing the buzzer tone. Assume somebody now in the airlock, where pressure within and without is equalized. You have an inner door,' making a drawing.

'I see. It might be the butcher's boy, or a man selling insurance.'

'Or a friend. So you switch off your buzzer, and glance through the judas. If you've a customer you bring him in the office.

'But you're not the Town Hall Enquiries: you don't want just anybody dropping in. I think your advert carries a phone-

number. When that rings it could set off a recorded message,
after which it records an incoming voice, until so-and-so puts
the phone down.'

'Why can't I just answer the phone?' asked the well-trained
Doctor's wife.

'My dear girl, are you a footman? You're in the bath, or
walking your dog. This is standard for anyone without a full-
time secretary.'

'Isn't it over-sophisticated?'

'I agree that offices bristle with these devices and it's easy to
have too many, but you must have some protection. Drunks,
lunatics, anonymous obscenities, possessive husbands, neur-
otics of every sort. Come to think of it,' said Arthur, suddenly
serious, 'when alone here you must have some physical protection too. You may be making some undesirable acquaint-
ances.'

'Oh Quatsch,' she said. 'I was a cop's wife; I know how to
look after myself.'

Arthur poured himself a cup of coffee and stirred it length-
ily.

'So you can. After other people too: it goes together. In
some ways too you're a protected, sheltered woman. All to the
good; you aren't case-hardened. You've a quality of innocence
that's most valuable.

'There's a lot of violence about, though. More imbecile than
insane, but still . . . I'll talk to the Commissaire of Police: we
need anyhow his permission and approval. I want you to go to
the police gymnasium for self-protection lessons, and it's
necessary to have a gun licence.' Arlette was looking extremely
mulish.

'I refuse totally to have a gun.'

'Quite rightly so.'

'Violence simply breeds violence.'

'Absolutely. There are, indeed, few situations in which a gun
is of any real use. None the less you have to have one. The
Commissaire, you'll see, will agree.'

'But I do not.'

42

'My dear girl. Consider gold, in the vaults of the Bank of France. Quite useless, you'll say. But in obscure ways, necessary to the stability of the currency.'

'Utter nonsense,' she said. 'The stability of the currency depends on not spending more than you earn. But tell that to governments ... don't dare admit it: all the economists would be out of jobs.'

'Damn the Americans,' said Arthur. 'Their neurosis about guns is on a par with numerous other idiot inventions, like new maths, or credit cards: causes no end of trouble. I'm not going to argue.'

One married this woman, thought Arthur, knowing there would be endless arguments. One did not bother about how many arguments one would win. Male power-principles, banging on the table and saying 'This one I'm going to win', were useless in female-dominated societies, which were the ones where all the men carried guns. The Swiss do not have complexes about guns.

Am I in an Arlette-dominated society, Arthur asked himself, grinning.

8. 'Fringes of Professionalism'

She thought she had won this particular argument, until quelled by the Commissaire of Police, a type she recognized. He did not look in the least like a cop, and she knew enough cops to know that very few, and those mostly the bad ones, resemble cinema cops. The general characteristic is that they look anything but.

He was so soft-spoken that she had to sharpen her ears. He had a nice rug on the floor of an office utterly unlike the usual police office: there were plain sunshiney curtains on the (clean) windows; attractive pictures on his walls: in fact the only thing suggesting cop was the face that old priests get, which comes from listening to a lot of confessions. It could have been the office of a Geneva private-banker: the walls had heard as many secret turpitudes. When he smiled, which was not often, it was like sun glancing off his gold-rimmed glasses. he wore a plain grey suit cut narrow to a narrow body, with a waistcoat, and it was quite impossible to imagine him carrying a gun.

'Here is your authority,' giving her a piece of paper. 'Professor Davidson and I had a long talk. I have to know what agencies operate in my city. There are a number of charlatans whom our notions of liberty, and present legislation, allow to flourish. Now you know your rights, and liberties, and their limits. Mm, the responsibilities have their limits, too.

'Very nice,' studying her, apparently with approval: with pleasure or not was impossible to say. 'It is good to meet you. We may meet from time to time, within or without definitions of my professional competence.

'There is also – here – a sort of credit card. Designed by Professor Davidson and myself. It lends a certain professionalism – not altogether spurious – to your amateur standing. You are upon the fringe of professional standing. There is nothing official about this. It carries though my stamp and my signature. A responsibility I accept. You are not upon oath; and are a purely private citizen. I should like you to carry this card. Notify me of any loss or misappropriation. Like a bank. Yes.

'It will help establish your good faith with some people. You may also from time to time be pestered with jacks-in-office. In, or out, of uniform.

'Here also is a gun permit. I know of your scruples. They do you honour.' And that was all; a tone managing to be so flat as well as perfectly polite that there was no argument. Her mouth had opened but – well dear, try not to leave it open.

'You don't wish to be a kind of policewoman. Quite rightly. I have a few girls in my services. Not enough. Yes.

44

Among other things they do simple gymnastics. Come around and they'll show you. Good for the figure. And how to use the gun; meaning not to. The Secretary will arrange it. He's perfectly discreet. What by the way did you adopt as an advertising slogan?'

'Arlette van der Valk.' Odd it did sound to her, now. 'Counsel and aid: personal and family problems.' The Commissaire appeared to approve.

'That's not too much. These things get around by word of mouth. Good; I can rely upon you to know police business when you see it.' He wrote on a calling card. 'That's my home telephone. If you get beyond the depth of your discretion and judgment. Much like the gun. Not designed as a court of higher appeal.' And the thin perilous smile. Getting up, to show politely that the conversation was now over. Escorting her courteously to the end of the passage.

There was an envelope on the kitchen table at home, with a tape in it and a scribble from Arthur. 'This is quite good now, I think.'

Her voice, a quiet contralto, came over Arthur's high-fidelity speakers, sounding better than it would on the phone. She had heard it innumerable times before the wording, pitch, and timing had been got right and he'd taken the tape to cut and splice. She'd been so concentrated on the technical exigencies that the words had become meaningless.

"This is a recorded message by Arlette van der Valk. At the end, the line will remain open to record your message, which will be in confidence. Please give your name, a number to reach you, and the time that suits you best. This is necessary; to make an appointment without keeping you waiting. You can speak now."

She felt weak in the knees. It sounded serious, no longer a party game. It had all been academic yesterday: too long or too short; too businesslike, or not enough so. Detached and impersonal, and now neither. This was her, putting her finger between toothed wheels. What was she meddling with?

A day or so ago a boy had been killed. Like Isadora Duncan.

45

Wearing a long scarf, the end of which had caught in the back wheel of his scooter. The boy had been ripped off the bike, and slowly asphyxiated. There had been witnesses, but none with a knife. A cop had come at last, sawed through the tough thick wool, tried resuscitation but failed. The ambulance came too late.

That appalling commissaire of police. He had not laughed or treated her contemptuously. Just . . . been businesslike.

Good God, there her handbag lay on the kitchen table; a gun clanking about in it. A short-barrelled revolver of blue steel. Like a large size alarm pistol. With a permit, to show the armourer when buying ammunition. Businesslike.

She looked around, at her nice new kitchen. Stay in it? She could tell the hospital she'd changed her mind. Put it down to newly married caprice.

Arthur had left her quietly to make her own mind up. She had only to say sorry, this was absurd.

There was shopping to do. An eatable supper to produce. Female tasks, for which she was quite adequate. Arthur would understand.

'So what changed your mind back?' asked Arthur, professionally curious.

'I told myself you counted on me. And your pal, that awful commissaire – he took you seriously. A gun . . . as though it were a box of matches. No, those are all pretexts. It seemed – unprofessional; to refuse. And idiotic to be frightened.'

'Not idiotic.'

'What else could I do? I have no choice, really.'

'That's my girl.'

'What have I done, to deserve this fortune? I've lived my life; it's been a pretty good one. I've brought up three children. I was left a widow: that happens, and the way it happened. I had a job here, a place to live. A pension, and in fat heavy Dutch guilders. I could feel satisfied, couldn't I? And then a man comes running after me, with this fantastic notion. I get this flat and everything. I just haven't earned it. Am I to be memsahib? Arrange the flowers, clap my hands for the boy?

46

Give little parties from time to time, where the food of course will be exceptional. Bed and the kitchen; woman's job. To learn it? – come sit here next to Nellie, she's been on the same sewing-machine thirty years, you'll learn it all just watching her go through the motions. Well fuck that,' breaking into angry tears. 'Look now: useless cow starts to cry. Cretin. What else could I do then?'

'Hush. There is more to it. The man, too, wonders what he's doing, in that idiot tower of babel. A social-sciences expert, dear God. And paid, my God, paid. These European bureaucracies are extremely expensive luxuries. That Palace affair is so ugly really because it looks so cheap, and so plainly wasn't.'

'But you don't work there, do you?'

'No, the University gives me house-room. But the Council has commissioned me. Still,' said Arthur thoughtfully, 'I do quite a lot of good work. By the way, clothes. If I can bring you to agree, you should be feminine in the office. And pretty; that's no strain. If you happen to take your gun, one has these trouser suits, rather dashing and they suit you.'

'The police girls are going to show me. Not that it's any business of yours.'

'Only offering suggestions,' said Arthur humbly. 'And oh, I'd nearly forgotten. Carried away as I was, in the turmoil of your emotions. I have a car for you. On the street outside. Here are the keys. What the female private operative drives. Discreetly dowdy; tweed coat and skirt. I have hopes of being allowed to borrow it from time to time.'

'Good God,' she said looking out of the window. 'That almond green thing? What is it?'

'What is it?' pretending to be shocked. 'A small but suitable Lancia.' She was not a woman for raucous screams but she did, he saw with satisfaction, have her mouth open.

'I'd try it now,' wistful, 'but dinner's almost ready.'

'You may drive me to the office, this afternoon.' Where he began to laugh uncontrollably until it went on too long: his secretary looked at this hilarity and tapped her forehead.

'Sorry, Sylvie. Where's my pipe? Damn; I've left it at home.'

47

These men, thought Arlette. That policeman with his gun. 'Do you mind showing me your hand? And pulling up your sleeve a moment? Thank you – that'll do nicely.' She was driving the Lancia with appropriate awe, cross with every other driver who did not give her at least thirty metres interval, the way everyone drives who has just taken possession of a new car. This part of it has rewards, all right. The Council of Europe and the United Nations put together could not be more lavish. It was like a perpetual birthday.

She bought clothes. The carpenter came: more unheard-of still, he worked. The greatest miracle, he cleaned up after himself, with a dustpan and brush. One of these days there will be a liberated male carpenter, pushing the vacuum-cleaner.

The electrician came, installed things, gave her long explan-ations she had difficulty following. She drove the car. Really Arthur was very clever.

9. 'The Thin Man's Wife'

Without being noticed, the little advertisement slipped into place in the local paper, among fortune-tellers, marriage bureaux, the man with aquariums, terrariums, vivariums. Nothing happened: Arlette told herself that this was what she had secretly expected. Nothing ever would. Things did happen, but of the sort Arthur prophesied. Oafs, lumpenpack. People who ring the fire brigade on New Year's Eve to wish them a happy year and giggle at the wit. Drunks, frustrated folk. A person sounding too good to be true who said "Oh; well; really, you know, darling, balls, rather," and rang off. A lot with warmth and limited vocabularies saying this was no business for a woman. Rudeness, cant, ignorance, violence and hypocrisy abounded in the city of Strasbourg, but that one had known already. Odd though, the number of folk who have nothing better to do. The tape was always full of rubbish, and she turned it patiently to Delete, and thought that Arthur had wasted a lot of money. He seemed quite unperturbed.

Rain? It was pouring; three on the tape together. Arlette did not feel nervous, though green and inexperienced. Here it was . . .

In the silence the tape, hearing nothing, jumped forward. Clicks; someone had trouble digesting all that recorded-message crap and was starting again. Then a quiet sensible voice said in English, "Couldn't make much head or tail of that, sorry . . . I'm afraid I can only talk English, see? Take a chance on your understanding that." Bit of a giggle, realizing she was being ridiculous. "I don't know what to say, really . . . Oh well, I got the address all right. I reckon I'll come along just the same. What have I to lose? Don't even know if anyone can hear me on this thing." Giggle. "Look, I'll get a bus . . . Don't know how long that'll take," from some experience of Strasbourg public transport, an enterprise of feeble mind. "Don't know even where it is, exactly. Nev'mind: do me best, okay? Sorry about that: bye."

Arlette pushed Stop, and wondered how to be business-like. She reached for the diary or the casebook or whatever it was called, and wrote the time down. What use was that? – she didn't know how far this weird party had to come, and the bus service . . . Funny accent – north of England. 'Arthur, I speak English, and some German, and of course Dutch – put that in the ad?' She switched the tape on again.

Man's voice, very curt and businesslike. Ring this number, ask for Dupont. Male aggressivity, disguising someone vulnerable? Don't theorize ahead of your data, girl, ring up and find out. She did.

'Monsieur Dupont? Arlette van der Valk.' 'Who? Oh yes,' as though he'd forgotten. Self-reassurance trick, so commonplace as not to be worth noticing. Chief-executive voice. 'I don't intend though to discuss my affairs with anyone before knowing a good deal more about whom I'm talking to, right?'

'You can come here and see. Ask any question you wish then.' She felt lamentably green but how did one gain experience? Ring up people to practise on? Tell them sorry, but you see, you're the first I've ever had?

'No, I don't wish that.'

'Is it your office you're calling from?'

'No, that won't do either. This is a personal matter. Wait, you live by the Observatoire, right? Meet me on the street in the neighbourhood, all right? Six this evening or a little after, by the statue of Jeanne d'Arc, all right?'

'Very well, if that's what you want,' wondering whether it was all right but not about to turn down the chance.

'What charge do you make for that?' still tough.

'None at all, until I know what I could do.'

'Fair enough. Uh – navy blue coat, brown hat.'

The third voice on the tape was that of a youngish girl. Self-assured, but obviously under strain.

"This is Marie-Line Siegel. I live in the Meinau – no, I don't think it's any use giving you the address, or not yet. I wish I knew – I'll just have to hope you can suggest something; there's a terrific fuss each time about what I've been doing and where I've been. Listen; I need to come and see you, but I don't know exactly when I can make it. This afternoon – sorry but I can't risk your ringing me at home; this is a public box. My father . . . – shit, I hope I can make you see. No, it's useless to talk: look, around two if I can make it, and I ask you to excuse me if I'm late or anything." Rang off abruptly.

Siegel in the Meinau. Arlette reached for the phone book and shrugged; it was a common enough name. The girl had been hurried and flustered, and not particularly coherent. The clear educated voice of the well-brought-up, but some trouble at home, seemingly. One could only hope she would persevere and follow it up: nothing one could do for the moment.

The day was full, in a tiresome manner. This English

50

woman, any time now, may be. A girl who might or might not appear in the early afternoon. And this Dupont, whatever his name was, at six by the Saint Maurice church. Only two minutes' walk along the road: one wouldn't take the car. All of them vague and awkward: nothing definite.

Was that the pattern things would take? She shrugged. The very first working day. And if she'd wanted it cut and dried like a dentist . . .

Start in the kitchen, where every woman begins.

The cleaning woman, a bow-legged little soul from Portugal, was having a cup of coffee: she worked well and hard, as long as she could down a strong one at quarter-hour intervals. We all have our little fads, huh. Arlette had one too, and put her overall on.

Arthur would have to cook the supper. If this Dupont wanted to talk, as seemed likely, she might not be home for some time. Get something out of the freezer. Sorry, but food is important. All those years in Holland Arlette had never understood those women who threw away twenty pairs of shoes as good as new, while their idea of a meal was a frozen chicken, improved with bits of tinned pineapple. Arthur, mercifully, took food seriously.

And something fairly rapid for now. Too bad if it was a bit late. Mm, that Dupont. Sounded the kind of man that comes in and turns the television straight on, because of that hard day at the office, and heaven help the wife if there isn't solid grub ready, dead on time. She was about halfway through, when the buzzer went. She took her overall off with one hand and combed her hair with the other. The judas showed a young woman in black, glancing in a surprised way around the 'waiting room'.

Arlette was pleased with the waiting room. Partition off a lump of corridor, even a wide one, and the result is a box, hard though you pretend it isn't. She had decided to admit the box. It was lined with pine boarding kept pale, hung with simple, pretty flower prints, and given spotlights and ventilation in the false ceiling. Not claustrophobic a bit: cosy as a womb, said

51

Arthur admiringly. She whipped into the office and opened the door with a desire to say 'Next'. This was the first – the very first.

A pale face that would have been pretty but was both fattish and haggard, but managed to be better than plain.

'I say, I hope you talk English. I just can't manage to learn French, sorry.'

'Take your coat off and be comfortable.' Dear Berlitz School. Rough, cough, bough and dough. And people say Russian is hard.

The woman had had nobody to talk to for ages, and spitting it all out was what she wanted more than anything. A listener. If sympathetic, so much the better. If there were any intelligent suggestions, that would be better still. Not that Arlette could think of many. You're in a mess, my good soul. You got into it out of goodhearted stupidity, and the best way out, indeed the only way out I can see, honest, is to bugger off quickish.

Her name was Norma and she came from Salford. Her husband could be said to have deserted her. Not technically perhaps; not on such-and-such a date. A sailor, seen at intervals that got longer and longer until one realized one day with only a slight sense of shock that Jackie was gone for good. Leaving her with three children: did that much work at home. Divorced?

'No. Got me pride, you see.'

Made any effort to trace Jackie?

'Not really. Where's the point in that?'

Well, to recall him to a sense of his responsibilities.

'Yah, he hasn't any. Oh, he was all right. Quite kind, not a bad father really, on the whole. Just slack like.' She'd managed okay. No real grievances.

One could see the point; nobody was a whole lot worse off for the lack of such as Jackie. Amiable hedonist. Arlette made a conscientious note: Danish, there must be a Danish consulate somewhere in Strasbourg which could catch up with Master Jackie, though he'd been left in peace a long time, too long she suspected for a court to get excited about conjugal

52

rights. And what good was anyone naturally a bit slack-like, brought back sullenly – by the slack of his trousers? Be off again in five minutes, as Norma said sensibly.

Some women were born victims, but she liked Norma, who had a certain tough gallantry. One called it dignity, and generosity, and other things quite out of fashion.

'I'll make a cup of tea, shall I?' The symbol of solidarity in England, and it touched Norma.

The trouble with women, Arlette knew well, is that they will insist on making fools of themselves over the same kind of man.

Robert had been around a couple of years, with a job in the Manchester area. Good job. Spoke good English for a Frenchman, near as good as you. Good chap; quiet, domesticated, liked the children, got on well with everyone. Solid chap, what.

She could suppose it. Men were infernally plausible. Anyhow, he'd had no bother gliding into bed with Norma.

Well, the job in Manchester came to an end. Robert, by now accustomed to domestic comforts, proposed bringing her back with him to Strasbourg. Well, what was to hold her? Her sister to be sure had been against it: what, over there, all among the Frogs? But her sister'd always been a wet blanket. What's different in France? Schools there too, aren't there? You go where your man is.

And how had that worked out? Plainly it hadn't, but apart from getting the necessary details Norma had to be given the chance to pour herself empty.

Started fine. Strasbourg was lovely. Robert had a nice little flat, quiet, with green spaces round and trees. Hautepierre is fine. The children liked it too. Didn't speak any French, any more than her, but kids never worry about that. Made friends everywhere; loads of kids in the quarter. They'd gone to school; the woman had been real kind, fixed them with a lot of Vietnamese children that didn't speak French either. Had that worked? Not too terribly; mean to say, the kids learned a lot of Chinese but no French . . . Still, they rubbed along.

Like her; she managed, shopping and stuff. Hell, she knew how to get along. Not like we were blacks, Paks or something, eating special grub and wearing turbans. Did the children look any different to the French? Did she? Learn the names of a few things, fromahdge, and you're home. Honest, I love it here. No kidding: you should see Salford, love.

Arlette's heart warmed to Norma. She'd had just the same herself in Amsterdam and found it rough going. The Dutch called the fromahdge kahss, put it on their bread with margarine and cut the result with a knife and fork: weird, and you learned to call the vinaigrette slahsowse.

No, the fly in the ointment is this bleeding Robert. Not the same as in England. They never are, thought Arlette gloomily – even dear old Piet . . .

Robert had gone real funny. Suspicious and jealous, my gawd. Look, the other day he got a rifle, and lined them all up against the wall, and said he'd shoot the lot if ever she looked at another man. Not that she had, but he wasn't kidding, and it frightened her, you know. Another thing; he'd got so goddamned mean. Had always refused to give her a weekly allowance, but a banknote here and there from his pocket.

'I'm used enough to making do. Always been poor, not ashamed of it or frightened of it. But giving you a ten-franc note, expecting the day's food to come out of that for five persons, that's just daft. I'm not just a prostitute love, honest. Keep his house, and I keep it clean, and put his food on the table. I've got to clothe the children – not right, is it?'

Plainly, the first thing was to get ol' Norma's morale up. She poured a second cup of tea, found a pack of Virginia cigarettes, and talked hearteningly for ten minutes. This is nonsense, girl. Entitled to Social Security like anyone else. Of course you must have money of your own; there are the children's allowances, and the woman-on-the-hearth, and a whole lot more. I'll find out exactly what your entitlement is, help fill in forms, lot of paper. No, you write down 'concubine' and the hell with it. Makes no difference; nor does being English. And I'll help you sort the school out.

54

But more important, you have to stand on your own feet; have some independence. This is serfdom, and the sooner Robert gets that into his head . . . Any trade? Barmaid? Well, you can earn good money at that, and better still in Germany. How old are the children? Seven, eleven, fifteen? Old enough to stand on their own feet. Hard work and awkward hours, but you're not workshy.

Sure thing, said Norma sturdily, but bleeding Robert's that jealous. Barmaid . . . !

Arlette had seen this snag coming, and could see more, too, but right now . . .

'Look, can I come and see you? Maybe tomorrow? I need to give this some thought, see what I can work out.'

'Sure. I'm always there. But – what about the payment? The kids saw your advert. You aren't the Sally Army, love, are you though?' Looking round at the office, which did look quite expensive, and at Arlette who did too. As Arthur said, they had to.

'You'll pay me what you can afford, when you can. Like an agent. Ten per cent of a month's money, if I find you a job. Is that fair?'

'Sure. You've done me good. I'm frightened though, about Robert. Violent . . .'

'But I'm not.' No. Because Robert can't do anything to me. He might beat up this defenceless woman though, or worse, a child. She'd have to be cautious. 'Say nothing to him yet.'

'No-o. Thanks for the tea. Did me good.'

'See you then. I'll talk too to my husband if I may. He might have some good advice.' And she could guess what it would be.

'Sure.'

Janey it's nearly lunchtime. Never mind, you can get out of trouble with the pressure-cooker. Poor old Norma had to bus all the way back to Hautepierre. Three children staving off pangs with bread and jam. But you won't help the woman just by being sorry for her, you know.

Arthur listened with patience.

'You want no advice, and I'm not giving you any. It's one

55

for the welfare worker, but she speaks no English and you do. Poor cow's helpless, quite. So what's the obvious? Don't just help them, that's no use; back next day for more. But give them some leverage to help themselves, sure. Your question has to be, are you biting off more than she can chew? Or you'd be laying up a heap of grief for her.'

'That's what I thought. Want some fromahdge?'

'You buy this Brie? Hacked out of the limestone is all I can say.'

'Yes sorry, it's supermarket.'

Arthur grumbled, but he did give a hand with the washing up. Things are wrong somehow, she thought.

10. 'The Meinau Marie-Line'

For the brave bourgeoisie of the city Hautepierre exists by hearsay: one would never think of setting foot there. If not actually a waste inhabited by dragons it is terra incognita: one is uncertain even of how to get there, assuming one wanted to try. It exists: that's enough. The Meinau is a different matter. People 'whom we know' live there. A little uneasily, a little apologetically now, but there's no quarter of Strasbourg now as it used to be. There's hardly anywhere one gets one's moneysworth nowadays. Everywhere is under siege.

If you were a student, whether of sociology, or urban psychology, or architecture, or simply the morals of provincial cities, and Arlette was all these things, the Meinau would be worth study: a residential suburb in South Strasbourg, classic in being ramshackle and piecemeal.

Before the war – ah, the good old days – land was cheap and building permits available for a bit of palm grease. There were none of these damned controls; socialism was for the poor and was called the French Section of the Workers Inter-

56

national. Laughable. An enterprising capitalist could do wonders, cut his coat generously. Buy up a farm, cut it into lots, plan a street grid, lay on a bit of electricity, and you were in a snug way of business. Equipment in the paving and sewage line was perfunctory, very, but that had never bothered anyone. In the Meinau, a rural part of the world along the main road to Colmar, there was an excellent precedent. Schulmeister, a Napoleonic adventurer who had flourished exceedingly selling dubious information to governments and cardboard boots to the army, had carved out a huge estate there, palace and park.

Houses in bad pretentious taste shot up and surrounded themselves with little trees and flowering bushes. All very nice. You were conveniently close to the town and to business, yet peacefully free of the hurlyburly: the old urban quarters along the Avenue des Vosges were getting alarmingly dirty and noisy. Even in the fifties the volume of motor traffic was becoming quite impossible: everybody said so. The Meinau, bordered by little serpentine waterways and rustic allotment gardens, was ideal: no roads led anywhere, and values kept going up: lovely.

It was in the sixties that alarming things began. There was a football stadium on waste ground just across the railway line to Germany: stadiums are low. Much worse, the municipality laid violent hands upon the Schulmeister estate and built controlled-rent blocks for the poor around the park and the 'Canardière' pond: decidedly low. The Route de Colmar became a vulgar brawl of congested traffic bordered by filling stations, all the way out to Illkirch: frightful. Last and worst, to relieve the traffic of heavy freight, seeking a way west out of Germany while avoiding the saturated city centre, the awful planners are driving new ring roads. The heavy articulated 'street trains' come galloping through the rustic orchards, stinking and squealing past one's own front door.

There are still a dozen placid, outwardly unwrinkled streets of desirable residences in the Meinau. But the noose is drawn tight: they are fighting asphyxiation.

One would sell, but values have flattened out. And it's the same everywhere; you have somewhere nice and the poor appear alongside you. Where do all the poor come from? Why can't the municipality, run after all by our friends, do better at hustling them off to weird places like Hautepierre with the Spanish and the Arabs? There are flesh-creeping tales of these blocks, of urine-stained elevators, ten-year-old gangsters and women raped in underground garages. Maddened invalid pensioners shooting from their prison windows with .22 rifles. The horde of greasy unisex hornets on motorbicycles.

Arlette was ironing Arthur's shirts, a complicated syllogism. Ironing is female servitude, right? But no civilized man wears synthetic shirts. While cotton shirts must be ironed. You can send them to the laundry, but this is not economical. Men iron, if at all, clumsily and incompetently.

Lamentable conclusion: if the men are not to be laughing-stocks the women iron the shirts. All wrong.

She was curious about Marie-Line. A bourgeois offspring from the Meinau. The sociopathic conditions seemed to Arlette just as menacing as those of the noisy smelly barracks of Neuhof or the Elsau. She knew these houses only from the outside; she was guessing.

A solid core of solid ugly villas, divided into two, maybe three flats now there are no servants any more. Polished bellpushes and clipped hedges. Veneer drinks' cupboards and real leather sofas. Italian-tiled bathrooms and matched-unit kitchens. Basement garages shielding well-washed and waxed cars.

These people have arrived. They are by God going to stay arrived. They will fight tooth and nail to ensure that their children do not lose class, face, standing. The marxist cliché is that capitalism is on its last legs. Maybe; tough ol' legs though. Marching about chanting slogans produces tight-lipped grins behind the lace curtains, while the money flees quietly to Switzerland. The bourgeois are well fortified against riots by the ruck. What they fear most is the creeping attack from treachery within. Today's anarchists are rarely tubercular orphans in damp cellars. Most are expensively educated well-brought-up adolescents in rude health. The old-style Marie-Lines came from physical slums: the new ones from moral slums.

Well after two o'clock. Damn this tiresome child. Arlette thumped crossly with the iron. A lovely day outside. Mid-autumn was best of all. When the mists lift – there are rather too many river-valleys in the Strasbourg area – the sherry-coloured light is full of mellow fruitfulness. Keats' truism is altogether too bland and feeble for the grape harvest in Central Europe, for the splendid cocktail of acrid invigorating smells. Who'd be indoors?

The buzzer went.

Marie-Line was still a child; thin bony fingers; flat boy's behind. The features well formed, the voice poised, the move-ments graceful. Almost, not quite, an adult.

It took no skill to see she was in a nervous state. Bit fiercely at her fingers, smoked greedily, fidgeted with her feet. As tall as herself and well nourished. Golden corn hair, pale face made paler by too much whitish make-up but set off nicely by a black sweater and a violet scarf. Very pretty face. Might coarsen and thicken disconcertingly soon, even without beer and fried potatoes. Marvellous classic nose, thought Arlette, her own twitching: that wasn't beer. Child has been at the whisky bottle.

She'd looked around, coming in, with a knowing air at the newness and selfconscious rawness of the place. 'Interviewing' people at a desk takes practice: Arlette didn't have it yet. The girl seemed to know that. She'd taken a cigarette out of the box without being asked, and picked languidly at a punished finger. One can look very world-weary at eighteen.

'I'm Marie-Line Siegel,' she'd said coming in. 'Sorry about being a bit late.' Irritated at having been uncontrolled and vulnerable on the phone.

'D'you need that thing on?' stabbing a finger at the tape recorder.

'Not if you prefer it off,' said Arlette.

'I don't mind. Irritating that's all; thing going round. But what's the use of coming at all, unless I'm prepared to trust you? I don't know you. But one must trust somebody.'

'What made you decide to trust me?'

'I don't know. You're a woman, I suppose. Not that that . . . skip it. Are there woman detectives; I mean are there many?'

'I have no idea.'

'Then what – oh well, let's not quibble.'

'Let's come to the point.'

'You're so right. Anyhow, my father's Doctor Armand Siegel.'

'What sort of doctor?'

'Dentist. Lots and lots of sophisticated equipment. Great big panoramic radiograph. Squads of assistants and nurses, eligible females. Boy, do you appreciate it when the bill comes in, typed in a beautiful huge IBM typeface. Sorry; gassing rather. Sorry too, bit uptight about my father on the whole.'

'And your mother?'

'Is, better said was, Véronique Ulrich; that's another great doctor dynasty. She was a disgrace though; ran away. I kept on being told how wicked and ungrateful. I don't see her, so don't know how wicked she is. Average, I suppose. Leaves me alone; that was part of the bargain.'

'Divorce bargain?'

'No, you don't know my family; they don't divorce. Too Christian and forgiving and suffering. Divorce is shocking. Be a sight better if they did. Then he could marry his exceedingly respectable mistress, Catherine-Rose Pelletier, who's in the cabinet of the Prefect, a career woman you see, pure and single-minded.'

'You sound a bit uptight about her too.'

'Cathy's all right. Makes rather a fuss about being cultural; Bach and stuff. But she doesn't pretend she's my new mummy. Quite cool and detached. Loathes me, I dare say, but too Christian to allow that. All these people are very honourable, but they're to piss on, you know.'

60

'Why?'

The abruptness made the girl give a short uneasy laugh, turned adroitly into airy.

'You're right, I'm being unfair. And talking too much. And sounding sorry for myself?'

'Be as sorry for yourself as you like if you deserve it.'

'Just that this is all very hupperclawss Strasbourg. Very right wing. You very right wing?

'You mean do I vote for all those people calling themselves Republicans? No. Will I show you credentials? No. Take me as you find me.'

The girl laughed with less tension.

'Good. Sorry. You know, that's how one gets corrupted. They want to know who you are, meaning where you fit in, meaning how they'll behave. Wouldn't do to upstage somebody who might have a brother-in-law in Paris, knowing people.'

'I don't. But where do you fit in?'

'I like you,' with a real laugh. Big compliment.

'Great.'

'Oh, I'm still at school, in the last class, terminal A you know, philo and languages. Should be in C, where the bright ones are supposed to be, doing maths, if I'd been willing to do medicine. It wouldn't have been looked at askance, if you get me. Biology or something, that's suitable enough for a woman; they'd have admitted that. I wouldn't be seen dead with it, and maths bores me silly. Or I could have done B. Economic sciences you know, like Cathy. Frankly, they're the dropouts from both C and A. D of course is unspeakable; that's all the commercial ones who're going to make money.' One knew more now about Marie-Line, as well as about the school selection system.

'They all want to make money. Normal in the circumstances.'

'Yes, but these think of nothing but marketing and the cash flow. The one true religion. Yes, I'm crude; I hear nothing

61

else all day. So you do a philo baccalaureat in A, and where are you?'

'You're in the Law Faculty,' said Arlette as though it were not rhetorical. 'Or you're in the big troop of Arts, an apprentice school teacher. Or you do the phony ones like Sociology or Psychology, and read Marx only nobody does, and Freud which everyone does, alas.'

'You know about it then.'

'Did it myself. You thought mostly then about getting a man.'

'We've come some way since then,' with the tolerant contempt of eighteen for fifty. 'The men can't afford to get married, to let themselves get crippled and distracted by some passive sofa cushion. There are the cheap lays, and of course the gang of nymphos and lezzies, but if you've brains you don't sit all obsessed with sex.'

Arlette was wondering where the point was and when would they reach it. Be patient. You got confidences, the greatest banalities, told you solemnly like the Dead Sea Scrolls had got deciphered, and you must not yawn. She'll get there. It's what, after all, she's come here for. I have to pass a test first, that I'm not sex-obsessed.

'I know a boy,' said Marie-Line abruptly, 'in the lycée. Doing Greek; slightly weird but he's interested in prehistory. He doesn't have it easy. He's from a poor family, they're not educated a bit, and while they're nice, and one respects them, they're pretty dense and kind of null. So he depends on me quite a lot. And I depend on him. It isn't jam and roses, this narrow sterilized background in a provincial flea-dump like Strasbourg.

'And we're economically dependent. I'd like to get a job only there's nothing I know. What's the use of that university anyway? Anyhow I'm up against it. I do what the daddy wants, which is get a right-honourable Bac and be a good girl, meaning cut Michel out of existence, or Dad and Uncle Freddy Ulrich will Take Steps.'

'What sort of steps?'

'Shut me up in some psychiatric clinic,' quietly.

11. 'Realities'

The quiet voice that is kept for bad news: 'it seems the tests
show a fairly massive cancer.' Arlette was startled.

'Really? Said openly as a threat?' She'd heard of it: there'd
been a notorious case a few years back. Arbitrary Sequestration, the Penal Code calls it. But if done in the family, carefully and legally, it was not easy to combat. She'd have to look
up the jurisprudence; there was a notorious hole in the legal
procedures for a declaration of insanity. Or was this girl
trying to make herself interesting?

'Made openly to me? Yes. I didn't pick it up listening at the
door.'

'Well . . . help you ask; help you shall get. I don't know
what yet, nor how. I must have time to think. Intervening
clumsily would make things worse. How urgent – immediate –
is all this?' The girl looked at her with a sour smile, as though
able to see a certain acid humour in it all.

'Not all that immediate. The threat's supposed to be
enough. Quite a comprehensive threat. Enough for me. I'm
frightened by it,' bleakly.

'Yes.'

One no longer cut disobedient children off with a penny:
they told you where to stuff your penny.

'Does anybody else know about this threat?'

'Michel you mean? I haven't told him – he'd do something
wild. How would it help him, being saddled with thinking it
was his fault? I tell you. Who else would I tell – doctors?'
with contempt. 'Priests maybe?' She looked at Arlette. 'You
don't believe me.'

'Don't be silly. That's not the point. It sounds like a legal
problem. Like pleading rape: you must know it's notoriously
difficult to plead rape. Who was there, who's to say you
weren't the willing partner they claim?'

Vistas were opening, and happening too fast. If a medical opinion said one was neurotic and in need of psychiatric care – to contradict that, did one have to apply to a tribunal for an independent expert?

'Like if you're raped you get a specialist lawyer, who knows the loopholes.'

'You'd sure as hell get no lawyer here to touch this. Who's to pay it anyhow? I don't even know how to pay you. I've plenty in the savings bank, but I can't touch it.'

'You don't have to worry about that yet. You – we – must gain some time. You must be meek for a few days. You can reach me here. But I must have somewhere to reach you, to leave a note or a message.'

'*Mauricette* – the pub in the Boulevard de la Victoire: we go there. Just write Marie-Line on the envelope.'

'That'll do nicely.'

'I've been here too long,' looking at her watch. Good watch, real gold. First Communion present in a bourgeois family. Pass your exam and you can have a motorbike.

'Whatever you told me here is in confidence; you can rely on that. Have I your permission to ask my husband's advice?'

'He's that professor of sociology isn't he? – whose name's on the door? Sociologists! – taking bribes from the government to say yes, that's a good place for an autoroute.' Must remember this adolescent definition – Arthur would like this!

'You've only my word that he doesn't. But I take yours.'

'All right,' with a sudden smile, unexpectedly sweet.

Hm, thought Arlette. Not though about to suspect herself of getting sentimental about young girls and their problems.

This was serious. Young girls and their problems couldn't be taken frivolously, either. One couldn't interfere irresponsibly. She'd have to talk to the parents – to this father – and that would not be easy. He would regard it as interference by a stranger in a family matter. And the girl would regard her confidence as betrayed. One false step and . . .

What did she know, what qualification had she? Neither

64

legal nor medical. You've been a cop's wife but what do you know about something of this sort? The fundamental vagueness and fatal ambiguity of the idea still troubled her. She wasn't a shelter for battered wives, despite Norma. Nor a citizens' advice bureau. Nor, heaven help us, a 'detective agency' . . .

'You'll learn what you are, by experience,' Arthur had said. 'You're all these things. Sometimes you can't do as well as they could, and you send people on to the competent authority. But sometimes you can do a lot better. Because you're just one person, and you bring individual effort and understanding, and that's what people want.'

Norma – yes. She could only give the same advice, and maybe help in filling out forms, as the Social Worker. But she could talk English and give a cup of tea. And that really was what Norma needed.

But Marie-Line . . . She could look up the legal texts, but had no experience in their interpretation nor skill in preparing an argument. As for a medical opinion on a neurosis . . . Surely anybody with common sense could see that the child was a problem, and under stress. At this age they always are a problem. The broken family pattern accounted for the rest. The girl just wasn't getting enough affection. Call it a neurosis if you like. But to suggest that a psychiatric clinic would be any good, however skilled and sympathetic, is bullshit.

Look, you know nothing about medicine. You're fifty years old: you've brought up three children. There is in fact little you don't know.

Is it enough? You have never, for example, had to face violence. Secondhand, oh yes, plenty. But you were always sheltered and protected. You followed the rules.

Rules exactly as in childhood, about talking to strangers or opening the door to people you don't know. Rules of schoolgirlhood, of student days. What does it amount to? The Metro is a place where you get your bottom pinched . . . Dirty old men can be all ages: quite normal people can get neurotic about female flesh: oh, quite . . . Don't get drunk and don't get isolated: keep visible and invisible means of support; oh yes, quite ...

Realities were harsher things.

She'd had to appreciate the wisdom of her police commissaire. She'd been sent on to Corinne, an inspector in the street patrol brigade, a tired and overworked woman, but solid, simple, quiet about it all. They got on well.

'It's quite pathetic,' said Corinne. 'This July there were four of us passed out as potential commissaires. Get put in charge no doubt of some Lost Dogs Home in the department of the Doubs. As of the first of January this year you know how many of us there were in the whole of France? Women I mean with inspector's rank? Three hundred and thirty-two. As with everything else – thirty years behind the times. You look at Denmark or Norway. Here they expect us to be something like on television, superb blondes with marble tits when your blouse gets ripped in the heat of battle. The realities ...

'Old Joe send you down to learn something about that unarmed combat crap? Oh well ... if you've finished your coffee, we've a gym at the back here.'

Square and sturdy in a track suit, Corinne threw mats around in the male atmosphere of socks and stale sweat.

'Lesson number one, invariably I'm afraid, is not getting raped. So I'll start raping you shall I? – Sorry; not much fun for either of us.'

'I'd like to meet, frankly, the man who's going to rape me,' said Arlette as she generally did: wasn't this all a bit of a nonsense?

'I'm afraid you might,' said Corinne unsmiling. 'I said the same. Healthy strong determined woman, kick his crutch in, claw his eye. Oh yeah. Look,' producing a horrible knuckleduster, 'this is now a man's fist. Sorry, but I hit you straight in the face with it and you're a gone goose. They don't stop to worry about your looks. I beg your pardon but interested only in this,' slapping her pelvis, 'while you're semi-conscious with a crushed jaw and cheekbone. Look, I'm starting with the very worst. But there was an English policewoman, I can tell

66

you she was no softy, went out as bait for a violent one – and went the same way as the others. He bashed her, strangled her, fucked her: one, two, three. If you don't like this, now's the time to say.'

'You've been told, haven't you, to show me I'm just a wet amateur,' said Arlette softly.

'By who – old Joe? No. He said you'd sense enough not to get into trouble, but to show you what could happen if you did.'

'I can get hit by a drunk in a car, even on my own side of the road doing twenty.'

'That's right, that's the professional way. Take the obvious, reasonable precautions first. Don't have long hair, necklaces, pendants on chains, ear-rings. But there it is. The best protection, frankly, is to have a man. Yes. I know, I know. But inevitably. Look, in a Latin country, and that's Paris or even Strasbourg, a woman without a man is public property. It's a whore or it's rapable. Once alone, in the street or the café or the train, she's regarded as belonging to anyone who takes a fancy. This attitude is one of the most primitive there is. We've barely scratched the surface. Woman is butcher's meat. I've got as far as educating the men in this office.'

'Now you are shocking me.'

'Believe me, I mean to. The women are as bad. How many rapes are there, really? We don't know. We guess that one in ten gets reported.'

'Go on,' said Arlette woodenly. 'I don't intend to be the one or the other nine.'

'That's the stuff. Right, we tend to say that nine of Them are just frightened little flashers. True, but a hard core is bulls. And they can all be physically strong. You're tall, and you've muscles, but you must learn this: you just haven't the strength.

'You know it, the one place where the biggest stud is vulnerable is his balls. So try to learn to go with it: don't fight. At all costs avoid his hitting you, breaking you. So frankly, try and make it look you're longing for it. Because that's what they want to believe so you must give them the illusion. Never

67

mind the shrink stuff about how timid they really are; that doesn't help you with your pants down.

'Set your teeth. Now: my hands are busy on you; where are your hands – make like you want to help me, get my trousers off. Don't worry; I'm hetero as hell. Talk, do a patter, heave about and wail like you're in a porno movie, darling I love it.

'Sorry, Arlette. I know this is hideous. But the thing is worse, you see. I've talked to certainly thirty women in two years who've been through it.

'Better ... We'll take a minute's rest now. Want a fag? We've done the worst. If you've a gun of course and your hands aren't pinned, then you're super-penis, but if you've dropped it, forgot it, can't get to it ... all right? – ready, again? Now if you're grabbed from the back.'

Realities. The world was very evil.

Monsieur Dupont hadn't sounded like a rapist on the phone. But, said Corinne, 'You're a woman. Take nothing for granted, anywhere.' There are violent emotions in the world. People did violent things, for violent hidden reasons. You don't grasp it, until you go out and learn professional attitudes.

'Quite right,' Arthur had said when told about life with Corinne. 'No sentimental attitudes about you; I approve most thoroughly of Corinne. 'In fact, in his dryest voice, 'quoting textually the interesting memoirs of Albert Pierrepoint the Home Office Hangman, I never knew what jealousy meant, until I became an Executioner. Even at that job you got sabotaged by the professional colleagues.'

'I'll remember that,' Arlette had said.

She was silent that evening, and the music she chose, to listen to, a long and to Arthur slightly trying piece by Mahler. He made no comments. It might be in the nature of a requiem for Mr van der Valk, whom he had not known, but understood, he thought, and fairly well. For whom he felt respect: a cop; not always a polished personality but neither oaf nor ruffian. He suspected that it was still more a requiem for the widow van der Valk, and was careful not to fidget.

She was remembering the Vosges countryside, and the toy-like white Citroën, and Ruth as a young teenager. The flat in The Hague, always rather dark, and seeming cramped whatever she tried. And the road to Scheveningen, where Piet had died on the pavement. Her 'dottiness': everyone who knew her agreed that she had been slightly psychotic throughout the entire wretched episode. 'Arlette's gone mataglap' as the thoroughly frightened Ruth told a friend. True: she remembered little of what had happened. There are mechanisms of mercy that obliterate such from the memory.

A peculiarly nasty person, whom she couldn't see, never had seen as a person. She could not remember his face, nor anything human about him: he had aroused in her an intense uncontrollable violence. She had done things she had not known were in her. And it had been a wretched creature, mean-minded and sadistic, eaten by vanity, incapable of anything himself, who had manipulated a harmless immature boy.

She had been driven by what she had seen as the apathy and cynicism of the police. Rushed to Amsterdam, done all those things she could not recall, did not wish to. Violence . . .

Arlette the Avenger; the Detective . . . no, and no: she'd never again risk travelling that road.

She looked across the room; her handbag, with a pistol in it. She'd accepted it. A symbol that she was no longer the Widow; she'd broken once and for all with the old life; not only in justice to Arthur, who deserved better than a palimpsest. She'd chosen a new road, set her feet upon it; had no intention of withdrawing. The pistol was a tool, like the waiting-room, like the recording gadget on the phone. But no violence: she'd leave that to policewomen. And any more of Arthur's jokes, about Marlowe or the Thin Man's Wife, would get snubbed.

The 'agency' existed, and for a purpose. It exists in the first place, she thought suddenly, to get rid of the Widow. A woman I have lived with for long enough. I am shaped, informed, ripened by my past, but it's not going to get up on my back and ride me around. Piet's legs, heavy-muscled, too hairy, wound round my neck strangling me . . . thanks.

There was a small snort that might have been a snigger, so that Arthur glanced up for a second: the woman had a grin upon her face that seemed to have little to do with Mahler.

This woman . . . whose body is again being used. Very nice too. Disagreeable to have been reminded how many men perceived nothing but a brutish sex-object. It will be painful no doubt. The Widow got puritanical about Flypaper Sex, and was forever washing the stickiness off her hands. Not fair to Arthur, who is so extremely unselfish. The woman Corinne had reminded her brutally that this body, stupid forked carrot, was a thing people got boringly obsessed with: better remember it.

The slow movement came to an abrupt end: she got up with a jolt to turn the record.

12. Monsieur Dupont's Café Confidences

Arlette stood outside the church of Saint Maurice, in silent converse with a bad statue of Jeanne d'Arc on a horse. Not a bad patron saint for liberated women. It was rush hour: the Avenue de la Forêt Noire was full of noise and a bad smell. Even if seven months' pregnant in an orange raincoat and pushing a large shocking-pink pram, do not attempt crossing the road. In fact especially not then, and especially not at a pedestrian crossing. Even under the particular protection of Jeanne d'Arc. A Strasbourgeois in a car is a Hun: rather fond of raw meat under his saddle.

Just then a woman with a pram did cross the road, sailing head high, indifferent to stalled fuming automobiles and a chorus of klaxons. She even made an overweight pig of a Mercedes back up. Ah well, she was young and pretty. No gesture of thanks to the driver, grinning all galant'uomo out of his prison window at her. Arlette, entertained, missed M. Dupont's arrival.

'Madame is it, or Mademoiselle?'

'Madame if it's of importance.' Efforts have been made to struggle with Mzz in French. Little velours hat: he noticed her staring at it and lifted it.

'Err, my car is parked. You've no objection to err, some café?' There was a tolerably dismal specimen of bistrot down the side street. *Aux Merlets de Lorraine.*

'What will you drink? Waiter, a quarter Perrier and err, I'll have a whisky.' Not a beer man or a pastis man. Petty-bourgeois-man drinks whisky even if he loathes the taste: a Correct drink.

'You smoke?' Packet of Camels, another affectation. Well-built enough. Shoulders a bit round, when he took his coat off. Tallish, quite a good head, brown hair, nice blue eyes when he made his mind up to take off the sunglasses. He rummaged in the pockets of a business suit for a lighter. Completely normal looking. A small tic puckered the bridge of his nose and between the eyes, giving him a moment's puzzled glare every few seconds, but it was nothing disturbing.

'D'you mind telling me your real name?'

'Demazis, Albert Demazis, it doesn't matter. Look, I'll give you a card; I take you into my confidence, but disregard these addresses and numbers will you? I'd rather you didn't contact me at home either.' He had to recover male superiority. 'This must remain confidential.'

'You have my word. If that wasn't good I wouldn't be in business.'

'And how long have you been in this uh, business?'

'I was a police officer's wife, Monsieur Demazis, for twenty years.'

'Oh. Um – that's no longer so?'

'He died. I settled here. I remarried. Liberal profession.' Always let them know you've a man, as Corinne recommended. And as Arthur said dryly, always say liberal profession, there's

71

nothing the French respect more. Top of the earnings' ladder. Say a professor, and sociology at that, they start looking for the holes in your socks.

'I see. I beg your pardon.' She seemed established as bona fide, though even if reassured Monsieur Demazis was not at ease. Smoking in a greedy way, putting the cigarette in the centre of a fleshy mouth and sucking hard, getting the most out of each puff; fidgeting with his glass. And the eyes roamed. What was this idiot Dupont act anyhow? What harm could it do to say your name?

The café was peaceful enough. A couple of groups of students guffawing round cups of cold coffee; two or three old men ritually enjoying their usuals: a workman or two having a quick one at the bar and prolonging it with gossip. The patronne languidly rubbing at chrome on the coffee machine and the boy, probably her son, gazing vacantly. All present looked innocent: any KBG men were well under cover.

'Now what about fees?' businesslike. A piece of patter she had not yet practised.

'You haven't told me what you want. I made it clear, I think, that this costs you nothing. Thereafter the same rate as any specialist consultation. I do nothing financial, so no percentage. If it's something needing research or enquiry we can agree a daily rate. The usual expenses, travel or whatever.'

'That's um, reasonable,' stubbing his cigarette and taking at once a fresh one. 'Waiter – same again. This . . . is difficult, very delicate. Concerns too my wife . . .'

'You realize I'm not a lawyer? If you want to stop a divorce I might be able to help. If you're looking for one, I'd suggest the usual enquiry bureau.'

'No, no – nothing like that.'

'You must give me something to go on, you know.' The waiter brought his drink and looked at Arlette, who shook her head.

'I'm being menaced,' he said abruptly. 'I've reason to believe my life's in danger.' Oh dear. One of those. She felt let down. Wasting her time, here. Still, one must play fair.

72

'Why?'

'I've had messages,' unwillingly. 'Nothing written that would leave a trace. Peculiar telephone calls.'

'Anybody you know?'

'Perfect strangers. I don't like it at all.'

'You mentioned your wife – how is she concerned?'

'She's been acting oddly – saying funny things.'

'Are you on a course of treatment for any illness?'

'What? You mean pills or something?'

'Some chemicals set up funny reactions.'

'You mean I'm having hallucinations? Ridiculous. You're no help to me if you don't believe me.'

'One must eliminate the obvious. No health problems?'

'Like anybody else. I've a sensitive throat liable to infection.' The implication hit him. 'You're not suggesting I've some psychiatric trouble?' not pleased at all.

'How should I know? It could be a commonplace thing. Depression symptom; too much work – over-fatigue.'

'I'm well on top of my work. I'd go to a doctor if it was as you suggest.' Irritably. 'Don't let's be absurd.'

'With that out of the way, how long have you had this sensation?'

'A week or two – three. I didn't take it seriously at first: someone with ideas of being funny. Or with a grudge, and neurotic about that. Disgruntled employee.'

'But you can't ascribe it to anything definite?'

'Explain yourself.'

'If you become irritated each time, Monsieur Demazis, we can't make progress. I'm in the dark; I seek light where I can find it. You've nothing on your conscience? – knowledge of or even involvement in something you'd rather stayed concealed? Just to take an instance, that you'd rather not take to the police?'

'Of course not. What good would the police be? They'd just laugh. Who trusts them anyhow? Come bursting into the office, asking when my books were last audited. No discretion.

73

Why d'you think I come to you? After, be it said, much hesitation. You're an enquiry agent aren't you?'

'Not in the ordinary sense. Would that be more use?'

'No. Extortionists: every pretext for wanting more money. Like lawyers; wring a thousand francs out of you and then sit on their hands. Nosy too. Credit status – every sort of backstairs manoeuvre.'

'You're not being asked for money?'

'No,' with a snap.

'Some nosiness is inevitable,' she said mildly. 'I've experience enough of police work,' boldly mendacious, 'and whoever you ask for help has to ask some personal questions. Is it going to be me?'

'I have to confide in somebody,' staring down into his glass and remembering it, drinking it off, wanting a third but deciding it might make him too loose of tongue besides not looking well. 'I can't see clearly around this. It's worrying me; it upsets my life all round. Even my wife . . .'

'You don't trust her?'

'A fortnight ago I'd have said yes. That's just the point.'

'Do you gamble at all?' He smiled bleakly. Still, it was a smile.

'With my employers' funds you mean? No. A lotto ticket now and again just for amusement.'

'Extra-marital entanglement?'

'No,' flushing.

'Forget I'm a woman. Political activities? Membership of a group perhaps with some political motivation.'

'No.'

'Well . . . lastly then for now. Do you possess confidential information – like at work? Something that could interest a commercial rival?'

'I'm an accountant. Figures are confidential of course. But nothing there could justify a threat of some sort.'

'Yes. I'll want to know more about the threats, and their nature. But not here. Well then, Monsieur Demazis, as far as

74

we've gone, do you want me to go further? I'd have to ask a lot of things, and do I inspire your confidence?'

'As far as I've gone . . . Seems to me I've small choice in the matter.'

'I'd give you what advice I could. And tell you frankly whether I saw any chance of helping.'

'Yes. That's quite fair, I suppose. I suppose I'm a secretive person, by training and inclination, and this isn't easy.'

'Would you like to come to my office? Now, even? Or would you prefer to think things over?'

He frowned and looked at his watch.

'I've thought things over. But no, that's impossible now. Euh, I don't want to arouse curiosity about my movements. Tomorrow it could be arranged. Five-thirty say, or a little after. I know where you live. That all right?'

'I'd ask you to sign a simple form of agreement, stating that I'm working on your behalf. You'd pay me a sum – nothing like a thousand. Three hundred say, covering a few hours of work. You'd get a detailed note of my activities: my agreement is that I respect your confidences entirely, divulging nothing to anyone without your express permission, saving discovery of a legal obligation.'

'What's that mean?' with the angry, puzzled twitch.

'Look, if I see someone with appendicitis I might recommend more or less urgently that he have his stomach looked at. But if I acquire knowledge of say a criminal act I can't conceal that without sharing in the guilt. Suppose you have knowledge of such, maybe something that hasn't taken place but might. I'm not suggesting that. But either you'd have to conceal it from me or accept that I'd take it further.'

'I want to think this over,' said Demazis. 'But it's all right; I mean the money side and the form.'

'I have to have an authorization,' she said, wondering whether she was being melodramatic and making a silly fuss. But Arthur had told her to be careful. 'Outside the police there's no proper code for enquiries. Anybody can call himself a detective. I don't. Those who do, you'll find, ask for all sorts of safeguards.'

'I suppose so. I've no real experience of the situation.'

'I have,' firmly. 'Till tomorrow then?'

'It's agreed,' said Demazis making up his mind, getting up heavily and putting his jaunty little hat on. 'I'll settle up. I'll see you then. Goodnight.'

'Goodnight.'

Arlette stayed a moment. Nobody was taking interest in her and her activities. Their voices had been low, and thoroughly covered by background music playing from a jukebox: the students were laughing loudly. She had a notebook in her bag.

"Monsieur Demazis is in a nervous state of high tension, and certainly seems uneasy or frightened about something he'd like to shuffle off – a need to confide in somebody. He's not quite sure himself, perhaps, whether this is something criminal or not? He doesn't trust his wife: feels obliged to account to her for his time?

"What's he trying to rope me into?"

She went home. It had begun to rain outside, but she had not far to go.

13. 'Mise au point'

Arthur, wearing her apron, was cooking; looking pleased with himself.

'Ho. There you are. Moist and delicious: nothing like a bit of rain to improve a woman. You may talk but not interrupt; this is going to be delectable.' Only a half chicken that she had taken out of the freezer that afternoon, but she'd hoped it would stimulate his imagination.

'I'm in business,' said Arlette grinning. 'Three all at once.'

'So? Tell all.'

'How fine you manage to chop those onions.' Having got the men into the kitchen, butter them up lavishly.

'A question of having the knife sharp, which women never do. Now don't stand there with your hands in your pockets: make the salad.'

'Monsieur Dupont he called himself. It'll do to go on with. I don't have the right to say much about him. As a case marked X...'

'Lemon juice please, not vinegar.'

'... so either he's pretty kinky or it's an elaborate trap one can't see the bottom of. Hardly for me; nobody knows me. So for whom? Why all the melodrama? Is your rice ready? – I'm starving.'

'Your sense of mystery makes it rather elliptical and tiresome. A whole category of scary stories written by women. Shudders and shrieks in the shuttered house. The species was described by Jacques Barzun as "Everything is Rather Frightening".'

'What's in this? Tomato and sherry I can recognize. Oh I see; grated orange peel, that's very snazzy. The nervous trick of glancing about doesn't mean he was frightened. I mean it's commonplace. But he was frightened.'

'A mythomaniac. You'd be well advised to leave it alone.'

'What, my first day? No, no more rice; I mustn't stuff. A myth for whose benefit? It might be police business; I made rather a fuss of warning him but he didn't blink. I said come to the office and cough it all up. If he doesn't then it's myth. Now these other two girls I'd like your opinion on.'

'Norma's the classic lame dog and as I told you this morning, helping over stiles is one thing, collecting lame dogs and getting saddled with them – that's rather an unhappy metaphor.' But he was pleased with Marie-Line.

'If you have a tame doctor, and of course he has plenty, nothing's easier. It wasn't the Russians who invented using the psychiatric clinic as a means of repression. I rather think we owe that one to Napoleon's fertile invention.'

77

'Can you think of anything more wicked? You need no brainwashing. You're refusing a young girl control over her own body. It's a rape.'

'There I'm with you –' Arthur pulled up crossly. 'Manipulating young girls is indeed wicked.'

'We'll do the washing-up first,' said Arlette firmly.

'Exactly like porn photos: now open your legs dear, so Joe can get a good shot at your pussy. They do it, silly little things. But it's a rape. They are profoundly humiliated and wounded even while telling themselves it's of no consequence. And some shrinks sit there canting that porn is good for you.'

'Male shrinks,' bored at this labouring of the obvious.

'You've only her word for it all though. Beware of these young girls – fearful little actresses.'

'Of course. I have to make some contact with the parents. If I go to Hautepierre tomorrow I'll make a detour, spy out the land a bit.'

'Ah yes,' said Arthur sentimentally. 'Phil Marlowe the shop-soiled Galahad goes out tomorrow calling on General Sternwood. That marvellous house with the stained-glass window: the lady with no clothes on bound to the tree.'

'In Hautepierre?'.

'Yes, well who knows? Norma, I agree, bears no great resemblance to General Sternwood, but the Meinau is sinister. You might well find yourself among the pornographers on Laurel Canyon Drive. As long as Marie-Line doesn't start behaving like Carmen Sternwood, biting her thumb and looking coy.'

'Intensely funny,' she said, getting cross. 'Stop it.'

I'm at a crossroads, thought Arlette sleepily. She hitched her quilt to make herself comfortable.

'You're creating a draught,' muttered Arthur. Men ... turning round and round, like a dog ...

If I can make some sense out of these three people, then I shall be able to ... what? I don't quite know yet: not just sociology. Be fair to Arthur. He's trying to make sense of it all too. The whole structure of our civilization is on its last

78

legs. Law, ethics; meaningless phrases. Professionals, clacking away about methodology. Helpless, and too stupid to know it. More and more techniques, complications, sophisticated tools. Simplify, simplify . . .

She was asleep.

Arthur brought her a cup of coffee in bed. Ignominiously, she fell asleep again over it, woke, rushed out in a panic. Arthur was gone to work. The cassette 'pocket memo' lay on the kitchen table.

'Coffee,' said Arthur's voice. 'And aluminium foil. It occurred to me, if you're going to Hautepierre, you might stop at the Italian grocer.' In the little Italian car, right. Sausage. Ham. Forty thousand types of sausage in Strasbourg and none that's eatable. Arthur was good at housekeeping. Remember Piet, very old-fashioned and male, not to say old-woman Dutch fusspot. Couldn't scramble an egg, but fond now and then of 'pulling the women up about their household accounts'. Meaning complaints about the quantities of lavatory paper used for jobs like wiping out the omelette pan. Do I have to type it all out in triplicate?

While Arthur would thread a needle and sew his buttons back on. Sighing, sucking the thread heavily, holding it all up to the light to get it through the blasted loop. He took his glasses off for this job; she put hers on. Otherwise there was not much difference.

That wash-basin takes a long time emptying: must be hair blocking it. If Arthur can thread a needle I can unscrew a siphon. Need big pincers and where are the big pincers? Not in the broom cupboard where they ought to be. She found them in the electricity cupboard and thought herself a good detective. Wrote down light bulbs, 75 watt, screw and bayonet. Left some instructions on the tape for the cleaning woman. Whip out smartish to the Italian grocer.

'Do you mean you leave your cleaning woman the KEYS!' marvelled a silly bourgeois woman. 'You'll get everything pinched.'

'There's nothing worth pinching,' said Arthur comfortably. They all worried so about burglars. Life was too short.

She walked as far as the Italian grocer. Not a hope of finding anywhere to park around here. The more roads they built the more they needed.

One could think, while cooking. Consommé is a long job. She got the bones out of the oven, drained the fat off, deglazed the pot and set it to simmer, turned the fan on to get rid of the smell of blackened onions, put in one clove and a quarter of a bay leaf. When it boiled she would turn the gas down, skim for ten minutes, add the onions and their skins, a carrot, a bit of celery, a few parsley stalks. Put the lid on and let it simmer till tonight. Tomorrow it would be cold; one would peel the fat off, strain the stock, and put it on again to clarify with minced beef and an eggwhite. Result, after another hour or so – consommé. If only her other jobs were that simple.

Norma was fixed, more or less. As long as she stuck to it, and really made a clean break. She'd made her own decision; Arlette hadn't made it for her.

No problem then, there. Albert Demazis . . . That was several different kinds of problem and one had no idea what, nor how many. She didn't intend to let it bother her. Whatever loony notion he'd had in his mind ringing her up, going through all the rigmarole, and then going back on it all – she probably would never set eyes on him again, and if she did she'd be rather cold and curt. The mystifications are not appreciated, and I'm not interested in the money either.

Marie-Line. Had worked herself up into a great stew, and quite likely that pop-eyed Françoise, enjoying all this rather, was making the most of it. A dose of cold water was needed, and perhaps a dose of castor oil too. She'd go see the parents. This evening; better waste no more time.

The pot with the bones, Arthur's chicken carcase, some odds and ends found in the fridge had quietened to a gentle simmer, and so had she. Dinner was going to be simple; she'd bought big bicycle-tyre macaronis from the Italian shop, as well as ham that was not soaked in water to make it weigh heavier . . .

She went into the office, peaceful with the light beginning to fade and the big seascape looking kindly at her, its smoky blues getting deeper and smokier as the afternoon wore on. There was nothing on her tape.

Two days of work and it seemed to have frittered away again into the incoherent nonsenses that had been on the tape for a week. Nothing to show. No penny either. But no, she was not in the least discouraged. This was the way it went. You sat in the office. If anybody came it would be small and unimportant people with small unimportant stories. Like Norma. But that was exactly what she was here for.

14. A Slightly Unwished-for Houseguest

There was a tremendous peal at the front-door buzzer, startling in the hermitage atmosphere of meditation. It could only be a telegraph boy or the gas-meter man. An unnecessary double ring at her own door confirmed this: she pressed the release and prepared to be leisurely and reproving. Opening she found herself face to face with Marie-Line.

'Heavens.'

'What's the matter?'

'Nothing. You seem a bit windblown and stormtossed. Come on in then; I've nobody.'

'Thanks, no. Sorry to have troubled you.'

'Don't be absurd.'

'I can tell when I'm unwelcome.'

'My dear girl, I thought you were the gas man, pealing like that, so I'd put on a telling-off expression. I'd no idea it was you: didn't you get my note?'

81

'Yes, Françoise brought it round. That's why I came. If you were out I was going to wait *Chez Mauricette*.'

'Sit down then. But is this a good idea? – I thought you were supposed to stay put.'

'Everybody tells me to stay put. Till I can be shot in the arm and put in the car without protest. They're coming for me this evening. I thought of Germany and I thought of Switzerland, but there are so many cops with an eye out for terrorists I'd be asked for my papers at once, and I felt sure if I made for Paris they'd have notified the police before I got there. And hitch-hiking on one's own . . .'

'None of those things would have done at all. I'm glad you came to me. Though . . .' Arlette realized she was still standing. This wouldn't do: the 'office' atmosphere was wrong. 'Come on into the flat'. She looked at her watch; nearly half past five. 'There was a man coming but he rang to put it off.'

'Arlette – can I stay with you?'

'You could do with a drink, I think. Yes you can.' It was decidedly "I'm a big girl but I promise I don't take up much room in the bed". But what else could one answer? 'Do sit down and unwind.'

'I just want to pick up . . .' She scuttled out on to the landing and returned with a leather sack of sorts.

'Oh I see,' said Arlette a bit dry. 'I was just wondering whether my pyjamas would fit you.'

'I've nowhere to go,' apologetically. 'Michel or any of the boys – that would just be asking for trouble. Françoise or any other girl I know, their parents would be quacking down the telephone before you could say knife.'

'Nonsense. It's what I'm here for,' reflecting ruefully that yes, it was, and wondering in the same breath whether there was enough ham. Arthur would have to go without a second helping: we must all learn to make sacrifices. Be touchy, possibly, at being asked to cook again. But plainly there was no time to lose. She needed a drink herself; tinkling among the ice-cubes gave her time to think.

82

'What time does your father get home. And Cathy?'

'Cathy any time, unless she went on somewhere. Pa not till six-thirty counting rush hour. I see what you mean.'

'People don't go ringing up the police and stuff in that much of a hurry. But he's due for an explanation and he has to be given one. Above all we mustn't have you put further in the wrong. Don't worry, my husband will be here.'

At this moment indeed through the open living-room door a clatter of keys could be heard and an English voice upraised in melody.

'It's only me from over the sea.

Said Bollocky Bill the Sailor . . . oh, I beg your pardon.'

'Arthur this is Marie-Line Siegel: my husband Doctor Davidson. I mentioned her name, you might recall. She's in some trouble at home and is staying for supper and the night, okay?'

'Very much okay, by the look of things,' not too offensively flirtatious. 'Do you play chess? Splendid. Do these explanations have to be given to anyone else?'

'Well yes; I have to go and see Marie-Line's parents. I'll be back for supper if you'll very kindly cope.'

'Delighted as long as it doesn't involve chopping parsley which I admit bores me.'

'I can chop parsley,' said Marie-Line with a little too much vivacity. Really, thought Arlette, he's only exacting a small mild vengeance and watching to see do I get indignant and make some spiteful remark about four-handed piano playing.

'There's macaroni, and that nice Italian ham, and any sort of sauce you like except tomato. Smitane maybe, and there are endives ready. There's soup but it won't be ready till to-morrow; leave it ticking.'

'It shall be done,' said Arthur helping himself to ice-cubes.

She went into the bedroom to change. Passing back along the hallway she heard, 'I have the greatest possible dislike of parting with even the wretchedest of pawns, but what must be will at least leave me a scrap less constipated.' Right my lad: force her to concentrate.

Despite rush hour, she was in the Meinau before half past six. Either the Jaguar wasn't home yet, or put away already in the garage. No sign of the little Fiat. She wasn't going to hang about.

The gate clicked open to her ring; the porch light went on. She had a sensation of being examined on the step before the door opened and an elderly female in a white apron said, 'You want?' with abruptness and a strong Alsatian accent.

'Doctor Siegel, if he's home yet. My business is personal, you could say, and concerns his daughter.'

'This way.' The hall was an impression of solid mahogany and grandfather clocks. She was shown into a room chill with heating turned off, diamond-paned bookcases full of forbidding volumes and a stuffy atmosphere of the windows not having been opened that day. There was the sort of desk at which a man does cheques for the insurance, and old dark green curtains with a lot of cords and tassels. No time for more; a slight cough and she turned. Doctor Siegel in a brown suit and an air of cold rage. To show how controlled he was he shut the door quietly and advanced as far as the hearthrug, where he put his hands together behind his back, bowed slightly and said, 'I'm told you have some information as to the whereabouts of my daughter? I don't believe I've had the pleasure of meeting you before?'

'No. Madame van der Valk. Marie-Line's quite all right. She came to me in a nervous distraught state, so I asked her to stay to supper. I left her playing chess with my husband, which should have a calming effect,' smiling. 'I thought it right to come and see you instead of telephoning – less needless explaining to do.'

Doctor Siegel made another stiffish little bow but did not smile.

'That was kind of you – and your husband. I don't I'm afraid altogether understand: My daughter is a friend of yours?'

'She confided in me. Girls that age, with a lot on their chest – they want, and it's natural, to be able to talk to someone, not

84

necessarily family.' Arlette felt at once that it could have been worded better.

'I have not yet grasped,' his tone was quite polite, 'how you come to be – acquainted – with my daughter.' There was certainly no point in disguising it. Just the little flick of inexperience that hindered, however slightly, the smoothly worked form of wording.

'I run an advice bureau. Any member of the public is free to consult me. What is said is in confidence.'

'An advice bureau,' handling the word delicately, with little dentistry tweezers. But something corrupt, that if one got any closer would not smell very nice. 'I see,' putting it down on a glass table to be referred to in a minute. The probe: we'll just make sure there's no area of infection. 'Then I can take it that this uncontrolled spasm once calmed, you'll advise her to return home, promptly.'

'Is that wise, do you think, so soon? I think perhaps she might be given a day or so to get over the upset. It's only emotional but –'

'You'll allow me, perhaps, to be the judge of that.'

'You haven't asked me to sit down,' said Arlette amiably.

'I beg your pardon. There's a chair behind you.'

'There's a bit more to be said, isn't there.'

'May I ask just what my daughter has been telling you? I didn't, I'm afraid, realize that there was any call for discussion of this matter. I'm not sure I do now.'

'Doctor Siegel, I wished to say only that having been myself a doctor's wife for twenty years I've had a lot of people on my doorstep who needed or thought they needed medical care. I've some experience in the matter.'

He unbent slightly, as though in courtesy between members of the confraternity, but not that it removed the prickles.

'You'll excuse me. I thought I knew at least by name . . .'

'No: he practised in Holland.'

'But you're not yourself qualified? I feel justified in saying that within the family there are those who are, most adequately

85

as I can assure you. My relation, Doctor Frederic Ulrich, is – you might not be aware.'

'Marie-Line mentioned her uncle. I don't want you to think I'm in any way hostile. She feels in conflict with her family, and she has real or imagined terrors.'

Doctor Siegel gave this ten seconds' consideration, his eyes examining Arlette.

'Madame, I must thank you for your good offices, but I must tell you that I am the sole judge of what concerns my daughter, and also that I feel a distaste for discussing family affairs. To put you to no further trouble, I think I had better come and fetch her home.'

'Isn't that going back to square one, rather? She came to me and asked counsel: wasn't that sensible? Next time, she might do something sillier and more damaging.'

'Apparently I haven't made myself clear,' said Siegel from a lipless mouth. 'If you have encouraged this child in an attitude of direct disobedience I cannot congratulate you. It goes without saying that I permit no interference by well-meaning persons in my affairs.'

'I can't go the whole way with you on that; I'm sorry. The girl is vulnerable, and deserves consideration. I didn't come here to fight a battle, but to find common ground. Your hostility is misplaced.'

'There is no hostility. To speak plainly, I don't know what an "advice bureau" is. When the advice consists of abetting a foolish girl in rebellion against her parent and legal guardian, I am free to interpret that as an effort to turn this situation to your profit.'

'I'm not looking for money, Monsieur Siegel.' Arlette had wanted to smile and say it lightly, but found herself too tightly strung. Her hand was trembling a little, on the straps of her bag.

'I'm glad to hear it.'

'Marie-Line told me that you threatened her with a suggestion I found hard to credit. I thought that if you had said such a thing it must have been in anger, and felt sure you would agree that anger had passed.'

86

'For the last time I will not discuss it. Now will you have the kindness to tell me where my daughter is to be found?'

She got up, opened her handbag, and found a card. She put it on the desk and said, 'This is where I live.' She started to walk towards the door. Siegel did not move but shot a finger out.

'One moment. Are you attempting to show me defiance? You will answer for it.'

Native obstinacy helped her.

'I had hoped to hear you contradict that quite shocking notion of denying her liberty. She asked me for shelter and that I give her.' Siegel had recovered himself.

'This looks to me uncommonly like arbitrary sequestration. A criminal offence.'

'I'm not at all sure that doesn't apply to what you propose.' She did not know why she should feel frightened going out, but she did. Nobody chased her, but she felt better once she got home.

The chess game had finished: nobody said who had won. Arthur was lying horizontal with his pipe and his feet up; Marie-Line sat straight and well brought up with her knees together, and they were listening to Count Basie.

15. 'Diverse Deeds'

The dictionary gives 'divers' as sundry, several, more than one, with the forbidding note 'archaic or jocular'. This is the meaning all right of the French phrase 'faits divers' which comprise the small change in a local newspaper, but not the sense. The behaviour of the population is to be sure very often both archaic and jocular. So at least said Arthur, the kind of person whose curiosity leads him to consult the Concise Oxford at the breakfast table: goes well with Coopers Marmalade.

'And "diverse"?' asked Arlette.

'Unlike in nature or qualities; varied or changeful. Dictionaries, as the French say, leave one upon one's hunger,' turning cheerfully to the toaster. 'People go on doing the same silly things,' with a crunching noise. Since *Monde* only arrived with the postman it was the *Dernières Nouvelles d'Alsace* which divides handily into sections suitable for breakfast reading. Marie-Line still in bed?'

'Let her lie. What are we to do with her?'

'To a large degree, I think you've made your point. This dentist may be still grinding his teeth – ho, apposite – this morning, but he'll simmer down. He'll realize that his fell design wouldn't work very well, because the fact that we know about it means that some unpleasant publicity could be created. He wouldn't want to find himself a diverse deed in this,' generously pushing across 'Strasbourg and Environs' slightly smeared with butter.

'I thought of trying the woman at the Préfecture: the girl gets on quite well with her. One has to get the tension out of the situation: the child must go back to school – a day makes no odds but she can't stay. I'll see what I can cook up. One must avoid litigation. Everyone having been rigid can afford to give way a little.'

'You should be on the Israeli frontier, wearing a white helmet,' cheerfully. 'I'm off to work, but if you need a peace emissary, give me a buzz.'

'Okay,' she said, picking up the paper. What were the diverse deeds this morning in dear old Strasbourg? "Fatal Imprudence" ran the headline.

"Around nine-thirty to ten last night an inhabitant of Neudorf committed the grave imprudence of walking along the metalled way of the S.N.C.F. main line between France and Germany, apparently with the purpose of exercising his dog. In, it is surmised, an effort to control the dog alarmed or excited by the approach of a train, he stepped onto the rails and was fatally injured by the locomotive." Really, as Arthur said, people go on doing the same imbecilic things.

'Black Spot.'

'We must recall that in this same area, close to the bridge crossing the Rue de Soultz, a child while playing met a similar tragic end some few months ago. A spokesman for the S.N.C.F. at the time, it will be remembered, denounced the indifference of the public. *'It is impossible'* he then stated *'to protect the entire length of this sector. While emphasizing our total refusal to accept responsibility under these circumstances we again address an appeal to the populace as a whole to exercise some collective discipline.'* Fat hope you have, mate.

'Alarm raised by dog.'

'The alert was sounded as we learn by the dog, a German shepherd, whining and barking at the apartment entrance. The wife of the unhappy victim, since named as Albert Demazis –' Suddenly she found herself trembling violently. She put out a hand for a cigarette. There weren't any. She got up and hunted for one. Good God.

'. . . forty-three, described as an accountant, of an address in the Rue de Labaroche, alarmed at this behaviour, called the police. After a fruitless search of the streets of the quarter, enquiry was directed to the railway line, where the unfortunate victim was found, atrociously mutilated. The hypothesis of the dog's escape from control was supported by the pathetic fact of Monsieur Demazis clutching still in his hand the dog's lead. This, and his health which was normal in every respect, seems to rule out giddiness or cardiac collapse, but it was pointed out that yesterday's rain may have made the rails and sleepers, treacherously slippery, and a stumble with fatal consequence would seem only too easy.

'Once more, this newspaper underlines the extreme danger of such practices.'

Even in the laughable prose of the local paper, she got the message.

At this moment Marie-Line appeared in pyjamas, cheerful, and Arlette had to bottle up shock. It was just as well, she told herself. One can't go flying off the handle. Odd expression,

89

Arthur would say. Presumably an axe or hammer-head. Who do you risk most damage to – yourself or all the admiring bystanders?

They are familiar to everyone, these days: evil-eye days. From the tiny, petty frustrations; the zip that sticks, the thread that snaps; in crescendo everything goes wrong. Oneself is stricken by impenetrable stupidity: why else does the milk boil over, why else a fingernail break and a new pair of tights ladder for no reason? What is this stain upon fabric that would just have to be both pale-coloured and delicate? You look at yourself in the glass, and are greatly depressed by what you see.

To the well known malignance of inanimate objects, upon which any comedian can rouse a guffaw, is added the obtuseness of the human race: the world is peopled by cheerful imbeciles. In the post is a letter from the Minister of Finance, nasty in tone. And everywhere, hanging in the air like an acrid smell, is brutishness, the Barbarian, a pleasure taken in suffering inflicted.

The girl hung around irritatingly, occupying the bathroom for an age. Why have I this tiresome old-fashioned flat? Everybody else has two bathrooms: it is the minimum for civilized living.

The Préfecture of Strasbourg has two faces. One is the Préfecture itself, an ugly building on the Place de la République where there is never room to park one's car, full of governmental instances from automobile registrations to permits for aliens. Everyone there has the extreme unwillingness proper to bureaucrats ever to do any business. They're always trying to persuade you to go up several flights and try Room 304. You are always in the wrong. You never have enough photostats of documents or photographs of your beautiful self, without which the State cannot function, and you cannot get out again without buying many fiscal stamps for odd, arbitrary, large sums of money. This is the face shown to the public.

The private face is back across the False Rampart in the old town: the Quai Lezay-Marnesia next door to the Opera. This is the Hôtel du Préfet, eighteenth-century palace in a pretty garden. Not for the public. Policemen loiter at the gate to stop you; the sort of bemedalled chevronned policeman with an elderly weary Corsican face whose great age and infirmity has ensured that he will never again do any work, though he is still capable of stopping other people doing any. This majestic pest is an obstacle. Arlette was viewed with suspicion and practically stripped on the spot to make sure she had no bombs about her. This kind of policeman is always very tired, but a well of cynicism. Slipping them a bottle of Chivas Regal is kind of crude.

She was aware of having fallen into a small neat trap. Madame Pelletier, on the telephone, when one finally got her, had been bored and perfunctory.

'Oh yes,' vaguely. 'Well . . . come and see me at the office, why don't you.' Arlette was kept kicking her heels a good deal. The machinery of government is quiet hereabouts, and very leisurely. One supposes important things behind the padded doors, private lines direct to the Ministry of the Interior, but everybody seemed to be reading the *Canard Enchainé* and making private jokes of exquisitely honed venom. Damn it, this Pelletier was only in the Service of Statistics.

There is a sub-préfecture down in Colmar where some farmer, told to wait while a functionary finished the cross-word, just wandered off, and was eventually discovered peace-fully having a bath in the Sub-Prefect's private suite. Arlette thought of this with pleasure.

Cathy-Rose Pelletier, run to earth, was pretty, neatly coiffed and dressed, smelt nice, appeared bright, and behaved amiably. She did not make faces at Arlette's introducing herself, she did not frown at mention of Marie-Line. But one did not get hold of her. She was polished to glassy slipperiness like the ballroom floor, and one saw only one's own reflection.

'Yes. You mustn't believe everything Marie-Line says, you know.'

'Of course not. Lazy, insolent, full of affectations and

91

comedies. A great nuisance, probably. Weren't we too, at that age?'

'I have great affection for her which she treats with contempt. Bossy you know, and schoolmarm. Finding fault with all around her.'

'I can imagine. It's the usual adolescent girl, isn't it? And she wants attention, and goes to great lengths to get it. And without pretending to any insight, her father is a rigid person, impatient and perfectionist, who is conscious of inadequacies, and wants to be proud of his daughter, and gets very angry when he feels she lets him down. I know this must be superficial, and I'd be glad to hear I was wrong.'

'I can't say, you know. I don't want to discuss personalities. I'm in a special position: I don't know whether Marie-Line has been voluble on the subject. She doesn't of course approve of me at all.'

'No. She said she liked you. That's all.'

'Her father is a good and fine man.'

'I don't doubt it for an instant. Please believe me; I want to see her go home and lose no time over it. And I'll do all in my power to persuade her. But she surely needs to feel less isolated. Not of course pretending to be young and girlish, but the understanding that comes from sympathy. You must agree that the notion of putting her in a clinic is outrageous.'

'You know that Marie-Line drinks a lot?'

'I wouldn't be surprised to hear there's a problem there.'

'And has been caught taking drugs? In justice to her not, as we believe, anything as yet really dangerous. But smoking certainly, when they get it. And what they call popping pills. And one thing slides, imperceptibly, into another?'

'Again, I'd loathe to come out with glib little bits of psychology, but isn't that all the same – a bad feeling of being disapproved of and even disliked? She's a warm-hearted thing, and reads a lot of rubbish in school texts, and thinks of herself as rejected, and builds that up into a dramatization.'

'I dare say there's truth in what you say. I'll do what I can for Marie-Line, and I'm glad to have met you, for it must be

92

good for her to find in you a sympathetic audience. Perhaps I might go as far as giving you a friendly – well no, we won't use the word warning. A little signal? Her father's not a man that brooks anything he sees as interference. I rather doubt if in the end this sympathetic interest you're taking – or thinking of taking – would really go far towards helping her, you know? I've already said too much. I know him quite well, you see? You've, shall I say, made your point? But having made it – well, you must make your own mind up. Marie-Line imagines things vividly. You know, I do have rather a lot to catch up on: I know you'll forgive me. I'm so pleased to have met you. Can you find your way in this labyrinth, or shall I come with you?'

Marie-Line was missing when she got home. That whisky-bottle too had been fuller this morning, she felt sure. For the tenth time she wondered if she hadn't been a little over-spontaneous.

She ran the tape.

'Oh this is Françoise. Sorry Madame, I just wanted to say is Marie-Line with you? I'm supposing she is, because she wasn't at class this morning, and that's a lot of absences and the Censor is muttering and asked very sharply where she was: little note'll be going off to Pa, I'd guess. If you see her, perhaps you'd tell her better not show herself at home awhile because I saw the old man's face this morning and stormy weather! That's all I suppose, but I'll be *Chez Mauricette* if you or she want to get in touch . . .

'Scheffer, officer of municipal police. I've been trying to get in touch with you, Madame, affair concerning you, your cleaning woman tells me you'll be back before lunchtime, I'd like to say I'd be grateful if you'd arrange to be at home in the early after-noon and I'll call before three o'clock or would you otherwise please ring to make an appointment at headquarters. Thank you . . .

'Press here, Jean-Claude Bouillon. I'm anxious to make contact, Madame, to arrange a short interview on the subject of a report that's circulating, and we'd like to get that this after-noon at the latest, so perhaps you wouldn't mind ringing me

at the office to confirm. or if I'm not there the desk, to say
when it'll be convenient, and please don't put that off or we'd
have to say you know, you weren't available for comment, and
that never looks well, so it'd only be prejudicing your own
interest. So hoping to hear from you by lunch if poss., right?'

She switched on the phone and at that moment it buzzed.

'Arlette van der Valk.'

'Bouillon here. Did you get my message?'

'I have just heard it. Whatever this is, I'd be glad to clear it
up as soon as may be because I'm about to be extremely busy,
so I'd be obliged if you could arrange to call here within a
quarter of an hour.'

'That's okay, be right with you, Rue de l'Observatoire,
right? Yes, I've the number noted; five mins.'

She clicked the receiver and dialled.

'Arthur? Could you arrange to leave the office a little early?
I'm a bit under siege. Press on the doorstep and cops: it looks
as though an attack has been launched.'

'Really? Well, we'll deal with that. Is your press literally on
the step? – Stall him till I get there.'

'No, I can handle it. I'd like to have your broad bosom
handy so I can rest a cheek if I feel that way. Have you by the
way any notion of Marie-Line's whereabouts?'

'Yes, she was here learning how sociology's done. I told her
a few truths which staggered her a little: she tapped me for ten
francs and made tracks I believe for the pub. Ten minutes
about, I'll be home.'

16. Divers Facts

The Press was young and bit its nails. Seemed fairly clean. Inclined to be noisy. Had experience enough to listen, but fonder
of the sound of its own voice. Made itself very much at home.

'Rather snug you are, here,' glancing about at the panelled 'waiting-room'. The same quick glance round the white walls of the office. He strolled up to the big seascape and said, 'Not bad that. Paint's put on nicely. Funny how representational is coming back.'

'I wasn't thinking of following a fashion. Sit down, then.' He had already.

'Madame van der Valk, that's your right name isn't it?'

'Correct.'

'You speak good French.' Nice, to have one's accent as well as one's pictures thought well of.

'I am French.'

'You're married to Doctor Davidson, right?'

'I don't use his name; he's a professional man. And now let's hear from you.'

'What? Oh,' laughing merrily, 'this is just routine interview stuff, you know.'

'Let's get it straight. I've no wish to become a divers fact in your paper, and no particular need for a write-up. Suppose you tell me the purpose of your visit.'

'Ah; a certain distaste for publicity, is that right?'

'I'm neither courting it nor avoiding it, and please be careful not to misrepresent me.'

'No need to worry. Now aid bureau, perhaps you can tell me what that is exactly.' Arlette was determined to keep her head. Be rude to this young man and he will find ways of being unpleasant.

'We like things labelled in this country. Our famous Cartesian spirit of system. There are a lot of help organizations devoted to a particular purpose: I don't address myself to any type in particular.'

'A penny here and a penny there, so to speak. Do you have any particular qualification, d'you mind telling me?'

'Monsieur Bouillon, we're beating round the bush. You spoke of a report that's circulating. Will you tell me what it is?'

95

'That's right; I'll come to that in a sec. You were just say-ing, about your qualifications.'

'I have a variety of diplomas in medical and social work, which I do not pin on the wall. If I see out of a broad experi-ence that anyone consulting me would be better served elsewhere I send them on. Whether that be to a psychiatrist or a fortune teller.'

'So let's suppose I come in, Madame, and ask you for help, what then?'

'Are you in trouble with your employer, your syndicate, your family, your debts, or your car? The best advice I can give you without knowing you better is to be very careful what you print, and especially what you insinuate.'

He smiled.

'Not bad at all. No insinuation, just a straightforward question, so no need to take offence: have any of your activi-ties been the subject of a complaint, let's say, to any legal or judicial authority?'

'If you like to go down to the police, Monsieur Bouillon, and ask the commissaire, I dare say he'll answer that.'

'But I'm asking for yours.'

'Not to my knowledge. If any complaint is made, I'm there to answer it. Since this is the subject of your visit, it's my turn to ask you.'

'No notion, I'm sorry. You'll have to ask them at the desk. I believe that some query turned up. They just asked me to pop along and get a general picture, you know. Which I have. No need to be sore at me, you know. Just doing the job.'

'I'm aware,' she said. She got up. 'I've my lunch to cook. Okay? As long as you're careful, you know, about supposi-tions. I know you'll be careful about facts.'

'One last question then on a fact. You're sheltering a young girl under your roof here, as I'm given to understand.'

'That is true. She came to me yesterday in a state of anxiety. She's free to go as and when she pleases. I don't intend to discuss it. That would not be acting in her interest.'

'But you're advising her not to go home, is that right?'

'No comment, Monsieur Bouillon, and no suggestions, please.'

Arthur was in the living-room, with a stiff drink and a frown.

'Pestering you?' he asked. 'I'll admit I've been finding self-control rather difficult. A tendency to eavesdrop . . .'

'It wasn't very easy. I'm not used to them. I tried to behave as though it were anyone else. But patronizing, rather offensive, and, of course, provincial. Anything without a clearly written label that's not within their experience, they're unable to grasp. He told me I spoke good French: I was much touched. Thought I was Dutch I suppose.'

Arthur shrugged.

'If need be I'll go down to their office and set them straight. They will be pretty careful what they print. It's plainly this Siegel stirring them up.'

'No, I prefer to fight my own battle – if battle there's to be. I've a notion what they might do is refuse my advert.'

'My dear girl, I won't interfere at all, but if there's any harassment, I'll make it quite clear to them that you're not unsupported. There's quite a lot of cooperation they get from various sources which they value.'

'I see. That sounds comforting. It rather makes one think – I mean supposing one didn't have any influential friends, or a certain social standing.'

'Then one would be bullied. A fact of life that's universal. By the way,' changing the subject firmly. 'It occurred to me – but I don't know yet how you got on this morning?'

'The Pelletier woman. She's all right. A bit distant. Call it selfish, if one likes, but only to be expected. She's neutral. Refuses to intervene either way.'

'Act according to the way one's bread is buttered, specially when it's thick. Yes, well, most people are like that: acting out of interest is the world's chief occupation. With that in mind, how about getting a shrink's opinion on Marie-Line just in case they try any hanky-pank when she goes home? Now, while she's free of emotional pressure. We have to get her to go home; can't have her hanging round here.'

'Yes, but isn't that a bit drastic? – might she get worked up about that and start one of her comedies? She's healthy as a tree, and absolutely normal, but if she gets the idea that we think she needs an expert opinion, I wouldn't put it past her to act up to it.'

'No: apart from anyone competent being able to recognize that, I told her with some bluntness this morning not to be a little ass. She swallowed and gulped a bit, and said she'd be good. Shpss, there she is.'

Just in time really. Arlette was a bit indignant with Arthur. Tact with Marie-Line, over lunch.

'I'd a bit of a chat with Cathy. She's quite sympathetic. You know . . . doesn't want to be the interfering step-ma. And she's really rather frightened of you: under the impression you take a slightly poisonous view of her.'

'That's crap, honestly. I've never resented her at all. But it's an excuse for her, you see. She acts all independent and the intellectual executive stuff, but she's bossed about by the men both at home and at work and likes it. Pretending I disapprove of her lets her agree with them, while pretending to be neutral.' Arthur laughed, and Arlette had to grin.

'You aren't far out, I dare say. A bit crude, but we aren't going to psychoanalyse Cathy. Nor you either, come to that, but Arthur's made a suggestion and there might be something in it, and that's to ask a shrink to give you a rapid check-up; the result of which would be of course that you're resoundingly well-balanced. This would cancel any subsequent suggestion that you weren't at any moment. Like last night. A bit emotionally het-up, which is far from being neurotic. You don't have to, of course.'

'I don't mind a bit. Will you come with me?'

'No, I'd prefer you handled it by yourself: it's only a formality and if it comes from you it has more weight. I don't want it said that I'm whispering suggestions at you. I can ring up for you.'

98

'Why bother?' asked Arthur. 'Perfectly good neighbour down one flight.'

'No, I'd like to leave old Rauschenbach as a neighbour, and no more. A completely independent evaluation is best.'

Arlette went into the office and tried three or four numbers of psychiatrists at lunch-time. Everybody was most polite but all full up today, teddibly sorry. Lordy lordy, she hadn't known there were so many Strasbourgeois with neuroses. There's a clinic of course at the hospital, yes, yes, quite. Wait all morning, and by that time anybody'd be neurotic.

All right then. She slipped downstairs to Doctor Joachim Rauschenbach, an elderly gentleman who was having a post-prandial cigar in his living room, who greeted her cordially and gave her a cup of coffee. Ma Rauschenbach said hallo, and vanished into the kitchen, the way she always did: one of those effacing women that haven't anything to say with a man present.

Arlette was on good terms with her neighbours, had been since going down at moving-in time to apologize for all the damn hammering.

'I've come to ask a favour, tiresomely – a matter of could you fit someone in for half an hour without upsetting your appointments.'

'Oh, that's probably no great strain. One often has cancellations; even if not, I could squeeze a half-hour if that's all it is: who is it, you?' grinning.

'A girl who came round with a family problem. I wouldn't dream of bothering you, and don't intend setting any precedents, you know? I want her to go home as soon as maybe, but she's a bit scared to: the parents are – so she says – threatening her with a psychiatrist simply because of a few behavioural problems, and I thought it would reassure her if she had a word with the expert, and get told, I imagine, that she's nothing to worry about.'

'I see. You mean something quite rapid and superficial, without a physical or any tests? Bit of fatherly chat? That's easy enough. I might want her to come back. What's her name?'

'Marie-Line Siegel. I don't suppose there's any problem about coming back, if you wanted it more thorough.'

'Siegel, ah. The name's familiar: I wonder, am I mistaken – colleague of sorts?'

'That's right. Dentist.'

'Ahah, that's it.' The old boy was looking at her and rubbing his jaw. 'You're putting me in some slight embarrassment, my dear Madame Davidson. I'd be delighted to do as you ask, but hereabouts I'm not too sure. Professional colleague you know: I don't know him socially but we sit on a committee together. I'm wondering whether what you suggest mightn't be a wee bit ticklish.'

'Yes, I see,' said Arlette at once, knowing it was hopeless to press it. 'Not ethics but perhaps etiquette?'

'Some such protocol expressions. He's a bit stiff, you know, and old-fashioned. The father whom I knew as a young man was exceedingly Victorian. It might be taken amiss, y'know.'

'No strain,' said Arlette, 'and forgive my bothering you.'

Arthur was doing the washing-up, with Marie-Line to help, when she came strolling in falsely negligent, hands in pockets and cigarette in mouth, looking, said Arthur, 'just like John Wayne at a discouraging moment'.

'It looks rather, children, as though we've been anticipated. All the shrinks in Strasbourg are unaccountably preoccupied. The old fruit downstairs was mortified. I almost think he'd had a phone call.'

'That wouldn't surprise me at all,' said Marie-Line portentously.

'Quite a conspiracy,' squinting along the cigarette and blowing ash on the floor. 'The press this morning, with broad hints that I'm a charlatan. There's a cop coming this afternoon, probably wanting to know whether I've got you locked in an attic, my girl. Ludicrous. I don't quite know what I've done to deserve all this.'

Arthur had been drying the draining-board, meticulously lining up all his little mops and sponges.

'Something of a campaign to discredit you,' he said. 'Some

woman challenges his authority, undermines his leverage, unheard of. Who's she? Some extortionist, some fortune-teller. Piffling but possible. This is still a small town in many ways, encouraging delusions of grandeur. A friend here and there, in the Préfecture or on the paper. How many consultant psychiatrists are there in Strasbourg – Twenty? Well, if you want one, you go to Paris and get one.' Marie-Line looked delighted with this idea.

'No,' said Arlette. 'Running to Paris every time we can't get something done here; idiotic. We defend ourselves right here.' Sounding intensely obstinate.

'That's my John Wayne,' said Arthur. 'I must admit that a certain native tenacity, horribly Brit., takes possession of me, and with apologies to you, Marie-Line, your old man's rather a pest.'

17. 'Pressure'

Mr Scheffer was stolid, middle-aged, and blunt of feature, with a jacket that needed brushing and a red box of tiny cigars. He wore ankle-length suède boots that zipped up the front, with thick crêpe soles, and had thick square fingernails, curved and yellowish.

He was roundabout, with an irritating way of saying 'Now Madame, I beg you not to be aggressive', ending by making Arlette feel aggressive, which would have been a mistake and she had trouble with it.

The cutting phrase, the stinging retort, etcetera, doesn't do at all for the police.

'It's difficult to know how to satisfy you,' she said patiently. 'You talk vaguely about a complaint, and you won't tell me the nature of the complaint or where it originates. In a way I welcome your visit, since you can go back and file a report stating that I've nothing to hide and less still to be ashamed of. Whatever the complaint is, it's nothing criminal. You're not accusing me of fraudulent extortion of money, or illegal practice of medicine, anything like that. Anyway, Commissaire Berger is aware of my activities and gives me a certificate of moral health or whatever you care to call it.'

'May I see it?'

'Certainly. So all right?'

'Quite in order, Madame,' with no change in expression.

'There's no municipal regulation being flouted that I'm aware of. Taxes or hygiene or fire-escapes or something?' The thick fingers waved all this aside and squashed a butt out carefully in the ashtray. 'I'm a thoroughly respectable person, my antecedents are impeccable, and my husband, who does scientific work in the interests of the Council of Europe, is hardly to be thought of as irresponsible.'

'Na good,' he said after waiting patiently for the end of the tirade. One of the paternal Alsatian expressions; he had the powerful singsong accent and pronounced it 'gut'. 'You've been quite open with me even though I could wish you needn't feel so aggressive about it. I'll be open with you.' Generally an indication that they'll be the contrary, but he puffed peaceably on a new cigar and said, 'Just a shadow of disquiet about this girl. Who's missing from home, see, and whose legally appointed guardian, the most normal thing in the world, entrusts us to make sure she's not frequenting bad company. Mark me well, I suggest nothing of the sort. No corruption of a minor or anything like that, just maybe inciting a minor towards quitting the paternal roof, maybe rebellion.'

'Come off it, she's eighteen and she's free to go home whenever she likes. I don't try to keep her. In view of her father's autocratic attitude, I believe I'm justified in thinking that at this moment home isn't the best place for her.'

'Where is she now?'

'Gone to the cinema with my husband. Do her no harm to take her mind off things for an hour or two.'

'Mm. She ought to be at school, no? What legally constitutes a major is subject to interpretation. The texts aren't too
clear. A young girl still at school, living with her family and
dependent upon them . . . Well, I'll go back and consult –' The
phone rang.

'Excuse me a second.'

'Arlette van der Valk.' There was an odd sighing sound
along the line, so that she looked to see whether the switch
was on record but no, it was through to her. 'Who is calling,
please?' The sighing sound continued; was it a sort of deep
asthmatic breathing? 'Have you got the right number?' A
hoarse deep whisper, sounding male but one could not be sure
– disembodied and as though distorted – said 'You'll be sorry
about it, dear, sorry about it,' and nothing again but the
breathing, and then at last the click and buzz of an open line.
She put the phone down and said, 'Somebody clueless.
Sorry.'

'Like I was saying, it might be cleverer to conquer your
scruples, don't you know, and send the girl home because you
know, the matter might get more complicated. Like I'm not
saying anything now but I might find myself sending you out a
summons, you know, and you'd maybe find yourself at the
Magistrates' Court with something to answer for. Well,'
getting to his feet, 'I'll be off.' He didn't apologize for taking
up her time, but the police never do.

Lot of bullshit about Magistrates' Courts. She couldn't feel
sure, but that sounded like the cops disconcerted and kicking
up dust behind which they could retire in good order.

But what was that phone call?

That didn't sound like the worthy dentist. His idea of a
menace – she'd had plenty of proof, no? – was more bureaucratic.

But was it the sort of call Albert Demazis said he'd had –
before he died?

One couldn't tell: Albert had been vague. He'd talked about
menaces, and used some expression like 'funny phone calls', or
maybe 'anonymous calls'.

103

She didn't know whether she was frightened or not. On the one hand, not. It was the kind of thing one would expect of Arthur, if Arthur had been the quite unspeakable type of Englishman that thought practical jokes funny. There – hadn't Albert said he thought, at first, it was somebody playing a joke . . .?

I mean really . . . You were supposed to tremble, and for goodness' sake, you didn't go trembling at some loony on the phone. She'd had plenty of loonies already, either direct on the phone or on the recorder, and no reason to suppose she'd exhausted all the ways there are of being loony. Any telephone girl, surely, would have ripe tales on the subject: it was as standard as having your bottom pinched on the Metro.

It stayed though in her mind, like a grain of grit. Albert Demazis was dead, and wasn't it too much of a coincidence? Police business? When the phone rang again she felt an aversion, a slight creeping of the flesh which she had to conquer, and it was a relief to hear Arthur, sounding crisp.

'Silly film. I'm having a cup of tea with the child, more for her enjoyment than mine. I'll bring her home; I've some letters to sign at the office. I was thinking – during the silly film. Might get a legal opinion. I thought of somebody good – Paul Friedmann. I phoned him; he was at the Palais pleading but I caught him, and he said he'd be through around five and intended to go home, so if you'd like to have a chat with him you could pick him up at the Palais, and it might be a bright thing to do. Bye; my tea's getting cold.'

Arlette had a stew in the oven simmering nicely, so she picked up the cassette and said, 'Take the stew out about a quarter to seven if I'm not back, and I think plain boil those spuds. Would you be a love and cook me the spinach, it's all washed and ready.' She shot out into the Lancia; Arthur and the girl had taken the bus.

The Palace of Justice in Strasbourg is gloomily neo-classic outside in a Teutonic way, vaguely Nuremberg, and a dirty yellow within, huge edifice constructed as though of Marseille soap. There is a gigantic staircase with lions, something be-

104

tween Rome and Egypt seen on a drizzling day through a dirty bus window after too much lunch.

Maître Friedmann was discovered in a criminal corner full of lockers, disrobing, smoking a little cigar like Monsieur Scheffer, but not looking a bit like him. Handsome, young, Jewish, sparkling in that particular Jewish fashion with lovely blue-black hair that would never need brushing, magnificent eyes, a lovely grey suit, everything lovely. And a person needing no damned explaining.

'Hallo there, you're Arlette, how splendidly you've timed your arrival. My car's in front, insolently, is yours too? Double parked, wicked cow, we'd better take both, no, of course not that ghastly office, home, I'm dying for a cup of coffee – I'm a coffee maniac.'

He drove very fast in a white Alfa Romeo as far as one of the flats near the Orangerie that she fancied but couldn't afford. All very modern.

'Claire! Claire . . . blast the cow, she's gone out. Make yourself comfortable.' He was very quick. Arlette had scarcely time to close her eyes hard and breathe deeply and wish herself into a state of calm when whisk, he was back from the kitchen with a coffee-maker and a bowl of ice-blocks. Whisk, in her hand was a big glass of ice and something colourless which turned out to be Cointreau and delicious. The tornado sat down opposite with a large china mug, which had a gaudy picture of a satyr on it and read, "You'll tell the Vicar? I AM the Vicar", and became still.

'Tell,' he said. He stayed perfectly still. He did not interrupt once. He asked no questions. The smell of coffee mixed deliciously with that of Cointreau. The expression on his face did not change even when she rambled and became aware she was rambling. Without his having moved at all a pad of yellow paper appeared on his knee, a yellow pencil, and a page of neat small writing had taken shape.

He took a swig of coffee.

'Right. Now we don't want to bother you with a lot of legal dinkydoo, so I leave that out. You're being harassed and I'll put a stop to that. I guarantee you'll hear no more from the cops. This Scheffer, that's a load of unmitigated cock. They're always telling you what the law is, and they don't know themselves. The Statute book pours forth simply mountains of texts, endless amendments to this or that, all so ambiguous and so badly drafted that the law is what anybody chooses to say it is. So you challenge a point. Plead it, get it disentangled, get a bit of proper jurisprudence on it.

'Matter of psychology. Who pleads it? I do. Tell you why. Get a juicy rape case, or even, as here, matter of parental control over a young girl, and you're dead right, that's rape. People think, get a sharp woman down from Paris, sexist, feminist, pretty, and she'll plead like a fury; you horrible old men, it's me you're raping.

'Court sees her coming from afar with her knickers aflame. Question like this, matter of male machismo, man's got to plead it. Court's terribly bad, you think, dirty old men, one half yids one half protty old Huguenots nodding away there: yes yes, support parental discipline; young girl's giving backchat, lock her up in the convent.

'Wrong in fact. Court can be surprisingly supple and sympathetic. All a matter of choosing the right moment, hitting the nail, but how hard d'you hit the nail? Most successful advocacy's this question of timing.

'Now I can see you coming. Oh dear, firebrand young yid, just longing to stir up a fuss, blasted eager boy wanting to make a name for himself. Dragging you into court amidst a wilderness of interjections and injunctions, rejoinders and counter-rejoinders. Blaze of publicity, rebounding to credit of brilliant young advocate, what? Not on your life.

'Don't want a lot of confrontation with this old hound of a dentist. If we have to, nothing easier. May-it-please-the-Court, let this old cowskin stand up and show cause why he should be thought fit to have parental control over his own socks: as first witness we'll call the housemaid he was screwing last week in the broom cupboard.

'But would that be doing you any good? Or Marie-Line?

106

She's the one concerned – is it such a splendid idea for her to be a bone of contention? She'd enjoy it no doubt, but you don't think so and neither do I. Two little girls of my own.

'Tact, and a light hand. I'll pin this dentist's ears back enough to give him pause. Comes to Court I can drive a bus up and down his spine.

'Stopping the harassment of yourself, easy; he's already overreached himself badly. Newspaper will be pretty careful. Print a piece that's not objective reporting, it's practically paid publicity, and they'll footnote it with a legal disclaimer refusing responsibility. You've a legal "right to reply" if you want to use it.

'Marie-Line's presence in your house is a weakness and an embarrassment. We must get her out from underneath your feet. Send her over to us here; Claire will enjoy that. I won't mind it. Got my domestic moo, two calves, what's a heifer more or less?'

Arlette was about to voice a mild protest at this ruminant classification of all the women, when the 'domestic moo' arrived herself, scooting the children to their rooms to do their homework and drifting in, delicately built but looking durable; slim, quiet, vastly pretty.

'What's he on about now? Calling us all cows again? Oh I know, simply awful, as though one's bra was soaking with milk: when the children were tiny he'd come cuddling up and say "Give me a licky too".'

Put firmly thus back in his place Maître Friedmann grinned and said 'Have we got room for a ravishing blonde of eighteen? Arlette's got one she needs to get rid of.'

'I daresay,' said Claire comfortably.

It was darkening rapidly out, and was dark by the time she got home. She parked on the pavement opposite, under the trees of the Observatory garden, turned her light out, set her handbrake and began collecting female attributes, like a high-heeled shoe one couldn't wear while driving and which had slid under the seat: she was doubled up awkwardly when there was a loud noise.

A complex noise, that she could not understand. There seemed to be a loud clap and a duller thud. An impact there had been: the car quivered on its suspension. She unfolded herself puzzled. The windscreen had frosted across.

'Oh damn, oh damn,' said Arlette crossly. Her brand new and cherished – had some fool bumped her? No – a catapulted stone from a passing truck? She banged her hand in fury on the back of the seat beside her and took her hand away as though scorched. The upholstery was torn and broken. She put her fingers back carefully with the glove off. Feeling about in the ripped padding she found a small hard object. Crumpled and bent, a slug half squashed and nauseating, so that she shuddered as though it still writhed, dropped it and brushed her cringing hand on her skirt. The car had been shot. She felt it as though shot herself.

Mustn't sit here to be potted like some paralysed rabbit. She got out and slammed the door angrily, not feeling frightened, too angry to ask herself why. Glared around. Nothing to be made of that. The Rue de l'Observatoire at night, dim reflections on patterns of window and balcony; skyscape and roofscape lit by the orange glow of the city at night; the dapple of darker trees, leaves beginning to fall. Everything silent and still down to the passing traffic on the Boulevard de la Victoire. Her hand was not shaking at all as she locked the car and strode over to her front door.

Arthur narrow and English in a waistcoat, back straight, holding a fan of cards up high and to one side, teaching Marie-Line to play piquet. They looked at her startled.

'My dear girl.'

'I've been shot at. Here. Just now. On the street.'

'Call the police.'

'No. Nonsense. Give me a drink. Police Judiciaire if anything. No. Not that either. Sorry, I'm being silly. Don't look so saucer-eyed,' crossly at Marie-Line. 'Sorry. Bugger. Heaven's sake, don't let's dramatize. I can't drive you, that's all. Windscreen's starred up.'

'Let me look.'

108

'Arthur – heaven's sake what will you see? You Scotland
Yard or what? Just ring Paul Friedmann, apologize, ask him
to come across. Forgive me Marie-Line, I'll explain in just a
tick, this is a friend who kindly asks you to come and stay a
day or so; he's very nice. Give me a cigarette somebody.'

18. 'Grace under pressure'

'Intimidation,' said Paul. 'Rather odd.' The two men had
pottered about, masculine and important, as always when
something has happened to a car.
'But of course. I worked that out; if anybody wanted to
shoot me they'd wait till I was out of the car.'
'Good,' said Arthur. 'We worked it out just like Police-
Whoever. You're parked nose a bit out – across the street,
about twenty metres, in the shade of those bushes that need
clipping, on the pavement. Flat trajectory. Might have been
standing or crouching. Bullet might have been deflected a bit
by the safety glass, tumbled a bit and smacked the seat back.
Wouldn't have hit you – far right-hand corner. Twenty-two
rifle.'
'I was bending down. Lost my glove. I've had time to think;
I don't believe it has anything to do with this at all. Or put it
another way, Paul, I don't think anyone will shoot at you.'
'Assassination attempt upon popular young advocate – I
feel quite regretful. Look, ring me in the morning. Come on
Marie-Line. Let's affront these sinister highways.'
'Nothing to it really,' said Arthur. 'Get the garage to replace
the windscreen tomorrow. No other serious damage. Legally
of course one's supposed to report these things, and the police
might be cross if we don't.'
'Yes. Arthur, am I getting badly out of my depth?'
'No no, this is just a nastiness of some evil-minded small

boy. Whatever the good dentist gets up to he doesn't creep about at night with his air pistol.'

'No, of course not. Listen, there was a man, and he made me promise to keep his confidence, even to you. So I did. And he's dead. Death cancels that kind of promise, doesn't it?'

'Yes, it does.'

'I got a queer phone call. But then I get lots of queer phone calls. It's all too Chandlerish for words.'

'Everything is Rather Frightening? You've had a shock.'

'Yes, I want to go to bed. I don't mean taken to bed, I mean Go to bed. I'm icy, would you put my blanket on full for me?'

'Yes; d'you want a pill?'

'No, I never want any pills.'

'I know: boiling hot lime tea.'

'Yes, that'd be nice. Warmth and comfort. Oh dear, what a foolish cow.'

'Vastly incompetent? Fumble-butter-finger?'

'Yes.'

'My dear, Paul and I were wide-eyed with admiration and Marie-Line simply thrilled.'

'Tiresome girl, I wish I'd never laid eyes on her.'

She fell asleep like a block, and Arthur had to push her to stop her snoring.

'Very well, I won't interfere,' said Arthur. She was already scribbling actively at a scratch-pad with the coffee-cup pushed back. The daily paper lay between them. 'Take my advice, draft it now while you're red hot. Let it rest. Rewrite it when cool: you've the whole day before you. I've taken by the way all the glass out; a foul job it was. Need no plastic, it's a lovely morning.'

'I'm going to fight this out, first.'

Get Maître Friedmann to handle it, Arthur had suggested. No, she said, it's my pigeon. And Paul will be quite expensive enough as it is.

Only insinuation . . . A letter to a paper . . .

"A correspondent writes to complain of what, as he sees it,

110

amounts to misleading and mischievous advertising in this journal. In printing his views, we need hardly add, in fairness to public opinion, we must emphasize once more that while we take pains to ensure that publicity announcements in the advertisement columns are as far as can be ascertained *bona fide*, we cannot be held responsible for any claims made by the advertiser. We have frequently warned our readers that fraudulent publicity is a matter coming under the Criminal Code, and complaint should be made to the appropriate authority.

"It is understood, in the consequence, that the editors of this journal do not necessarily associate themselves with the opinions expressed in letters received, and that such are printed in obedience only to our avowed duty to inform.

"It is a public scandal" (writes our reader) "that while the sale, especially to minors, of weapons, drugs or pornography is in theory at least regulated, persons should be free to announce 'services' in your journal that may be equally noxious. As father of a family, and a citizen holding a position of public trust, I protest energetically against the appearance of advertisements offering so-called 'aid or counsel' which to all responsible people are nothing but an impudent method of gaining confidence, and perhaps extorting funds. I have nothing to say in criticism of the approved charitable organizations. Such operations, however, as the one described are to be regarded as nothing but enticement, and it is to be hoped that the legislator's attention can be drawn to a deplorable gap in the regulation of offers made to the public.' (Editorial note: our correspondent's letter is too long to reproduce in its entirety.)

"Our reporter, naturally, took pains to verify the announcement complained of. The person apparently concerned, a certain Madame V, at an address in the University district. would neither confirm nor deny the allegation made by our reader. 'I have nothing to reproach myself with,' she stated when interviewed. 'I ask for no payments in advance, and I give no advice to anyone, minors or otherwise, that is not in their own interest and in that of their family.' When asked to explain herself in greater detail, Madame V. refused to comment further."

After much scratching and scribbling out, Arlette went downcast to Arthur, who was finishing shaving.

'I'm supposed to be an educated woman trained in putting a simple piece of prose on paper, but whatever I say sounds wrong.'

'My poor heart – overcome your scruples, leave it to me, I'll bring it you at lunchtime. Any so-called sociologist can draft a piece of pomposity to squash this bug. I'll bring the car into the garage and back with me, okay? Don't worry. I've been on the phone to our friend Monsieur Berger. He says it's nothing to bother about, but if you'll pop over to the PJ office, and ask for Simon, he'll be pleased to listen to your tale in confidence.'

'You do me good,' said Arlette bleakly. 'I feel most deplorably the bumbling amateur, making a right balls of it.'

'You can't do everything all by yourself. Don't lash about in frenzy. Sincerity you know – a relative concept. If I leave the office for a haircut, do I say so? No, I say I've a most important business meeting. If I may humbly say, you are still a bit rigid in your guidelines. Don't, above all, get worked up.'

There were already a few anonymous folk on her tape, pleasurably stimulated by malice. She passed a bad moment, like a repentant drunk after a swig.

Inspector Simon at the PJ was much more like a cop than anyone else she'd met there: in that half an hour after leaving him she couldn't remember what he looked like. Broad, and with a navy blue shirt buttoned up. Polite and painstaking, and suggesting only in small tactful ways that women were frail and silly. Being classified with the scattered-wits sorority made her behave more stupidly than she usually did. It was as a courtesy, doubtless, to Arthur that she was being given time.

'Wait a sec; I haven't got it clear yet. He phoned you giving a false name. And he got in touch with you; you met him in

112

this pub. And he behaved oddly. You got the impression of a man with something on his mind.'

'A frightened man. Furtive, and glancing about.' It did all sound like Peter Lorre in an old movie.

'It seems consistent. If he was nervous about something, that would be the kind of person who didn't hear a train coming or got flustered when he did. Look at it, you're strolling along there, and you're pondering some deep problem, your figures have a way of coming out wrong or you've pain in your gall bladder, and all of a sudden you're startled, Yaysus there's a train almost on top of you; that's when you make a clumsy move and slip.'

'But his stomach or his ledger wrong wouldn't have brought him to me. Anyhow I asked him. I pointed out that I wasn't equipped to deal with anything medical or legal, or financial. He said it was nothing like that.'

Monsieur Simon sighed a little, patiently.

'One of the first things you learn in this trade is that people tell lies all the time. I don't just mean when they're caught breaking the window and say no no, it wasn't me. Or people who're not very bright in the head. Or systematized fantasies. Quite ordinary people, nothing to hide, nothing to feel guilty about. I saw this and I saw that, when it's obvious they saw nothing of the kind.' She felt unsure whether this was supposed to apply to Demazis, or to herself.

'People seeking to make themselves important, you mean? Something of the sort occurred to me.'

'That and not even that. Think about it, get a nasty crime, like we get too often, with blood and violence; a lot of people reading about it get knocked off their balance. The ones whose screws are a bit loose but not so's you'd notice, become neurotic. Those are the ones who confess to it, seek to copy it even. A whole lot more, who aren't abnormal but who have a dull humdrum existence, want to share in the vicarious excitement. A bit sick, and a notorious great obstruction to us, but one has to learn to expect it.'

113

'The gawpers you mean, who'll get in the car and drive an hour to the scene of a bad accident, just to see?'

'That's right. See and share and enjoy. Sadism in us all, the shrink says, huh?'

'I thought of all this; and somehow it wasn't like that. He was too diffident, not wanting to confide at all and getting cold feet about it. He promised to come and talk to me, and rang up cancelling it in an awkward, silly way.'

Mr Simon sighed again, scratched his thick brown hair with his ball point, lit a cigarette and picked a thin folder off his table.

'Look here, this has nothing to do with us, you realize. We're at the disposal of the Proc, as you know, and we act on his word. This matter like any violent death, traffic accident or suicide or what, got the treatment, all proper, from urban brigade being within city limits; measurements, sketchplan all complete, observations made like anything untoward, weather conditions, visibility. They flipped the file over to me when I asked to see it, no strain. Doctor says – I spare you that, technical as well as gory . . .' She wanted to say Don't spare me that, I'm not a baby, but could find no grounds for objecting.

'Railway line. Rainy, a bit foggy. Track greasy and slippery. Loose ballast, you know the stuff, stone with sharp contours, doesn't slide about like smooth pebbles, but superficially unstable and uneven. Means you put your foot down, you can easily lurch a bit, because the loose bed forms hummocks and pockets. Narrow path, used by railmen, alongside. You can bicycle on it and they do, of course, but it's a hazard. This time of year, it's often obscured by summer growth of brambles, dead sticks. Easy to trip. Maintenance crews cut or burn this back, or they're supposed to, but mean to say Yaysus, it's a hazard, or why else warn people off the line? Fella shouldn't be there; damn dangerous situation. Likelihood of accident trebled, quadrupled.

'Time, late at night.' He dragged at his cigarette, turned the page of close conscientious typing. 'Statement taken from only

114

witness, to wit locomotive mechanic. Serious man, plenty years' service, no accidents, good record, clean of alcohol. You see? Quote verbatim: we always do keep a good lookout, standing orders and public notoriously undisciplined about trespassing. Het setera. Attention somewhat relaxed this late – that's fair enough. Signals clear, no untoward encounter expected – why indeed should it be? – visibility normal; that's lights he means, signals. Speed forty-five kayem hour, standard for the stretch. Right. He's taking regular mechanical looks at the line, but this is all dead routine, he's looking forward to getting off and going home and who blames him. Right, loco's a BB, I don't know how many tons that is but remarkably heavy. Slight but perceptible shock is what alerts him. No cry, but you're hit by a loco anywhere you're just dead, massive rupture, major bloodvessels. Doesn't have to decapitate you or hit your heart: colossal traumatic shock. Forty kayem, doesn't sound much, but even if a car hits you at that, you're a mess. He thought, he says, of an animal, a fox or a dog.'

'Is that a commonplace?'

'Deer or badgers or stuff in wooded country is, fairly much so. Less in city limits, natch, but there's woodland cover down to the Rhine in plenty; it's not unheard of. And of course boys and lunatics put logs and stones and stuff as obstructions, but that's a different kind of impact. Instructions are standard, stop and examine for damage or irregularity, which he does, and oh Yaysus, so of course he backs up, phones through; the first enquirers, firemen and S.N.C.F. security man were there in twenty minutes. One look sufficed to show him the fella's beyond help, and rightly his concern is then with railway security, there's an immobilized freight convoy on the line. Frequency of traffic on that line, anything between ten and thirty minutes.

'So what can we conclude? You take your dog walking maybe a fifteen-minute stretch along the line, you've a chance in one, two or three of meeting a train. Short odds. Conclusion, fatality due to imprudence and the likelihood of stumbling. Dog was not on leash but distracted him, or he was just

115

plain preoccupied, and you're a witness to a certain mental disturbance.'

'And there's no enquiry past that point?' asked Arlette.

'That's the technical enquiry,' said Mr Simon reprovingly, turning more pages. 'City Security makes of course the usual verification. One doesn't classify as suicide without a strong leader, which is why our statistics are cock, really, because hospitals will always mark accident out of consideration for relatives. Wife much distraught, unsurprisingly, states no ground for suicide. No outstanding heavy debts or obligations. Pattern of life normal. Books at work audited recently, director of firm categoric about everything normal. Quite frankly, the thing is classified and goes to the file: there's no earthly reason to keep it open.'

'It's necessarily quite superficial that, isn't it?' This sounded tactless. 'Not as though you had done it, for example,' she added hastily, making things no better.

'Listen, Mrs Davidson,' patiently. 'Your husband's a scientist, and a criminologist, and friends with the Commissaire. Normal, you feel there should be a thorough patient enquiry into this because it troubles you, and that's normal too. Why? Because you're personally involved, or feel so. You saw the fellow alive, and he's more than a statistic. Human; I understand it. But if we made an exhaustive enquiry on every death where would we be? Ask yourself that.'

'I'm grateful, and I'm ashamed to have taken up your time.'

'No, that's all right, it's nothing out of the way. You – you apologize. You should see how many pester us. Do they apologize – ever? Ho.'

'I suppose there wasn't an autopsy?' she said at the door.

'Autopsy!' said Simon, quite near breaking into manic laughter. 'Now, what are you looking at? Fellow's exploded, like he's jumped off the tenth storey. They shovelled him up. Second, why? Like he'd taken some drug or medicament, made him dizzy or sleepy? Standard question, put to wife,' turning pages back. 'Was your husband following a course of treatment? Or had he recently consulted a doctor? Answer, no and no. Not to the lady's knowledge. And she'd be the one to know, right?'

'Thanks' she said. The earnest amateur, worrying. The fusspot female, working itself up. Truth! 'Terewth? – what is Terewth?' as Arthur, quoting Mr Chadband, frequently said. 'Approximations, averages, and goosed-up statistics.' Like the man said, who knows really what the suicide rate is? People have already so many forms to fill in: suggest that they fill in a few more and they will find their consciences become elastic.

She walked home, across the tatty patch of open ground between the University campus and the Krutenau. It was sunny, warm and still. Students sat or strolled and chatted; a shirt-sleeved careless group played football. She came out by the students' cafeteria, crossed the Boulevard de la Victoire, and was as good as home.

What did it all amount to? Silly . . . housewifely . . . busybody . . . What had she managed to do? Given Norma some advice she didn't need. Complicated Marie-Line's existence by stiffening both father and daughter. And done no good at all to Albert Demazis. She'd failed to gain his confidence, and she'd failed to know anything about him.

Was he what Arthur had thought, and what the police plainly thought, a mildly neurotic person, not feeble-minded but what the shrink would call fragile-minded? Commonplace type, spinner of fantasies, teller of tales, who went a step further and began to act out his scenario?

Or as she had thought a sad and frightened man under a burden, who had not known how to bear it, asked for help, been disappointed, relapsed into a fatal indecisiveness, stretching as far as a death that was neither a true suicide nor a true accident.

She had been a flop either way.

Desolately she sat at home and had a drink; thought that

117

for some days now the grub had been a bit substandard and hadn't she better do something about that?

Was it only the alcohol that hardened her resolve? You will not cave in, she told herself.

Come on; show some grace under pressure.

19. 'You take the gun, Trelawney; you're the best shot'

But why had she been shot at? Such an idiotic thing to happen, so wildly melodramatic.

Paul Friedmann had been sceptical.

'Syllogism. Place is full of twenty-two rifles. They're not controlled – heaven knows why, since pistols are. Far more accurate and have a far greater range. Thus more dangerous. Typically French, this, like forbidding alcohol advertising, and importing more alcohol.

'Two, place is full of feeble-minded individuals with vague rancours and resentments against society.

'Conclusion; assemble the two sets of statistics and they overlap. People do let off rifles in the street, not aiming at anybody in particular. Does them good, if one may so put it, to make a bang and break some glass. Probably someone whose very old Renault got a flat tyre and who got extremely cross at you sailing by in that heavenly Lancia. Shit, even arouses my envy.'

'No,' said Arthur, after Paul had gone, bearing Marie-Line with him, a Marie-Line delighted with Paul, delighted with the white Alfa Romeo, delighted with adventures: wait till they heard about all this *Chez Mauricette* . . . 'No. Too much like an ambush. Too much premeditation. The shot was too carefully placed.'

Arthur had had a fright, and been cross about that. He had calmed down.

'"A voice called to him",' he said meditatively, '"to stand out of the moonlight or he would get some lead in him, and the same moment a bullet whistled close by his arm."'

'What's that?'

'*Treasure Island*,' said Arthur straight-faced.

'Intimidation?'

'It's been in my mind from the start. Anybody whose business is action, not academic speculation like mine, gets vague threats, feeble-minded vengeances, little nastinesses. I took that, as I thought, into consideration. You know, obscene phone calls. Hence various precautions, filter on the front door, peepholes etcetera, the recorder. But guns . . . I want to think about this.'

Arlette did some cooking, a bit desultory; she was restless. Prowled about. She hadn't had the nerve to tell Inspector Simon about the car windscreen. He would have raised his eyebrows, struck an attitude, and said 'Play it again, Sam'. Like Arthur.

'You take the gun, Trelawney, you're the best shot'. The phone call whispering to her was the same. These were the antics of mentally-retarded adolescents, surely.

Look dear, Dingus talks to you in a silly mysterious way, and a day later he slips on the railway line. You instantly get yourself worked up.

'No, no; NO,' she said crossly to the kitchen wall. 'I won't get worked up. But I'm not going to cave meekly in. I won't get told by some little peejay cop, that I'm a fragile-minded female and back to the saucepan, dear.' She went into the living-room, poured herself a whisky, and in mockery put the record of *My Defences are Low* on the player.

She stood in the window embrasure to watch for Arthur's arrival. Would somebody take a shot at the window? Let them! She was derisively aware that this was due to the size of the whisky, and didn't give a damn.

119

Arthur arrived driving the Lancia, with a spanking-new-sparkly-clean windscreen.

Arthur, however, was serious. He turned the player down a little, sat, started to fill his pipe and said, 'I'm wondering whether I haven't made a frivolous mistake, dragging you into all this.'

'You mean that I really did get shot at?'

'I mean that nobody knows much about violence. There are the obvious things like alcohol, people in urban high-density conditions, aggressivity on the road, stuff like that. A lot of fragmentary work has been done. It's a large, shapeless subject. It occurred to me that among other experiments this one would have value. Now I'm not so sure. Evil-minded persons can be nasty in small vicious ways. I think that you should not get involved with the hare-brained: perhaps after all we should leave it to the professionals.'

'I went through a stage of thinking the same thing. I've changed my mind. I was very uncertain and discouraged. But no – I'm not going to renounce.'

'What changed it?'

'The professionals. I was down at the P.J. I saw this Simon. He had the file on Demazis. They don't enter into it at all, because of course there's no earthly ground for supposing homicide. Municipal police. Railway police. Technically it's very thorough. I couldn't have done any of that.'

'But?'

'But, there are several buts. Like there's no background. They ask the wife whether he had dizzy spells, they ask his employer whether his books were straight. Nobody asks what he was doing on the railway line in the first instance. It's a silly, wild sort of thing to do. Like coming to me. Why doesn't he come again, he rings up and cancels, and next day he's dead on a railway line.

'The professionals are aware of these gaps. They're resigned to the fact that their machine which works very closely and competently on areas that interest them isn't adapted to the oddities. And there are too many oddities. I'm gabbling; I've had a lot of whisky.'

'Go on.'

'They shrug. Resigned to the fact that nobody enquires into the borderline of suicide or accident. Result, a lot of homicides go quite unsuspected. Simon, when I told him what I knew, said perfectly justly that you couldn't measure neurosis in a dead man. Like those car suicides where people who couldn't push themselves into jumping off the bridge provoke an accident. Dodging the responsibility as it were. To him this could be one of those. Mixture of bravado and cowardice.'

'Calling you up was a theatrical scenario to make it all more grand and important?'

'I don't want to speculate.'

'But can you ever find out?'

'I can try. The amateur can find areas that the professional doesn't bother with. I don't know what, yet. But if there was any intimidation, it simply stiffens my resolve.'

'Mm,' said Arthur. 'You mustn't take it so personally.'

'No. I won't make an obsession of it. Let's just keep our end up. Not be hustled by the likes of Siegel.'

'By the way, I drafted your letter. I can redo it this afternoon. If you don't like it, that is.'

'Marie-Line's worth an effort. And we mustn't let this wretched Siegel imagine the whole of Strasbourg stands tugging at its forelock. Show.'

"Your correspondent's letter is a distortion.

"The public has the right to seek advice and aid. Numerous organisations provide this in specific circumstances. By the nature of bureaucracy their action is belated, devious, often bewildering and frequently inefficient.

"The private advice bureau does not compete with state or municipal services. It may help in approach to them, or to simplify procedure.

"It functions where no competent authority exists: these cases are too numerous to mention.

"In all cases, it is to be judged on its merits.

"The accusation of fishing in troubled water for a profit motive is categorically denied. In my case, consultation costs nothing; in no instance do I ask payment before a problem has been explained and an action agreed upon.

"In professions offering services to the public a code of deontology, of ethical behaviour, must exist and be enforced. Where controlled by a governing body, malpractice may still exist and remain for long undetected. The private bureau, self-disciplined, must be judged by its practice. It exists to combat apathy, as much as to lessen abuse, and even corruption.

"No ethical practitioner will advise a minor unbeknown to the parents or guardians, recommend action contrary to known parental opinion, nor undertake action without parental consent, save where the interest of the minor, as in cases of ill-treatment, demands the intervention of authority.

"In accordance with the legal right of reply these words are addressed to the newspaper for insertion."

'Well,' said Arlette, 'You take the gun, Trelawney, you're the best shot.'

'Pompous enough? You could have done it just as well, you know.'

'So I could, no doubt. What counts with me is not that I could, but that you should.'

Arthur contemplated her, with pleasure.

'The Widow,' said Arlette, 'is now thoroughly married.'

'No need for Paul, though I'll get him to check it. I phoned the paper, belabouring them slightly with my own impressive professional titles. They were conciliatory, and promise full amends. They were jockeyed of course by Siegel: they won't admit he frightened them. Their legitimate claim is the right to campaign against shyster agencies. So we get that settled.'

'Is it necessary? I mean I was wondering whether to adopt dignified contemptuous silence.'

'No it's needed; failure to deny an accusation, in the public's eye, is tantamount to admitting its foundation. And it gives us a definition. I was vague myself on the point: I mean that a sociologist does not as a rule offer consultations to the public. I'm taking it up with Paul, to protect you if necessary. You don't, you see, offer legal or medical treatment, which is where there'd be an infringement and a charge of illegal practice. Paul was extremely funny about the jurisprudence involving faith-healers and witch-doctors.'

'Which is what I am.'

'Right. Advice does not constitute intervention. You advise your customer to seek where appropriate a professional course of treatment: the decision is up to him and the responsibility remains his. It's most important to have this clear. I hadn't thought of this,' laughing, 'but Paul thinks that Siegel might seek to entrap you, and the next attack might be a whole series of *agents provocateurs* with plausible tales.'

'Ho. So I don't offer Thai massage to tired businessmen.'

'No,' giggling. 'What Paul wants is to get a challenge, to put to the test, on what legally constitutes a minor. We're right on the ethics, and so any tribunal will confirm, so Siegel will back off. Think of it – a doctor seeking to force his own daughter into arbitrary psychiatric examination and treatment. If they get snotty about your ethics, that is exactly the ground where Paul would get most scornful about malpractice.'

'All right. You send the letter to the paper.'

'Is there anything you want to do?'

'Well, I'm like Kennedy with the Russians. If there's a confrontation, a frontal collision, one tries to probe round the edges a bit. While you clobber Siegel with deontology – good word, that – I'm thinking of Uncle Freddy Ulrich. Maybe he'd like a bit of Thai massage.'

'I won't enquire into that,' said Arthur cheerfully. 'I say, I'm fearfully hungry.'

'Those potatoes must be cooked by now. And thanks for getting my car fixed. And I'll try not to get shot at any more.'

'No, it would be a bad habit to get into. Down these mean streets strides Marlowe unafraid. Tripping occasionally over his own penis. Is this rabbit? Oh good.'

20. 'Solidarity'

Things happened fast. There was a timid little pip-pip at the front door bell, and in the same moment there was a loud terrifying shattering explosion.

Arthur, who had just put on a resigned 'I'll take it' expression, ran. Arlette ran. Everybody in the house was suddenly running. As in a movie when a swirl of patterns will freeze into sudden immobility they were all standing still, grouped in silly attitudes, hands and feet poised in mid-air, mouths open, at the bottom of the staircase. In the hallway was smoke, a sharp pungent smell of explosives, a tremendous mess. There were bits of paper and debris everywhere. The groundfloor tenant, Monsieur Lupescu, an inscrutable oriental gentleman who was an expert on East European languages, was standing unperturbed in his doorway. Doctor Joachim Rauschenberg, tall and thin, was arranged in a stork-like attitude, contemplating the unhappy follies of deranged humanity. The third floor, an impressive technical something in Electricité de France, was absent but the owner, from the top, known to Arthur as 'Little Miss Flite' because she had always a reticule stuffed with documents, was in hands-on-hips indignation. As is also usual everybody started talking at once.

'Somebody rang and I thought who on earth can that be at this hour . . .'

'Nothing like plastic; plastic leaves a disgusting mess.'

'Cops; journalists; I was just wondering what next?'

'Just like New Year's Eve. Horrible children put bangers in the letterboxes.'

'There was nothing in them anyhow but publicity rubbish.'

'They needed replacing anyhow, tatty old things.'

Nobody was worried, nobody looked accusingly at Arlette and said, 'This is your fault.'

'I'll get on to the carpenter straight away; obliging little man.'

'They won't try that again. However, one will keep one's eye open.'

'A nasty mess – it drew my attention, I thought well, I must tell Doctor Davidson –' Arlette, going back to get the vacuum cleaner and a wet rag, stopped dead at her freshly painted front door. A big smear of blood. A pinkish heap of guts or lungs. Somebody had asked the butcher for debris: somebody with lots of cats . . . It was much nastier than the bits of red paper from bangers tied in a bundle and dropped in a confined space.

She set her teeth, dumped the filth in the bucket, threw it down the lavatory and returned with disinfectant. When she got back she was touched to find Miss Flite picking up splinters, Mr Lupescu energetically pushing the vacuum-cleaner and Arthur scrubbing at the smoke stains. Doctor Rauschenberg was on her landing, taking a professional look at the woodwork.

'Not nice for you,' said Arlette, setting to.

'Oh my dear girl! That's nothing. Adolescent theatricals; if one allowed oneself to be shaken or intimidated by such things! Ask Madame Fuchs to tell you the tale of a rather tiresome patient of mine who pursued her all over the house with a loaded revolver. He was cross because I was away.'

'What did she do?' she asked, fascinated with this new light on Miss Flite.

'She asked him in, sat him down, talked uninterruptedly for three quarters of an hour and when rather naturally the poor chap fell asleep she crept out still as a mouse and called the police. This house has seen more. When you've finished that I'd be grateful if you'd find a moment to come in to me . . .

'You see, I owe you an apology. Would you like a kirsch? A

125

small cigar? I snubbed you over poor Siegel. Who's a good enough chap but tiresomely up-in-arms about all sorts of things, as I rather gather you've had cause to find out.

'You see, he came from quite a humble background, and is conscious, uncomfortably, of an arriviste streak. A smack of the nouveau riche? Marrying into the professor's family . . . he wanted very badly to acquire the life-style. He felt – this is important – dreadfully let down by the wife who ran away. Was that, just a bit, he wonders secretly and it eats him; due to his rigidity, to his straining to attain? You follow. He missed a professorship. Is it surprising that a certain rancour is trans-ferred, without his being in the least aware, to the girl? I recognized little whatsaname, Marie-Line isn't it, on your staircase. Remember seeing her as a child. You understand too, her being a girl was a disappointment.'

'Isn't there a brother?'

'There is indeed, a somewhat priggish young man, a goody-goody y'know, a model of virtue whom one instinctively desires to kick in the constipated fundament.'

'This becomes a classic.'

'But naturally. Now what I thought of asking – would it be of any service to you were I to ring Freddy Ulrich – in your presence – and ask him to have a word with you?'

'That would help a lot,' gratefully.

'You know where he lives?' dialling. 'That new block in the Contades. Doctor Ulrich please . . . Not my own taste, but . . . Freddy – Jo Rauschenberg. My friend and neighbour, Madame Davidson, would much like to exchange a word with you, on a subject you both have somewhat at heart. Be a good idea, I rather think? . . . Yes, I should think that would fit in fine; I'll ask her shall I? If you dash, he'll fit you in before his first patient – yes, that's splendid; right then: how's the world with you? Great, and my regards to Julie. Till one of these days then old boy.'

'That's very kind. Tell me, purely as a general opinion, people who make attacks like this – are they dangerous?'

'Dangerous – no. People who smear blood about the place,

126

would they commit a crime of blood; that could be difficult to say. In rare combinations one would have to say, possibly. But putting bundles of fireworks in the letterbox, no. Violent yes, in the sense of a personality unable to express itself through normal channels. Emotionally crippled and of course frequently intellectually retarded. Not the pattern of our friend Armand Siegel,' smiling. 'That'll settle down and sort itself out.'

'I'm really grateful.'

'Excellent,' approved Arthur. 'You whizz off and I'll hold the fort. Masculine presence, to soothe Miss Flite. Rather odd though,' added Doctor Davidson. 'Have to ask old Joachim. Things in the paper, quite small things, often provoke hostile manifestations, but this seemed too elaborately planned for that.'

'As long as nobody takes it seriously,' she said. 'It's awfully comforting to see everyone show such solidarity.'

'Us bourgeois my love, clubbing together instinctively. Off you go or Freddy'll be getting his duodenum in a twist.'

'I'm whizzing,' snapping her lipstick shut and making a bolt for the lavatory.

'Don't you drive too fast,' recommended Arthur.

21. 'A landed proprietor in heaven'

The 'park' of the Contades –really a public garden or square – is the centre of bourgeois Strasbourg. It is not particularly pretty, and indeed rather dull, though it has some fine trees and a nice little iron-work bandstand in Second Empire style. It is much favoured by the Jewish population because of the synagogue handily on the corner, and is generally full of solid matrons with little dogs and shrill energetic children, their skullcaps held on by hairgrips. Most of the architecture is

127

Hohenzollern, but one side, by the pretty little river Aar, is a fine example of Insurance-company-Investment Domestic, thoroughly deserving the hideous name of condominium. The building was madly overheated, which would have caused Arlette even acuter discomfort had not Doctor Frederic Ulrich not been so very very cold.

Not so much his manner, which was undoubtedly freezing, but not designed to freeze her out: it always was freezing. Physically: his was the coldest hand she had ever encountered. He was a specialist in the Digestive Apparatus. Thanks be to God, she thought, there's nothing wrong with my liver. That icy clutch exploring my tummy would be the obsidian knife offering me to the Plumed Serpent.

Not that Freddy looked in the least like a plumed serpent: he had the austerest of crewcuts and a beautiful midnight-blue suit in gabardine. His surroundings showed a devotion to Brancusi-like sculpture and the paintings of Sophie Tauber-Arp. His voice was low and soft, his manners impeccable. Courtly is the wrong word, sounding like Sir Leicester Dedlock. But yes – very like Sir Leicester faced with a Radical Rabble-Rouser. Life imitates art; she had learned it from her father – Proust's kitchenmaid who looked like Giotto's Charity. He used to read Dickens aloud to his children, which she hated. She had seen since how many French politicians adopted Mr Chadband's style of oratory, or how pop singers resembled Mr Guppy at the theatre, and now she was reminded in this hushed atmosphere that Sir Leicester thought of himself as 'a considerable landed proprietor in heaven'.

'I am glad to have this opportunity. You are both right and wrong. That Marie-Line misses, indubitably, the stabilizing influence a mother should provide, I should not seek to question. That you should set yourself up to arbitrate in family matters of which you know nothing is, to say the least, open to criticism. Your motives were generous. I believe I do you no injustice in saying that you were over-hasty, and imprudent.

'Since you have penetrated, unwittingly, into an old grief never properly healed, I may say this. My sister conducted

128

herself lamentably: my brother-in-law's behaviour compelled the respect in which I hold him.

'Marie-Line,' seeing that she made no reply, 'resembles her mother in much. Her father's anxiety concerning her should be the more understandable. That anxiety expresses itself in what I will allow to be an aggressive defensiveness. I would not, placed as I am, permit myself to criticize his attitude, originating in a painful emotional wound. I can however express my apologies, while seeking your understanding, for an over-hasty riposte to your abrupt challenge to his authority. I regret that assault, since such it was: an impugnment of your character. I wish you to realize that it arose from your over-readiness to take Marie-Line's – divagations – too literally.'

'Well, you hit me fairly there,' she said. 'I must apologize in turn, and will. I'll ask in turn, too, for you to understand that I never would encourage her to be hostile to her family. I wanted her to go back home; I still do.'

'I should hope so, indeed.'

'Please don't misunderstand me,' cross with herself at appearing to grovel. 'The first thing I did was to go and see Monsieur Siegel, to try and help Marie-Line to heal any rift that had come about and get her to see where she was at fault. I got a very – mistrustful – reception.'

'I accept that.'

'I got rather heated, and I was wrong, and I'm sorry for that. I do think – I feel bound to say – that surely he should – her father should realize that his anxiety, which is natural, exasperates her behaviour. Forgive me, I don't want to make a personal remark, Doctor Ulrich, but are the women in the family, even your own sister – is it fair to say that the women weren't very important, and treated as inferiors?'

His face did not alter.

'I will reply to you, as far as I reply at all, that my father belonged to an older generation and women in professions were then a relative rarity. Further I will not go. My sister did not have the type of capacity that lends itself readily to a professional formation. I am myself sufficiently old-fashioned

129

not to accept the upbringing my father gave us as a fit subject
of conversation with strangers.'

'Sorry again,' feeling the weight of the snub, 'it's relevant as
concerns this girl. Bluntly, she doesn't feel she gets treated on
her merits. I sympathize with her father's problems: shouldn't
we think of hers too? She's quite old enough to be lashing out:
it's not just an adolescent tantrum.'

Freddy said nothing for a long moment. Behind the eyes,
a highly disciplined mind swirled and came to a stop.

'Tell me,' he asked mildly, 'have you been much in her
company?'

'I've noticed that she drinks rather too much. She doesn't
look as healthy as she might.'

'Yes . . . It used to be thought that the use of one type of
artificial stimulant tended to inhibit an attraction – we will not
speak of addiction – towards others. The clinical picture is not
altogether clear, and I would question the causality, but
experience seems to show that the young adapt with discon-
certing facility to one stimulant from another.'

'She's been taking drugs?'

'We're in a realm of conjecture. The opium derivatives, at
least, are not accumulative. Even clinical tests might find it
hard to show whether, and to what extent . . . She has refused
to submit to any medical examination.'

'But is there any evidence?'

'Of taking stimulants, or possessing such – no. To wonder
what a girl of this age gets up to is to frighten oneself with
false fire. The fact is that both from her father and myself she
has stolen prescription forms. You're aware that they come
like cheque books, with counterfoils and carbons? These have
been abstracted, falsified. Oh, in no great number. There is of
course a traffic in such forged papers. We have taken precautions. We have said nothing. The circumstances did not
warrant a complaint to the authorities. There is no evidence
that she stole them for use or for profit. I should be obliged if
you treat what I tell you in the greatest confidence. Can I
count upon you?'

'You can.' I've got you there, thought Arlette; to conceal the theft of prescription forms is an offence. 'You think it more likely that she was doing a favour for a friend?'

'I think nothing at all. I should like to correct a view you may have formed, of her father's character, conceivably my own. I do not approve of forcing young persons into a clinic for the purpose of tests, against their will. I think it likely that as much harm as good might result. I believe that in her hostility towards her father, anything construable as a repressive action might be grave. But she's a worry, Madame, I don't attempt to hide it from you.'

'She didn't object to a suggestion that Doctor Rauschenberg take a look at her. Understandably, he disliked the idea without parental authorization.'

'Joachim Rauschenberg is an old friend and I see nothing amiss with that. It is not quite what I was turning over in my mind. I believe that nothing is to be gained by behaving as though you had not the interests of this girl – my niece – at heart. You have, I think, to some extent her confidence?'

'I showed her some commonplace kindness, gave her a sympathetic hearing but beyond that . . .'

'Your reticence does you credit,' with the first sketch of a smile. 'I am not proposing that you weasel confidences from her. Or spy upon her. I would suggest that you try to familiarize yourself with her friends, her haunts. On a confidential basis. Briefly, Madame, I seek to trust you. And trust me in your turn. I do not seek anything prejudicial to my sister's child, the more so that I have for many years lost sight of my sister.'

'That is fair.'

Freddy had not moved from behind his desk, exactly as though he were in his consulting room. He felt in his pocket, and unlocked a desk drawer.

'This should be put upon a professional basis. The best for all concerned. You should have some tangible evidence of this delicate trust. An authority, we may put it. Furthermore your time to consider, your expenses . . .' He opened a cheque book, wrote quickly, blotted it, tore it out: a cheque for a thousand francs. 'A basis for trust, Mrs Davidson.' One can't curtsy while sitting down.

'I'm afraid your patients will be waiting for you, Doctor Ulrich; I'd better set you free. You've set me free – and I'm grateful.'

'I have a good eye, clinically speaking,' said Freddy. 'If I may say so you have a healthy eye. I congratulate you upon it. Keep it.' He escorted her with formal courtesy. 'This, you must forgive my insistence, remains between us. I think it best if you make no approach to my brother-in-law.'

'I agree,' said Arlette with a small grin. 'Can I send her home, with no reproaches made? I'd like to see her back in a pattern as near possible normal.'

'That is sensible. You may rely on that.'

22. 'Arthur's War'

'These Premises are under Electronic Surveillance,' said Arthur.

'Are they?' asked Arlette, startled.

'Of course not. But if one put a big notice in the hall saying they were, enough people would believe it.'

'Aha. A deterrent.'

'Can't be done, alas. Rauschenberg's patients wouldn't like it. The Big Ear's listening to them. We think perhaps those bullseye convex mirrors of polished metal, set at an angle, like at blind corners you know? Periscope effect. How've you been getting on?'

'I'm employed by Freddy to enquire tactfully into Marie-Line's background because he thinks she might be taking drugs, and here's the proof. If she goes home by the way she won't be harassed.'

'That's to the good – splendid. Paul doesn't mind, but she pilfers ten-franc notes from Claire's bag.'

'She has a variety of tiresome little tricks one wouldn't want to live with for any length of time. Admire this. Do I frame it?'

'Paribas Bank, rather haughty. Cash it, you idiot; framing one's first pay-cheque is a cliché.' Nothing Arthur detested more than cliché. He sought them out, pounded upon them, took them by the scruff and kicked their arse.

'So much won from the capitalists.'

'Kiss it, don't spit on it. No such thing as laundered money nowadays. All stolen, every penny. What does old Flaubert say? – Be very bourgeois and conventional in your life, the better to concentrate the originality of your art in your work; I don't claim to paraphrase exactly.'

'Marie-Line taking drugs, or passing them – rather a cliché too?'

'You know, one must beware. I recall the first time I ever landed in America: Boston, the first thing I saw was a great huge Irish cop, gigantic belly soaked in sweat, all hung about with hickory sticks and forty-five guns, dangling handcuffs, western boots and John Wayne hat, the lot. Deplorable I thought, exactly like that Los Angeles chief that believes in setting up gallows at airports, hang any skyjackers on the spot. Cliché's a funny thing. Go to Chicago, of all places. You'll find a police chief that's highly civilized; thoughtful, soft-spoken, and black to boot. Clichés there all the time, deadening, brutalizing, tempting one into cheap crude prejudice.'

Cheap crude prejudice. The words fell on her like three blows of a stick. She felt too tired and stupefied to react. She sat heavy and passive on the nearest chair as though crouched at the foot of some rubbish heap. Let them pelt her then, with anything that came handy; cabbage stalks, empty beer cans, old roots, clods of soil. Bones, stones, lumps of guts: she could only cower there. She shut her eyes so as not to see the grinning faces: in an unconscious stylization she laid her hands flat alongside her face, as though she had to protect her head from

133

another hearty thwack. She felt quite unable to cry: how unfair that was; she needed to cry. Angry self-pity came to her aid and a nasty little hot tear oozed out. A gentle voice spoke to her.

'My poor girl, you're tired to death.' A gentle hand with a hanky wiped her face. This of course made her cry harder than ever.

'That's delayed shock,' said Arthur in a clinical tone. 'Hot tea.' He went away for a moment while she struggled and snuffled, and was just feeling that she was getting back on top of herself when she was rearranged and firmly cuddled, at which she went woo wah hah in an enormous crash, tumbling down from top to bottom of the rubbish heap and lay there like a mass of foolish dough, being petted and not deserving it. Then at last she sat up and said, 'That kettle's boiling its head off.'

There was silence for five minutes, broken only by small comforting household noises. The bump of the kettle put back on the stove, tinkle and roll of something small that fell, and a mild curse from Arthur at his clumsiness, musical tang of porcelain and plink of silver; sliding sound of a tray placed on the table; tock of a sugarlump in a cup and purring of tea poured out, the whee whee of a spoon stirring. She could not open her eyes.

'Easy now,' said Arthur's voice and the rim of the cup came hard and burning on her lips. She took a sip of scalding tea, choked, and began to cough without being able to stop. She went on coughing for about an hour until the voice said 'catch' and she got a handkerchief, a real lawn handkerchief agreeably drenched in eau de cologne, at which she gave a colossal sneeze, stopped coughing, mopped and blew her nose, sat up, drank her tea, and felt vastly better. Arthur was so Good. At this she had to cry again, but not for long. She made various attempts at smiling, blew her nose some more, took a huge gulp of tea to stop her teeth chattering, and declared that she felt much better and it had done her a world of good. Which, as Arthur instantly said, was the cliché to end all others.

'Catharsis. Which sounds like catheters somehow and not very nice. *Se casser les nerfs*, as the French say sensibly. I've locked the door, put the Back-Tomorrow thing on the phone thingy, and you will now go to bed and have a sleep.'

'I don't want to go to bed. I want another cup of tea. The rest is a good idea. I can't face anybody for another hour. God, I'm an incompetent old cunt.'

'Really? Not the way the object in question strikes me, but tastes differ. Don't tell me Freddy brandished. I must ring him up with a lecture then about his Hippocratic oath.' This idiotic chat braced her.

'I felt humiliated.'

'What, at being given a cheque! No French person is ever humiliated by receiving money.'

'Please stop being so annoyingly English. I was mortified at having a lot of preconceived ideas, and getting them kicked about my ears. Talk about selfish, insensitive bourgeois. Accurate description of myself. I know nothing, I'm fatuous, and I had the insolence to go in there looking down my nose.'

'*Ay de mi*,' said Arthur. 'Happens to us all. First book I ever wrote, a work of immense brilliance and no importance, should never have seen the light of day but for that fatal urge to see oneself in print, I was chided in the *Times Literary Supplement* for not being serious. Being young and foolish I sat down with that balm to vanity, the pen dipped in acid, and wrote a splendid letter showing that the reviewer was a reactionary imbecile, that he was motivated by personal animus, and that he was not in the least serious himself, having no knowledge whatever of the subject but was an accomplished mouthpiece for fashionable attitudes. All true. I then realized that from trivial, piteous and ignoble motives he had said something absolutely true. So I couldn't send the letter. But I had a great deal of fun writing it.'

'Yes,' said Arlette. 'The thing is, Freddy's not like that. Rigid, narrow, blinkered if you like, puritanical and viewing himself as Elect, and still capable of nobility. Like Sir Leicester Dedlock. And I felt like that revolting Esther, smarmy little bitch: everybody keeps telling her she's wonderful and is she ever pleased with herself in her tiny gentle ever-so-sweet little voice' bellowing. Arthur, tickled, got the giggles.

'The tiny sweet little voice,' wiping his eyes. 'May I die!' She became intensely uptight, and then got the giggles too.

'Listen,' said Arthur, who had been casting about for better sociological examples. 'I know nothing whatsoever about music, can just barely recognize a tune when it's thumped out. Now you – you have informed good taste and judgment. Who's the best conductor you ever heard?'

'Carlos Kleiber, without much hesitation.'

'Excellent. Now will you be kind enough to give me your views on the Herr von Karajan?'

'Yes, I understand. One is forced to admit, grudgingly, that he's not a charlatan. Can indeed be better than tolerable. But oh, oh, oh, the death in one's heart.'

'You see? You're able to apply honest standards of criticism to your self. It's a thing few can do.'

'I'd like to go out tonight,' said Arlette.

'Have you got tickets?' asked Arthur startled. 'Where to?'

'I didn't mean like that. I want to go and see that frau of my Mister Demazis.'

'I see. You find Inspector Simon a poor critic, and too easily satisfied with preconceived ideas?'

'Arthur, who shot at me? Silly phone calls are one thing – though Demazis told me he got weird phone calls. And vandalism, smearing blood on the door or blowing up the letterbox with bundles of bangers. You and Rauschenberg say that's just the result of the nonsense in the paper, the feeble-minded rallying to stamp on something that attracted an outcry. Is that true, you think?'

'You're not seriously thinking that Demazis was knocked off because of talking to you and having been told not to.'

'No. Nobody could know what he said to me, assuming he was followed or observed; nobody could know I took an interest. Nobody could assume I reacted. True, I went down to the PJ office but so what? They weren't even enquiring into

136

his death – it's classified. I'm a sleeping dog, so why should anybody stir me up? But suppose I stopped being a sleeping dog?'

Arthur thought.

'Woman, your time is your treasure to spend, as you see fit to spend it. As for these manifestations of violence or, it may be, hatred born of fear or misery, I'm like the man in the James Bond book. Two might be happenstance, but any more and I'd go to the cops. What good that would be likely to do I've no idea: it might relieve my conscience. Cops are like hospitals: you're apt to come out a great deal iller than you went in.'

'I don't understand that whatever I do – quite peaceful, conciliatory sort of things – I seem to arouse hostility. Ulrich showed me clearly enough that Siegel is a prickly defensive kind of person who feels vulnerable in all sorts of ways. But why did he have to strike at me so fiercely? And these other people – what have I done?'

Arthur dropped his joking manner.

'You're doing something new, that's all. There's an inherent mediocrity in human beings, a love of the lowest common denominator: hm, that's best left to the philosophers. The sociologist will tell you that it's fear. The slightest untoward happening sets off fear like a big choking cloud of gas. People fear in a big way that's obvious and understandable, like wars, plagues, typhoons, earthquakes. And they fear the unknown, the dark and the silence. You've been alone in a forest, at night? Or at sea? Ghosts and ghouls. This somehow never becomes a cliché, even if it's a truism. Harder to sympathize with are the small mean fears. Of losing one's position and one's standing, so painfully acquired and laboriously wriggled into. Fear of suddenly coming face to face with oneself in the cruel looking-glass. There's a fear of science, and a fear of art. Every work of art in any sense original arouses great hostility and even hatred: Yeats said that. Why? Fear of the unknown, or fear of catching sight of themselves? The dark hates the light, the hypocrite hates truth, the phony hates the real.

137

'Even me. I'm after nobody's job, I threaten nobody. Yet I'm surrounded by people plotting against me for fear I might push them off the narrow ledge. Granted there's nothing more obscurantist, cowardly and cringing than academic circles: I never fail to be astonished. You're paying the price of all this a little.'

'I don't understand altogether, but I understand I have to go on. For both of us.'

'*There's no discharge in the war*, as Kipling says. *Boots, boots, boots, boots, movin' up and down again.* One of the most terrible lines ever written, that.'

'When will the women put a stop to this?' asked Arlette. 'It's not going to be the libbers, the man-haters. One understands them, but they're such fools.'

'Don't let them hear you saying it,' said Arthur.

23. 'Women thinking, women talking'

Arlette walked out into a clear night, cold for October, the kind that in Central Europe tells you Russia is not far away. Strasbourg is closer to Prague than to Paris. The sky was saturated with stars, the air so vivid that she could forget the silts and oozes of the city, the marshy exhalations of her own and so many other bodies, the fear and the anxiety of the three hundred thousand soggy sardines buried down here in the mud.

Strasbourg is a couple of hundred metres above sea level; the Rhine has a long way to go before the mud-filled ditches of Holland. She didn't know how high; she knew it was the same height as the spire of the cathedral. But the Rue de l'Observatoire felt like the bottom of a canyon. She glanced through the railings into the garden, at the cupola of the observatory itself, silent and dark among the last of the leaves – the planes as usual holding out gallantly.

138

People! Why aren't you there observing? I should like to go over and knock on the door and climb up and take a look at something simply glorious like the Crab Nebula. They would tell her that it might look bright, but that in reality there was a thick blanket of filth caused by her and all her little cousins, and sorry, cousin. Stick to terrestrial observations, girl.

She climbed into the car. She had felt frightened coming out. It had cost her a lot to force herself through that door. She had come out like paint from an old dried twisted tube unwillingly, from the cosy nest of music and a smell of left-over veal curry. She had added some even-more-left-over tinned tunny in cream sauce. A classic marriage making a marvellous supper. Stay at home! Listen to Maria Callas! What songs the sirens sing.

She put the Lancia in gear; the new windscreen was already dirty. Through the Esplanade, over the Churchill bridge and the oily, glaucous canal, down into Neudorf.

Strasbourg is awfully flat. They built the cathedral on the only hillock there was. One superb result of this is that if you look back from twenty kilometres away the entire city disappears, and you only see the beautiful ship at anchor, naked in the mudflats. Neudorf is the flattest and muddiest, lying towards the Rhine, and up to a century ago tended to disappear under the Rhine each time the Alpine snows melted. Even today, Neudorf smells as though this still goes on.

It is not like the Meinau lying on its western flank. It is the old easterly high-road to the Rhine crossing. Here beside the Esplanade is Vauban's Citadel. Long before that, the city gate was that of the Ancienne Douane. Pedlars' road, Jews' road, bankers' road across to Augsburg, Nuremburg. On the river bank are the forges and mills of the Port du Rhin, and along the road you can trace the beginnings of the industrial revolution, the wooden sheds and hangars of artisan workshops still there between factories.

There is romance here, for those with a taste for it. Along the Route du Rhin the giant articulated road-freights come to rest, their lamps spattered with the mud of Turkey, Hungary,

Bulgaria, with enigmatic, cyrillic lettering along their sides. And on the top of the dyke built from the Alsace gravel pits, the Orient Express rattled by; the wheel spun; the Lady Vanished; Alfred Hitchcock smiled; Albert Demazis died. From the top windows in the Rue de Labaroche, where Albert lived, you can see this railway line.

Arlette drove down to the end, parked, crossed a footbridge over a tiny waterway, saw the embankment loom above her, followed a cyclists' path along it. Thin trees and bushes clothed the dyke. After a while her eyes grew accustomed to the starlight; she could see what she was looking for, a thin oblique path to the top. The railwaymen from the Port du Rhin station or the Neudorf freightyard rode their bikes along here, took short cuts down to their homes. Trembling from cold and fear she trudged up to the top, stood looking at the double row of silent metals, the worn path just wide enough for a bicycle or a man walking, his dog either in front, behind, or on the line.

Yes, there were brambles to trip on. Yes, if you stepped aside to avoid a muddy puddle there was loose ballast to slip on. If, anxious to miss these little traps in the dark you walked on the sleepers, the old baulks were worn and slippery, and set just too close together for a man's stride.

In the still air, the mutter of the city traffic now distant, one would hear anything coming a long way off. Would one though! Arlette, absorbed in detective pursuits, jumped back suddenly with her heart in her mouth. A loose locomotive had stolen round the curve silent as a ghost upon somebody absent-minded. Its lamps gleamed on her with an evil, oily yellow light and it tooted angrily as the big diesel thudded past her. From the cab a man shook his head and tapped his finger on his forehead, with no smile to her upturned, aghast face. Christ! Her heart thumped and she felt sweat in her armpits. The loco – perhaps the same loco – thudded round the curve out into silence, and in the silence a signal changed with a sharp snick and she jumped afresh. He might report her at the Port du Rhin a kilometre down. 'Now there's another one on

140

the line same place. Stupid cow of a woman.' Arlette fled guiltily.

Accident – my god, yes. Only too damned easy; proved it to herself Most adequately, thank you.

Only what the hell was he doing on the railway line at all? One didn't walk, or stroll, at all comfortably even by daylight. At night the streets were quiet and one recognized the other dog-walkers; smiled, nodded, said good-evening.

Was that it? If one didn't want to be seen, recognized, maybe remembered by other dog-walkers would one . . .? And if one didn't, why didn't one? A stupid, weary, profitless speculation.

Her mind had strayed into preposterous Hitchcock situations: spies, white slaves, crimson Orient-Express fantasies. A mysterious parcel was jerked out of the window to the man waiting in the shadowy bushes. Cary Grant, most athletic, dropped skilfully off the rear platform, like the man with the crutch in *Double Indemnity*. Back through the trees, Barbara Stanwyck blinked her headlights, twice. Joan Fontaine's face was seen an instant at the window, mouth open for a scream just before the chloroform pad was slapped over it. Arlette shook her head and tramped back to the Rue de Labaroche. She pushed the bell labelled 'Demazis'.

Pause, as of somebody getting up from in front of the television. 'Yes?' barked the little metal grille.

'Mrs Demazis? I'm sorry. I knew your husband, slightly. I wondered, could I have a word with you.'

Pause again, considering this, wondering what it meant. Curiosity overcame irritation. The intercom made a faint meaningless noise; the door clicked and buzzed. When she stepped out of the lift the landing door was open and the passage light was on: a woman stood in the doorway cautiously, peering to see who it could be late at night, ready to jump back and slam the door and ring the police to say there's an Intruder. Normal this tenseness, especially in a woman living by herself.

The woman waited. The lift-door slid shut and the lift trundled downward. Arlette was alone standing there.

141

'Yes?' said the woman again.

'I wanted again first to say I was sorry, and that I sympathize very much.'

'That's kind. And?'

'You see, Monsieur Demazis phoned me the day before. He didn't tell me exactly what he wanted; it was all a little confused. And when I read of his death like that I got a shock, naturally. And I wondered whether you know anything of it, and whether there was anything I could do to help.'

'Excuse me but – who are you?'

'My name is Arlette van der Valk. I run an advice bureau in the town.'

'An advice bureau?' thoughtfully, running her eyes doubtingly all over Arlette in that quick acute glance that prices your clothes, places you socially, knows to the hour when you had your hair last done. 'How very odd.' She hesitated, running her fingernail to and fro across her large even teeth. 'I think p'raps you'd better come in.'

'I'm sorry; perhaps I'm disturbing you?' Timid in the little hallway, conventionally neat with dark blue moquette, reddish veneer panelling on the cupboards, brassbound lighting, a stag's antlers for one's hat.

'No, no,' absently, moving on with quick supple movements over sturdy well-shaped legs. 'I'm alone. I was only looking at the box, nothing interesting.' In the living-room dancers vaguely waved scarves and wiggled over a blurry singer–saxophone duet; it all vanished together and the woman said, 'Please sit down,' politely.

Alsace comfort; furniture too large for the flat, too much wood with too much carving on it. Warm and bright, smelling clean and pleasant. It would be interesting to know where Albert had lived and how, but she had no time to stare about her. The woman sat opposite with the heavy supple gesture, face sharp and concentrated. A fraction shorter and thicker than herself, in a greyish silky buttonthrough frock half way to being housecoat. Leather slippers with a woolly fringe. Fair hair blonder and more metallic than her own, fading and

142

beginning to grey in much the same way, drawn loosely back and knotted in a bun. Large oval face that had been pretty, still was pretty, or handsome at the least; large well-shaped features, unpainted but for big pink lips heavy in their modelling. Big shell-shaped rimless glasses over big, perhaps magnified, protuberant eyes a vivid pale blue. Garnet studs in the pale fleshy lobes of the ears, and a necklace of garnet snowflakes to match: the throat was soft, heavy, fairly deeply lined. Cared-for white hands long and strong, unpainted. The smile was pleasant, and the face holding a little suspicion still, but mostly curiosity.

'I'm afraid I don't at all get this thing about an advice bureau. What's that?'

'Quite simple,' smiling. 'You know how officials are; they send you somewhere else. People go round and round and end by eating their own tail. Discouragement leads to frustration. I find I can help, quite often.'

'I can understand that. But my husband . . .'

'I thought it odd myself. As I told him, I don't do divorce and I know nothing about finance. You see why I've come to you,' smiling.

'Yes,' said the woman. She stared at the wall and said, 'Yes,' again. 'No, I can't account for that at all . . . You didn't actually meet him, did you say?'

It was rare, in Arlette's view of things, that one lost anything by telling the truth.

'Yes, we met; briefly. I told him approximately what I could do and couldn't: he said he'd think things over. He gave me no hint of what was troubling him.' The woman was running her necklace along her lips.

'And did you draw any conclusion?'

'I didn't have enough to go on. An impression perhaps; he seemed nervous. I wondered whether he'd been working too hard. I thought you'd know more about that.'

'The police asked that. They wondered I suppose whether suicide seemed a possibility. I mean, people do throw themselves under trains. All I could say was it didn't sound likely to

143

me. Working too hard – no. He was a very serious person, and he took his job very seriously. He was extremely meticulous, and if there was any small error in accounting somewhere he would get very annoyed until he found it.'

'If he found some employee cheating perhaps, he might worry? Case of conscience?'

'Oh no, he'd have gone straight to the boss. Why d'you ask?' suddenly. 'Did he suggest something like that?'

'Not in the least. I was casting about, looking for something that would fill the bill. You know, forced to sack the man but hoping I might help.'

The head turned to look at her, quite sharply.

'I never heard of anything like that.'

'People aren't always hardhearted. A man rang me yesterday. He wanted to employ a man with a prison record, and asked me to find out something more about him; family, background. I thought it nice of him. A lot just refuse, point-blank.'

'Anything at work,' said the woman flatly, 'Mr Tagland would know. He came to see me. To say, you know, how sorry he was and all that. Very nice man. And anything else, I'd know, wouldn't I?'

'Of course.'

'So I'm afraid I can't help you.'

'It was just an idea,' politely, getting up to go. 'Did he walk often on the railway line? Doesn't sound very safe.'

'I've no idea. As I told the police. He used to take the dog out, walking.'

'What happened to the dog?' The question seemed to disconcert her.

'I sent it to the animal shelter. I never liked it. It used to destroy the furniture.' She seemed to think something else was needed.

'It was an unhappy reminder.'

'Yes of course. I mustn't keep you. Very kind of you to talk to me.'

'I wouldn't worry any further. What's past is past.' She

144

brought Arlette as far as the lift, still putting the necklace between her fine teeth now and then, as though testing whether it were real.

Arlette got into the car. She glanced up while turning the key in the lock. The corner of a curtain was lifted. A thing most people did. Just checking up – idle curiosity.

Strange woman – hardish. Spoke about her husband with unusual detachment – a man who had been around the place, and now wasn't there any more. Like the dog, referred to as 'it'. Perhaps she had simply made up her mind to carve out a new life for herself. Being suddenly widowed – Arlette was aware – isn't the easiest of experiences. Your husband isn't there any more. You are still relatively young, and fairly attractive.

Arlette couldn't remember being that detached about a dead husband, less than a week afterward.

She didn't seem to have any children? Did she work?

A quiet woman. Easy circumstances. Just getting over the loss of a husband, learning to live with the widow. Conventional in conventional surroundings. No sign of anything outside a well-padded rut. So why is the woman so guarded? Wary . . . suspicious, even.

Does all this night air make one more observant, or simply more imaginative? There is such a thing as over-observing: a woman is naturally observant of another her own age. But which woman has been over-observant of the other?

24. 'An Irritating Nonchalance'

She drove back through the Esplanade but instead of turning to her own street went on down the Boulevard de la Marne, came out at the Orangerie and skirted it till she got to the highly superior apartment block where the elegant and dynamic young advocate, Maître Friedmann, lived with his pretty and charming young wife, their delightful children and a temporary lodger.

Paul let her in, glancing at his watch and frowning slightly.

'I'm sorry, am I shockingly late?' asked Arlette apologetically.

'Not in the least. Marie-Line is, though: I told her I wanted her back by ten. Is that unreasonable?'

'Not in the least.'

'I think of myself and old Clancy as the young swinging set, what. Young girls under one's roof, that's a responsibility. Not my own daughter, so the greater. Stop laughing, you cow.'

'Stop apologizing.'

'Have a drink.'

'Yes, I need one, rather. But I've come to take her off your hands, you'll be glad to hear.'

'No longer ashamed to say it'll be a relief,' admitted Claire, ravishing legs stretched out beyond a dashing batik print. 'A wonder there's any drink left to offer you.' Paul smiled.

'That's an exaggeration, but she does sip a bit slylike, and she pinches money from Claire's purse, all rather a trial so we tightened the belt and said it was in a good cause. The good cause seems to have collapsed – I had ol' Arthur on the phone, you wound these frightful doctors round your finger, I hear. Objectively rather a pity. No tighter closed shop than the medics with their lips sealed, except of course the Law Society: I was quite looking forward to a fast fifteen rounds with that Siegel, even though I've come in my heart to sympathize secretly.'

'That happened to me; I started feeling sorry for him. I'm bound to say that Freddy Ulrich was reasonable. He also gave me some money which is yours for all the trouble you took.'

'Stuff, I want no money, I did nothing. Keep it. But what did he give it you for – hoping you'd keep your mouth shut?'

'Don't be an ass. Tell you in a sec. The thing is, the coast's clear for Marie-Line, the old man has sworn mightily he won't pester her, and I think the sooner she's home the better.

146

Tonight, even. Then she can go to school in the morning, all normal and proper. Listen, before she gets here – is she taking any dope? I thought not. Booze yes, but nothing worse.'

'Wouldn't put it past her,' said Paul.

'Oh nonsense,' said Claire. 'That's most unfair. She's quite ordinary. She has this irritating nonchalance, but I keep thinking what I was like at nineteen, perfect little horror: she's just the same. Pestering one, you know, to assert herself. Never says where she's going and always late for meals. Talk to her she's not listening. Ask her to lend a hand tidying and she'll break all your good cups. Just when you're blissfully quiet suddenly turns the radio on full blast. Sings, skips, dances, and when you say something looks at you, as though just realizing you were in the room, and puts on the sad sack look as though sorry for you being so utterly wet. But absolutely nothing perturbed or disturbed or what does the shrink call it? Not like my children – now they're all deeply perturbed but they throw themselves into it, enjoy it. Tearing hair and shrieking. She's just goddamned nonchalant. I don't mind really but it drives Paul bats.'

'Just that I long to give her a slap. Big boots, little whip,' glaring and gibbering. 'Sadistic porn film: knickers down, you; I'll show you how we tame lions.' The women kept up the merry laughter with false enthusiasm as the door opened and Marie-Line slouched in. Not looking dissipated really; a bit smudgy, a bit messy.

'Hallo there,' said Arlette.

'Hi,' slumping on the sofa. 'Sorry I'm a bit late, I went to a movie.'

'Was it good?'

'No, shitty. I'm thirsty, can I have some lemonade?'

'Of course. In the fridge in a jug. Anybody else want some? Me a bit, Line, bring a second glass.' There was a loud crash in the kitchen.

'See what I mean?'

'Sorry, I let a glass drop. I swept it up,' virtuously.

'You'll be interested in this,' said Arlette – 'I had a lengthy,

147

and I'm glad to say helpful, session with your Uncle Freddy.'

Marie-Line didn't look a bit interested, picked at a thumbnail.

'I'm glad to say he's being reasonable, and I don't claim credit for that by any means. Your father agrees that he went too far. We mustn't try to force him to say so; on the contrary: do all we can to help him save face. He promises he'll not make you any reproach, and no more of this curfew business. Of course you can see your friends, and whom you like. Us too, we hope. What is asked of you is not much. To come in at a reasonable time, and let people know where you are – it was rude not to let Claire know you were going to a film. And, Marie-Line, you will agree, you can't avoid seeing it yourself, you're drinking much too much. That's ruinous to your health and it's spoiling your complexion. I'm not going to make a sermon. It's getting late too, and I promised you'd be home tonight.' Marie-Line who had just been looking sullen looked suddenly desolate. 'Cheer up, darling. That's not a hardship.'

'You were willing enough for me to leave before. They talked you round, huh?'

'To avoid a head-on clash, yes. Situation changes,' said Paul.

'No longer an avoidance but an evasion. I'd give anyone the same advice; shun litigation when the other side looks conciliatory. Arlette is absolutely right. Showing obstinacy would weaken your position, which is now strong.'

'And any time you feel isolated or need support, you know we're here.'

The girl made her mind up to put a good face on it.

'Thanks,' she said, giving Claire a kiss, 'you've been nice and I was horrid.'

'We've simply loved having you,' with equal gallantry.

'Arthur agrees,' said Arlette turning the car. 'The way he sees it, and I must say me too, that if you get down to it and pass your exam your father will be pleased, and feel rewarded. The exam is useless, nobody knows better than Arthur, but it

148

gives you freedom of movement. Whether you go to the university or not, you'd feel that these years haven't been altogether wasted, and I'm pretty sure we could get your father to agree then to your living away from home if you wanted.'

'Mmm.'

'I rather liked Cathy,' at the red light on the Boulevard d' Anvers. 'She may be a bit of a priss, and defensive about her precious standing, but I thought her basically a nice person.'

'Mmm.'

'I'm serious about not drinking so much, you know. One's character becomes vile and oneself unattractive.'

'Yes yes, I know,' crossly.

'That's right, I promised I wouldn't preach. Smoking the odd joint is nothing much to make a fuss about to my mind. Don't be tempted into anything harder.'

'I don't get any kick out of it: I just go a bit sleepy and silly.'

'Think yourself lucky. Nothing stupider anyhow than being pinched by the cops for possession. And nothing nastier than being sent for the cure. The psychiatric clinic would be a holiday in comparison.'

'Mmm.'

Arlette thought the subject best left unpursued.

'Your boy Michel – who does Greek, is that right? – sounds nice; I'd like to meet him.'

'He is nice. A bit weird,' making no offer to effect an introduction.

Warned off. It had been on the tip of her tongue to ask about the other Michel, who according to that girl Françoise was at the Beaux Arts. Quite possibly one or the other was a figment of imagination, or would they turn out to be one and the same?

After the heavy flow of traffic along the main road the 'bourgeois' corner of the Meinau was a haven of peace and respectability. Lights still burned in most of the houses: the street looked innocent and friendly. Doctor Siegel's desirable

149

residence had the porch light on, to show they were expected. Marie-Line scrabbled in her jacket for keys; Arlette stopped her and rang the bell.

'I must say a polite word, you see. I won't embarrass you.'

Siegel opened himself, youthful and unbuttoned in a silk dressing-gown which looked a bit staged.

'Sorry to be so late. Marie-Line had gone to the cinema, and I hadn't realized.'

'That's of no consequence. Well my girl,' with a paternal kiss on the forehead, received dutifully. 'You'll come in and have a drink.'

'For no more than a minute then, but nothing to drink thanks; I've still got to drive.'

'Wise of you. Never mind. I have at least the opportunity of thanking you, and to express my regret for some tempestuous remarks when last we met.' One must say this for a bourgeois upbringing: you learn to turn a handsome phrase.

'I was a bit of a virago, I'm sorry to say.'

'The fault was mine. You must allow me to make amends.'

A stiff little bow, and the hand came out of the pocket clutching the kind of little envelope that fits a calling card.

'Well,' said Arlette, falling absurdly into cliché, 'in the spirit it's offered, then. That's most generous of you.'

'We won't discuss it,' in quite the old voice, 'but my brother assures me there is now no misunderstanding between us. My daughter is very close to my heart.' It had a touching dignity.

'I can only say that in this short time we've grown fond of her. I'll say goodnight then. My regards to Madame Pelletier; I was happy to have met her. Sleep well, Marie-Line, and drop in any time you like.' She waved cheerfully and whisked down the path, Monsieur Siegel waiting correct and Japanese upon the doorstep until she was out of the gate. Well; that could have been a lot worse.

The amount of traffic there still was! The long-distance freight went on all night but the pub crowd was still thick on the road, and well tanked-up. Arlette drove with care. She wasn't used to being out late, and felt mindful of Arthur's counsels of prudence. She kept her doors locked and her windows wound up, and a wary eye on the rear-view mirror. But nobody seemed to be following her. In the Rue de l'Observatoire she parked a little way down, and spied out the land with some care, and walked rather too fast to her door, her heels making a fussy tap on the pavement. But no practical jokers tonight. A few students with loud cheerful voices.

Arthur had gone to bed, in a hedgehog mass as usual of books, pipes and bits of paper with useful notes upon them, folded into narrow spills and serving as markers. Why did he need all that – being intent upon something with a blonde on the cover? He did not speak but uttered grunts.

While undressing she discovered the little amend. Two carefully folded and pinned five-hundred franc notes. Now that is delicate, or would you call it cautious? No trace of anything changing hands. Doesn't appear, what, on Monsieur Siegel's income-tax returns. No, nor mine either.

Arlette went and got an orange and an apple, and climbed into bed.

'Stop making those greedy sucking sounds,' said Arthur.

25. 'Lycée Classique'

A peaceful morning, as well as wealthy. The local paper had a bland retraction of any nasty hints it might have dropped, studiedly airy, so that one needed to know how to read between the lines before realizing that Paul had thrown a fright into them and Siegel, after blowing up a large red balloon, had rather unfairly gone and popped it. Devout protests about not wishing to cast aspersions upon impeccable credentials.

This all had an immediate effect upon business. The phone rang; a woman sounding middle-aged and fairly excitable had

151

a problem. How urgent was the problem? Could it wait until tomorrow? Today was rather a busy day. Well all right, yes.

It spurred Arlette into thinking it Was a busy day, and she dressed in a hurry.

The Lycée Fustel de Coulanges looks much the same today as at the turn of the century. Or since the Revolution, come to that: the fine eighteenth-century façade, in the dark red and pale pink of Alsace sandstone, needs only the tide-mark at its foot removed – the seawrack of metal beercans and plastic yoghurt-pots. The visual impression left by parking cars in the Place du Château, between the Cathedral and the Rohan Palace, is deplorable.

Behind the façade the military quadrangle is equally unchanged: the uniformed boys changing class to the roll of the drum, just like V.M.I. or West Point, would not feel displaced. The scruffy horde in jeans, like the motorbikes outside, looks fragile and impermanent. Some are girls now, but it is not easy to tell which. 'May I just take your trousers down an instant?' begs the anthropologist politely. Lifting perhaps his solar topee.

The twin pillars of such an establishment, the Provost and the Dean, are unchanged too; remote gods behind padded doors, only appeased by human sacrifice. But you do not go to them for casual information about a pupil; you go to the director of studies. Arlette found the director in a small cluttered office papered entirely in work-charts and graphs, a big easy comfortable man. Face of severity, and of much kindness and humour. Framed in the large shaved jaw the mobile mouth was dangerous. Like a sea-anemone waving innocently. Small imprudent animals could find themselves caught. He had the enviable skill, while being at all times frantically busy, of appearing to have all the time in the world.

'What can I do for you, Madame?'

'I'm trying to identify, and get hold of a boy of whom I know very little. His name is Michel, he does Greek, and I think he's in the final year.'

'That's no problem. A child doing Greek is now a rare

152

species. This one I know well. Good pupil.' A turn half-left, a glance at a chart. 'Won't be in yet. No class before ten.' The door opened, a youngish overseer bustled in with a draught, said, 'Excuse me,' and dumped some dirty-looking papers on the crowded desk.

'What's that?' with distaste, not looking.

'That horrible Zissel.'

'Is he there? Shoot him in. Excuse me a moment, Madame,' as an inky boy was produced and stood limp and boneless. 'Zissel, you're a vile child,' mildly, big thumb turning over the dirty papers.

'Your father – you're aware?' The papers were covered in exasperated scrawls in red ink. 'Your professors are feeling ground down. So is your father. You're asking in fact for a monumental backhander. This work reeks of an immense capacity for not taking pains. You're putting a huge effort, Zissel, into persuading everybody that you are mentally deficient. I know you to be nothing of the sort. What have you to say?'

Shapeless mumble, totally inaudible.

'I see.' Another glance at his chart. 'You're free at four. Where does your mother work? You will go and wait for her, and you will give her this message with my compliments: will she have the kindness to come in and see me on her way home, and we'll have a talk. Concerning you. You have now three seconds to get from here to your classroom, while stopping on the way for a good wash. That will do, Zissel. I beg your pardon Madame, you were saying? Young Carlin who does Greek.'

'Who would know him best?'

'His work, his character? – makes no odds really. His principal professor is Monsieur Perregaux. Who is,' a swing half-right, to another set of charts '. . . as well nothing before ten: he'll be preparing his courses,' picking up a telephone without looking at it, the thick fingers agile on buttons, 'Perregaux there? Ask him could he manage to speak to a lady interested in one of his pupils. He can? Straight away if he likes. You'll find him at the foot of the stairs, Madame, by the concierge's office. Not in the least; enchanted to be of any service.' Wonderful, she thought. A man who wastes no second asking who I am and what my business is, takes one glance, decides I'm serious, and fixes it all within the half-minute, with young Zissel thrown into the bargain.

The nine o'clock bell, far worse than any drumroll – even that for an execution – took her back to her childhood along with the smells and the corridors full of children in crowds parting amiably, vaguely to let her pass without even a glance. Just a Mum, come to complain to the Surge about her Zissel.

Monsieur Perregaux was easily recognized, an elderly gentleman with round-shouldered academic bearing, this one a real figure from her childhood, the teacher with a master's degree and a doctorate, of terrifying erudition about the Bacchae of Euripedes. Unexpectedly sharp eye, shooting her an amused smile.

'Young Michel? A splendid boy. The rare bird at any time, rarest now when Mathematics is the New Latin. Has it struck you as funny? We based our criteria for excellence on the ability at the Latin Theme, we abandoned all that with horror as outdated élitism, and we now do exactly the same thing, with algebraic formulae substituting for Ciceronian pedantries. Both the same Chinese. Michel is one of the few to whom scholarship has meaning. Asks what the job is, instead of what it pays. I'm tempted to say he knows more about the Achaeans than I do.'

'Hot-house plant?'

'Oh yes, we still have our class preparing for Advanced Schools rather than that preposterous university, that Social Security knocking-shop with its courses in Envy and Calumny, the Gold Brick and the Polished Apple.' The old boy was funny, but she wasn't getting nearer Michel.

'Will you tell me what he's like?'

'I'm an old man. I no longer care what I say. I'm not to be relied upon. They're retiring me at the end of this year. High time, where they're concerned. Not modern, you know. Give me a chiming clock and a lot of polished speeches, forty years

154

of devoted collaboration, but glad to get rid of me. Hm, maybe I will tell you. But I've remnants of prudence. Who are you; why do you seek information from me?'

'I have a partly professional, partly friendly interest in a girl of his age, not one of your students, who has or had a friendship and perhaps an emotional relationship with this boy Michel. She's a little secretive and evasive about it. That's more or less all.'

'Is it?'

'All right. She's under some suspicion of handling or possessing drugs. Not officially, not a police matter. I've seen no sign of her using drugs, but it can be difficult to detect and I've not seen much of her. Getting to know something of her friends and associates is a step that's obvious. There's no point, quite frankly, in asking any official of the Lycée a question like that. Their interest is in hushing things, in keeping the parents from getting anxious. I've no complaint to make of that.'

The old man laughed silently.

'A social disgrace,' he said. 'Enquiry likewise fails as to how many have lice in their hair. Or gonorrhea. And all these people we have now? – school doctor, nurse, social and psychiatric counsellors – there seems no end to them.'

'All pretty superficial to my mind. And whatever I did would be not enough or too much. Make a polite murmur, the lips would be sealed. Shocked expressions, and they've never heard of such a thing. Push a bit harder and there'd be a hullabaloo, which I don't want.'

'And would the evidence be worth much? The children don't confide in these people, whom they view as the tame auxiliaries of authority, meaning repression. Nor I may say do they confide in me, but then I don't hang about sucking up to them. Well, well, I've answered my own question.

'Drugs? Yes of course. Shows up in their work. An anxiety, a febrile showiness. These children suffer from anxiety, and there is great pressure upon them to acquire social prestige – success in an examination. I've never paid much attention to

155

it in consequence. Use of hashish and opiates is a very old oriental tradition. Some modern pharmaceutic products, nasty things, adults all have cupboards full, doctors hand them out to all and sundry, how could you expect the children to do otherwise. Doesn't thus shock or surprise me. I've two or three in my classes mixing sedatives and stimulants. The parents wouldn't thank me for voicing my opinions.

'Michel? – no. He's not all that gifted intellectually; I've had lots much brainier. A good power of synthesis, a flexible gift of expression, a readily flowering imagination: not however the infant phenomenon. His precocity of development is shown more in an unusual sensitivity of observation, and a surprising maturity. Highly disciplined and a sharply focused ability to concentrate. What shall I say? – taken in isolation none of these talents would appear as exceptional. Taken together they're to my thinking of much promise. His analytic powers are lower. His philosophy professor has not as high an opinion of him as I have.

'Oh make no mistake, he's bright. And on the other hand I'm not seeing him as the young Proust.

'What he wants, he'll get. Tough of fibre, close of texture.

'For the rest, a quiet gentle boy. Can't abide brutality or cruelty. Patroclus rather than Achilles. Defensive, naturally, about this dreamy sensitive side. Puts on a bit of a tough act with the motorbicycle oafs. Repressive about romanticism. Suffers. Hum, I'm saying no more.'

'I couldn't have done better in a month of Sundays, as the English say.'

'Flattering of you. Well, I must go think about my courses.'

'How do you find the girls?'

'The girls? Ah – I enjoy them greatly. I like to smell their beautiful clean hair. When spotty and unwashed of course, even more pathetic than the adolescent male. And no less vulnerable. Ah me. The elderly pedagogue is not always pederast. Like Theseus, I've a taste for Amazons. Well: to shed light is my calling in life; I hope I've been of use: one so seldom is.'

156

26. 'The Flowering Suburb'

Follow the Route de Colmar out past the Meinau, and the tentacular suburbs of South Strasbourg seem to stretch on forever along a narrow congested road blocked with traffic lights every thirty seconds. The boring twin burgs of Illkirch-Graffenstaden have long given up the pretence of being villages. The housing promoters who have snapped up the last fields are lyrical about greenery and country air at 'less than fifteen minutes', means of transport unspecified, from the town centre. Very like the naked girls on television, ecstatic about the new shampoo they've just discovered.

Arlette could not understand it at all. 'Isn't it from this direction that the revolution will come?' she asked Arthur hopefully. 'How can they go on and on and on swallowing ever bigger and more blatant lies? Is the public so stunned, so brutalized and anaesthetized it simply does not notice? What is the limit of gullibility? How can anybody, ever, vote for any political party whatsoever? Who is it that sits starry-eyed sucking up the goo? The threshold of credibility has long ago been passed.'

Arthur smiled kindly. Dear girl! He got a smack for that: no male superiority here please.

'Poor France. They're even selling them cornflakes now.'

'Kindly answer the question.'

'There are seventeen answers, all interlocking. The market is continually renewed: the young simpletons replacing the cynical old. People are not more educated; they're if anything less so. Children look at publicity because it's more fun, they think rightly, than what goes on the rest of the time. More imaginative, technically more inventive, catchier rhymes and tunes. The copywriters don't expect to be taken seriously. They want only that you will remember the name of the product as you totter glassily along the supermarket shelf, and pop it in your basket. Politicians are there because of a void nothing else fills. Having once proclaimed that the people is sovereign and decides things they can sit back, knowing perfectly that the people which has been prevented from deciding anything whatever all these years isn't going to begin now. What more was there? Like everyone else, before reaching the end I've forgotten the beginning. What are you asking me for, anyhow? Your thoughts are as good as mine.'

Halfway down that long long road Arlette turned to the right, dodged about to avoid two more suburbs begging her to come and live in them, squeezed through an autoroute underpass and popped out in exurbia, otherwise known as Geispolsheim.

There are two. This was Geispolsheim-Gare, a commuter railway station around which has grown up a settlement of coyly rustic villas. Once you get out of this, with some difficulty, there is a quite countrified little road where you can see real fields, and there are crab-apple trees along the verges, of which motorists complain. Two kilometres farther is the village of Geispolsheim. Only a few years ago quiet and pleasant, with farmyard muckheaps and a steeple with a stork on it. The fields are filling fast with bungalows, and the airport looms disquietingly, and loudly. But there are still fields, and a tatty gate, and a notice needing repainting which says Taglang Horticultural Enterprises. A jumble of small old dirty glasshouses; a shiny new large glasshouse; a big rectangle of concrete with rusty sort of pillars sticking out of it, announcing one even bigger. The Enterprises were making plenty of money.

She had overshot: reversed, entered where it helpfully said Entrance, and came to rest on a boggy patch made muddier by several cars. If they're making that much money they could well invest in a few truckloads of gravel, thought Arlette, changing her shoes.

A high hedge, neatly clipped, and trees, and a fingerpost saying Office, through-here, and she turned the corner and found a bungalow, very large and super and stinkingly nouveau riche, with the New England clapboard bit tacked on to the California-Spanish bit, swimming-pool, patio, terrace, orange trees in gay wooden tubs and lemon trees in massive earthenware, Biot style. *Lots* of money being made. All this in the middle of the humble fields of Geispolsheim, and a V6 Jaguar, and a silver Porsche Carrera, and by gum a Maserati too, in Italian racing red. She felt hit on the head.

The office was the old part of the bungalow, now long outgrown, the former kitchen and living-room now tarted up with lavish Italian tiles and terrazzo, with many plants in pots. A girl with several telephones bade her good morning and said she'd try and find Mr Taglang.

He was a rumpled, friendly man in his forties; sports jacket, check shirt, flannels and cowboy boots, with an easy-going manner. She gave a rambling tale about business relations with Mr Demazis, said she'd learned of his sudden death with a shock – left a couple of loose ends.

'Left a couple here too,' making a lip. 'I'm the technician – he ran the financial end. Pretty snarled up, without him, but we're getting straight. What brought you out here then?'

'Oh, just vulgar curiosity, I guess. Was seeing somebody off at the airport.' Hands in pockets, legs crossed, casual; she hoped she wasn't overdoing it. The simple truth wouldn't do here. Lying was unsimple, and she must try not to embroider.

'What you in, then?' No suspicion. Like her, just vulgar curiosity.

'Oh, house property. You know. And any business is interesting, isn't it? One always takes a look. You're doing pretty well – I say with admiration.'

'Got to know how to find the right corner, specialize in the right thing,' with an attractive enthusiasm. 'Like to take a look?'

'Very much indeed.'

'I don't try to do the garden-centre thing. Matter of fact I don't do outside stuff at all, hardly. Always was interested in indoor plants. Got to have a gift for them. This market's hardly scratched. Should see the stuff they have in Holland:

159

ten times the varieties we have here. But we're catching up. Take a couple of basics, and work on ornamental varieties. Azaleas say, or hibiscus. Fella down the road has half the poinsettia market in Europe. The ecology kick helps us. Grow your own thing huh, even in a little flat. Coffee bean, pineapple top, avocado stone. People living in ghastly conditions, want something natural, something beautiful. Dies, as it nearly always does, they can replace it. Cheap.'

'Well of course. I do it myself, I understand perfectly. Bloody good luck, I say – you couldn't do better.'

Lightning tour, down a glassed passage, into a hothouse, out and into another. Some coolish, dry, others hot and humid. Close stifling smells of greenery. Quantities of turf mould and special soils, piles of little pots. Three or four earnest bearded young men doing the little, careful, handcraft chores with minute seedlings that were bathed in special light and heat, cosseted with automatic sprinklers, potioned with magic mixtures, flipped inside six weeks into sweet little bushes thick with flowers, all forced with skilful artifice. Frightful disappointment waiting. Three weeks later the darling thing blew its mind, languished and died. Well so what? You went back and bought another. They weren't dear. Cheaper than cut flowers.

'Fascinating,' she said, meaning it. 'Mail order, almost.'

'Not quite, because they're so fragile. But we deliver with the truck, all over. Germany, Switzerland, anywhere you like. Damn complicated. That was what Albert was so good at. We'll have to be getting a computer, ha.'

'How are you managing?' asked Arlette sympathetically.

'Ah, my wife used to do it,' said Mr Taglang. 'She laid off a few years ago – to have a family, you know. Got the main threads in her head still. Full-time job, though.' He seemed to enjoy talking to her.

Why not? People liked her, showed her confidence. Not just that she was a good listener. She was a happy person, said Arthur, and it showed. And a good person, he added. People feel this goodness. They feel they can rely upon you.

Pooh, good. What's that? Good as gold, people say. Gold will buy a lot? Won't lose its value? Is nice to work with? Ductile, a good conductor? Heavy, nice to touch and agreeable to wear? Warm, and solid? A golden mediocrity, that's me.

You have innocence, said Arthur.

I'm ready to believe good of people. I hope I don't lose that. Why always believe the worst, of everyone? Why always show suspicion and mistrust?

Mr Taglang was a nice person. People who are genuine enthusiasts always are. A man sunk in his work, loving it. These plants are more to him than a means of making money. The way he speaks of them: you can tell at once.

'What are these?'

'Camellias. They're resting. Mustn't bring them on too soon. Lovely things,' caressing the foliage. 'See them in bloom – come back in January. You see, that's when people need them most; in February when things are gloomiest. And these the azaleas. Ponticas and japonicas.'

'I never can tell the difference.'

'One is deciduous – look, just coming into leaf.'

'Most places this month are obsessed by those horrible chrysanthemums.'

'Yes of course, to put on graves for All Saints. Being marketed now – the work is finished. No, they're not horrible. I don't touch them though. One can't do everything. Some people do bulbous plants, lilies say. Roses, carnations. There's room for everybody.'

'The little lemons are sweet.'

'One of my main interests. Slow, and difficult. I'm working with some success on accelerating them, and on miniaturization. A full size orange tree is too much for people mostly. You can have a little mandarin though, fifty centimetres high in full fruit. Do the same with lemons – even grapefruit. Why not?'

And make lots of money doing so. Why not? Nothing wrong with that.

'All this glass – must be expensive. Big investment. Risk Capital.'

161

'Yes indeed,' seeming pleased. 'Costs a fortune. Got to take
the risk though.'

'Bank take a pretty favourable view?'

'M'yes.' Perhaps it was the one question too many, too nosy.
Or he didn't like to think of the mortgage the bank had on
him.

'I'd love to buy one of those.'

'Not those though. Too immature. Die if you took it out
now. Find you a natural one if you like. Won't bloom for you
till spring though. Too long to wait?'

'No, I enjoy the waiting and the wondering.'

'Most people are too impatient. Want it all now.' They had
come back to the outside of the office. 'This lot's been outdoors
all summer. Ready to move in, now.' A dark brown woman,
wearing a becoming shade of pink, could be seen through the
glass, telling the girl off by the gestures made. A camellia in
bloom. Pretty. That would be the wife.

'How about this? Quite a pretty shape.'

'Lovely,' feeling for her purse.

'Twenty francs. Ach – you were a friend of poor old
Albert's. Make you a present.'

'That's really kind. You'll miss him.'

'Yes indeed. The technical side – they're tricky you know,
like animals, they need constant care and attention – just
about swallows me. My wife looks after the packing and
shipping. All that indispensable voyaging about, Albert used to
do all that. I'll just get you a piece of paper for that.'

The woman was standing, looking at Arlette with curiosity.
Couldn't see much of her through the glass. Another man was
standing too, farther back; she couldn't make out the features.
Taglang crossed, carrying green tissue, a sheet of florists'
wrapping paper, stopped for a few words. Came out with the
pot wrapped.

'You are kind,' gratefully.

''S nothing. Bring it to the car for you.'

'Wouldn't have thought there'd be so much voyaging.' Just
to be saying something.

162

'Christ, yes. Holland, England. Stuff doesn't come up with
the rations. And the other way, the distribution. Frontier
taxes and so on. This yours? Pretty. I like these Lancias.'

'But you prefer a Jaguar,' laughing.

'No no,' laughing, 'that's my wife's. English taste! Mine's
the Porsche. You know what they say; that's not a car, it's a
way of life.'

'And that gorgeous thing – a Ferrari is it?'

'Maserati. Belongs to a friend. Associate,' abruptly. 'That's
okay lying. Don't stand it up. Branches are fragile; let it fall
and you'll spoil the shape. Okay? Glad to have met you.'

'It was fascinating. And I'll come in January. For a camellia.'

'You do that. Bye, now.'

Arlette drove back into town, thoughtful.

27. 'The Two Michels'

The student of Greek lived across the river from the lycée
and the Rohan palace. On the quay itself is a row of picturesque 'Alsacien' houses that feature on picture postcards, have
been elaborately restored, and are becoming snobbish, like the
Marais of Paris. But behind is the Sainte-Madeleine quarter,
stretching over to the Krutenau and the horrible 'Suisse'
streets, dank, lightless and cheerless. The church is nothing to
boast of and neither is the primary school, and neither is the
commercial college where girls troop to become office staff.

Lying in the middle of all this is a little rectangle with trees;
the Place des Orphelins. The houses are shabby, the trees few
and dispirited, the parked cars almost welded together. The
inhabitants have won, though, a notable victory. They have
forced the municipality to declare it a no-parking area, and
have already won a bit of terrain, roped it off, and have a good
plan for more trees, a bit of grass, a bit of peace, a few benches

where the old can sit quietly. Everyone is hoping, and Arthur Davidson one of the most hopeful, that the idea will spread. So many little squares like this. The idea of recovering tiny markets, artisanal workshops with outdoor show-spaces, the old pavement life under plane trees (and with orange trees?) could easily be twee and selfconscious. But one hopes. If the islands could spread and link – ah, this could still be a lovely town. Violence, fed and nourished by that hideous invention the automobile – ah . . .

Arlette found a shop, tiny, dark and smelly, where you can buy little cards of press-studs or hook-and-eyes, buttons, zips, bias binding or bra elastic. There was a tiny, dark, smelly little woman who looked on her with suspicion, spoke Alsacien, admitted without enthusiasm to speaking French. It is in these quarters that one realizes that Strasbourg is not French, any more than it is German. What did either country ever do for us, beyond a vague idea of making money somewhere from the deal, and acquiring a nonsensical prestige from pushing the frontier farther? Yet the cross-fertilization from both countries is exactly what makes the place interesting. There are those who would like to turn Alsace into yet another horrible little nation-state.

Michel lived upstairs: in fact the old biddy was his auntie.

These minute crooked houses, looking as though a poke would set them tumbling, built for dwarfs, are not very habitable. Nobody knew better than Arlette who had spent, by preference, years in the hideous Rue de Zurich. No heating, no sanitation, and you knock your head all the time. The younger generation – so incredibly tall – solves this problem with ingenuity. It takes up Japanese attitudes on the floor, throws out that clutter of tables and chairs that people born before the war need in order to be comfortable. Bed? – nonsense, a mattress will do. There is no space left on the floor? Hang it up like a birdcage. Michel had screwed things in the ceiling beams, secured planks with cords, slept up there airy among the geraniums.

Often there is no furniture at all, and they lie on the deck quite happy, a dictionary on one side and the record-player on the other. Michel, a thoughtful hammerer and tinkerer at bits of wood, made his own furniture. Who wants to buy any? Hideous, wretchedly thrown together, and fearfully expensive. Arlette was offered the only chair there was, a canvas one on an aluminium frame which served as spare bed, if anybody needed one.

He was the usual basket-ball-player's size, with Joan of Arc hair, a silky black moustache he had never bothered shaving, fierce eyebrows like Monsieur Pompidou's, aluminium glasses and candid gentle eyes. A very soft voice, an engaging casual hospitality.

The walls were full of pictures. A few of the expected ones, Toulouse-Lautrec posters, Cretan dolls, lovely broken columns not-quite-Doric and not-quite-Ionic, enough of both to be interesting, fifteenth century Persian miniatures, and so on. Much too that was less expected, Gothic, primitive – Flemish, very suitable to this architecture. He looked like a Clouet portrait himself, when the glasses were off, in a high-necked, long-sleeved black blouse with silver embroidery. Face very male, and yet feminine too as often at this age, and altogether a bit like Mary Queen of Scots with a moustache. He was sorry he hadn't any cigarettes: would she like a bottle of beer?

Here at least Arlette did not feel handicapped by her lack of experience. She had had two sons, on the whole successfully. Even the closed one, the difficult one, who never uttered, of whom his father complained that no contact was possible at all (since whatever you said he was never listening) and who treated you with negligent affection as though you were a lovable but mentally deficient dog, had never been the anxiety to her he'd been to everyone else. A man was always so defensive and selfconscious. They loathed that, and put on the bored look. That particular one used, when spoken to about anything serious, to let his jaw hang and his eyes go glassy, so that Pa, a monument of patience in all his professional dealings, became intensely irritable.

One had to avoid heavy-handed tact. Nothing but the truth will do, and that as plain and short as possible. Anything that smells of cant, humbug, hypocrisy or an ulterior motive, and you lose them. Michel took some convincing. Was she the cops or the social worker or the Ministry of Education? No? Then something governmental, departmental, municipal? Neither? Then, if he might ask without seeming rude, what the hell was she? The family! Because really, sorry you know, but he didn't want to get involved. Oh, she was just in it for the money? That was all right; didn't see anything wrong with that. But if they were paying her then she was kind of ambassador from the family, right?

'No, she came to me herself. The family wasn't pleased at all: in fact they were hostile. Once convinced that I wasn't trying to twist their arm, then they showed themselves anxious to help. Without her knowing about it. I'm not in a easy position: I don't want to do anything behind her back and I mustn't abuse her confidence. I come to you because you probably know her best.'

Michel, crosslegged on the floor, looked at her, and thought her over, shared a bottle of beer into two mustard glasses, and embarked on a sketch of Marie-Line.

'Une Paumée'; a duck with a malformation of the wing. An emotional one, safety valve jammed, brimming all the time and threatening to blow its boiler. A nice girl, a pretty girl, a warmhearted girl, and with a conspicuous talent for doing the wrong thing. He had liked her a lot: he still did. She'd some very good qualities. Didn't want to sound a prig, but she was a very entangling person and she slopped over. Vulnerable. Cramped and who'd blame her, with that goddam family. She'll be all right, if people let her alone a bit. They won't, and she goes on tumbling into disastrous situations, and getting a black eye, and one's got to build up her confidence. Not knock it down. People pick her up, and then drop her because she's a bloody bore, and that's all wrong. You might think me selfish, or coldblooded, and I don't care if you do, but I didn't want an emotional relationship with her because she's a mess,

166

on my account, and on hers because she's not able to handle it and she only gets wounded.

She's pretty, and she's highly attractive, and I did once go to bed with her, and that was wrong and highly foolish, and I tried to make it up to her, and I hope she feels she can rely on me. She drinks and becomes reckless. Dope of some sort, wouldn't be surprised. They're always experimenting with some rubbish. Not from me she never got any, I don't see any use in it and it's certainly bad for her. Reckless enough as it is.

This other Michel? An art student? I've heard of him. She's talked about him. Doesn't interest me, don't much like what I hear. Didn't welcome interference from me so I wasn't about to attempt any. That wouldn't do any good. Don't know where he lives; try the Beaux Arts.

Good that she has sense enough to ask for help; she needs it. And she's a valuable person. I'd hate to see her in trouble. I'll do what I can for her. But I've a lot of work. Not like that pissy baccalaureat. An entry class for a higher school; the competition's tough, you know: you're up against the Family Favourites from Louis le Grand and Henri Quatre; the Parisian Orchids.

Arlette thought him a valuable person too. Better able to defend himself than poor old Marie-Line. He knew where he was going.

She made a couple of false casts. The School of Decorative Arts was in the Krutenau, no distance: pleasant building with a nice garden. She got no help from a tiresome secretarial female who thought that students were a pest and shouldn't be allowed. And there were too many Michels, and all sounding or proving wrong. But there was a Michel – if you follow – whose surname was Michel. Jean-Luc Michel. No longer a student. Finished school. An artist now. Lives over in the Petite-France, one of those old houses.

It is the most picturesque part of Strasbourg. The engineer Vauban dammed the river here and sent it different ways, to make a moat around the fortified town: downstream of his

167

beautiful bridge is a weir and a millstream and backwaters, and crooked streets through the seventeenth-century huddle, and the city fathers are busy restoring a nostalgic atmosphere with cobblestones and antique gas lamps, and rather pathetic corners of greenery. The most tumbledown of the old blocks have been razed in favour of exceedingly expensive flats in suitably steep-roofed dove-cote style, but where they are pressed thickest and darkest, and dingiest, there you find the poor who live in highly insanitary and crowded fashion. The streets are blind, greasy old masonry alternating with heavily barred windows choked with a century of dust. The very word 'alsatia' seems to have been invented to describe these houses.

A door yielded to her push. Stone flags, remnants of ragged plaster, loud smells of Portuguese cooking and loud voices in what didn't sound like Portuguese. Might be Yugoslav, and so might the cooking. A stone stair mounted. But she'd got it right: a big plywood notice painted in bright blue said J-L. Michel, with an arrow and various mermaids, pointing upwards. Repeated on a smaller scale on the next landing. At the second was a door in the same violent ultramarine, and 'Michel' in script. A card said 'Come on in; faites comme chez vous', so she did.

Immense surprise. Instead of the darkness, the dirt, and the plaster chewed down to humid old stonework it was bright, white, beautiful. The walls had been fresh-plastered and whitewashed, the old wooden beams carefully stripped and restored. This was all attractive. Art, mostly looking bad but anyhow vigorous, stood and hung about in quantities; that was to be expected, but the floors had fresh planking and several largish green trees stood about in pots. As Arlette knew from only that morning, such things cost lots of money. A doorway was open to a kitchen. Also all modern. Tiles, two gleaming new fridges, a cooker grander than her own. Lots of bottles, bundles of herbs. Not that much money in art; fellow must have come into an inheritance. No owner of all this to be seen: she repressed the temptation to pinch a bottle of champagne and a few shallots in a plait and do a bunk with them.

'Monsieur Michel,' she bawled.

'In here,' a robust baritone bawled back. She pushed a very nice original oak door, and surprise heightened. Two rooms or maybe even three had been knocked into a narrow but splendid studio facing on the inner courtyard. The old windows replaced, in good taste, by much bigger ones. On a big table with two anglepoise working lamps the artist was doing things with acid to a copper sheet. The press for pulling prints stood against the far wall. The artist was tall and burly, with a bushy beard, a blue-jean suit, sandals, and a superduper-emperor-length cigarette.

'This is the grander for being so unexpected,' looking jealously at a lemon tree four times the size of the one Mr Taglang had given her.

He beamed with approval. Splendid-looking, and the looks suited the Bohemian get-up: the thick dark brown hair waved and curled naturally above well over six foot of muscular body, bright intelligent eyes and a good forehead. At first glance most impressive; almost the young Augustus John. At second glance a bit too pleased with himself.

'Yes, if I could do something about that damn entrance one could have a gallery here. But we have a permanent exhibition, me and a few chaps. And that's better than gallery space, and the bastard taking twenty or more of every per cent you earn. What can I do for you?' with an air of being ready for anything.

Arlette grinned.

'Not really in the market today, but could be another time.'

'Just window-shopping huh? Make yourself at home. The loose prints in the sheaf are really cheap, only three to seven hundred apiece. The walls three to five thousand, bar one or two of the biggies. A drink if you want it? White wine or a kir?'

'No thanks; I'll wander though.'

'Sure. I can't leave this, I'm afraid; got to time it carefully.'

169

The prints were commercial stuff; competent streetscapes on nice broad lines. Nothing to write home to Mother about, but look nice on the living-room wall of German tourist bourgeoisie, and that was what they were designed for. The Alsace wine towns, and the hill landscapes of the country round them. With the smells of the acid came an incensey smell of expensive male stuff to dab under the ear. The hands were too white. He was only twenty-two or three, but had already the practised patter. Another one who knew where he was going, and seemed well on the way with no time lost.

'See one of my posters?' he enquired.

'A girl I know mentioned you. Marie-Line Siegel.'

'Ah, yes. Doctor Siegel's friends don't buy many pictures, I'm sorry to say. I know the girl, of course. In fact she's a tiny bit amorous,' with a little laugh.

'Yes I know.'

'Really – how? She told you, I suppose. Well, don't take it too seriously. Not exactly a grand passion. She's not a minor, but I wouldn't want her father stamping about making a scene. She's a bit of a scene-maker herself.'

'Oh, I'm not an emissary; I just know her and like her, that's all. She worries me a bit. Drinks too much.'

'Ach,' casually, 'nothing very dreadful.'

'No, but a bit irresponsible. She has no mother and she's rather vulnerable.'

Variety of facial expressions; virtuous, affronted, irritable: the no-earthly-business-of-mine and the even-if-it-were-I-wouldn't-want-to-know.

'I detest people who preach.'

'The invariable excuse of the selfish and superficial.'

'Why don't you ask whether I sleep with her.'

'A satisfaction to your vanity, no doubt.'

'She's of age to make up her own mind. You people who moralize make me sick.'

'It must be true since it says so in Playboy. Have you been giving her drugs too?' He was silent for a moment, dabbing at the work in front of him with a rag, bending down and

170

squinting at it, making a to-do of the concentration involved.

'Got to make sure it's all neutralized,' chatty and relaxed. 'Has she been telling you these tales?' wiping his hands and throwing the rag in a corner. 'Totally untrue you know. I wouldn't mind, and it wouldn't have any importance, but that sort of malicious invention can make trouble. One wouldn't want to spread stories like that, and if I were you I'd advise her not to repeat them. Her word's not that trustworthy. What people do is no concern of mine, but if you start imagining orgies here, smoking grass and group sex and rubbish like that, it's total folklore. People always tell these tales about a studio. I've my living to make and it's important to me and believe me, I don't mix business with pleasure. I know plenty of these girls who hang around the art school but I tell you quite frankly they don't interest me. I don't want to say anything about Marie-Line. She's a nice girl. But it excites them to haunt studios, and it excites them to make up lurid tales. Better believe me – nothing in them. I've smoked marijuana occasionally, who hasn't, but I don't use drugs and don't have any here. Okay?'

'Perfectly okay. You're building it up rather, aren't you? I came to say that if you care about her, don't encourage her in anything silly. A bit of thought and you'll see this is right; nothing to do with morality. Having said that, nice to have met you, and good luck with the business.'

'Sure. No hard feelings. Sorry, just that people here imagine God knows what, all this haunt-of-vice stuff, don't stop to think a painter has something better to do – I suppose I'm sensitive. Come again – bring your friends!'

Arlette, whose car was parked miles away, walked into the town and stopped to phone Arthur.

28. 'A lavish expense-account lunch'

Arthur was mollified at her not getting home, delighted to have lunch bought him instead, and only produced an interminable argument about poisonous tourist restaurants in the town. It must be very lavish indeed; Chinese food – all right, agreed on that but it would take him some time because of the bicycle. Arlette, with time to kill, ambled up the Rue des Hallebardes, supposedly reserved for the stroller on foot but still full of delivery vans.

The old town of Argentoratum, squeezed in the loop of the Ill, became Strasbourg and was cut off on the other side by the fortified moat of the False Rampart. It has been split by broad modern roads, creating naturally a howling desert: the Place Kléber, desiccated concrete lid of an underground car-park, has no character left at all. Still, around the cathedral, while the Students, the Jews, or the Goldsmiths would not recognize the narrow medieval streets named for them, the proportions have not altered much. Little heaps of gaudily painted metal on rubber wheels replace the domestic dungheap, but the way is still obstructed, upsetting the city Fathers. The municipality hereabouts has made coy beginnings at a pedestrian sector. If it can steel its timid heart to make this universal as far as the waterside, where it speaks vaguely of planting greenery, the old town can be nursed back to life. Painfully, and expensively. But given devotion . . . much like the children Arlette had had to re-educate, after falling off their motorbikes. The end of the autumn was doing its best; a radiant warm day, perfect temperature for pottering. There were lots of German tourists having a shopping spree with blissful heavy marks at prices pushed up to compensate. You can buy some pretty things in the tourist district round the Rue des Hallebardes. You'd almost think you were in the Bahnhofstrasse in Zürich. On a day like this, with no smelly wet coats or umbrellas, Bay Street in Nassau after a cruise ship gets in.

Her eye was caught by something she'd seen that very morning. A car of extravagant Italian elegance, racing red, a little dusty from country roads. Mr Taglang's good customer. Retail outlet hereabouts – to be sure, the flower-shop on the corner. Tourists are not going to buy cut flowers much; an awkward parcel to carry around or leave in a hot car. But they're often taken with that cute little pineapple-palm, or growing your own coffee on a windowsill in Wiesbaden. She stopped by the window, and watched a stout mum having a mauve orchid pinned to her bosom, with much merry laughter, by a smiling girl in a pretty apple-green overall. Business was being done. Arlette looked at agreeable Carven clothes next door, without bothering about the price tags. Lunch was quite expensive enough as it was. Didn't even bother with a rose for Arthur's buttonhole: he'd be wearing that horrible corduroy jacket. She hurried on up to the Rue des Etudiants, or she'd be late. In fact he was already tucking into the white wine. Inclining, tiresomely, to be frivolous and gibber on about butterfly stew: she put a stop to this.

'I asked you out because I'm serious, and this is serious, or so I'm growing steadily convinced. I need your judgment, and advice.' Arthur looked serious, and listened carefully, and rubbed his hair, and ate through an enormous meal, and sent the boy for more tea, without getting his wits too clouded.

'Hm, this is getting altogether too much like eccentric English professors, detecting away while playing those games, Unreadable Books and Impossible Heroines: I'm getting perilously close to cliché in my behaviour and this is too close. Take it to the police.'

'Who'd be pardonably sarcastic about detectives. There's no evidence at all. Just try and make it add up.'

'Well, one might say that the likeliest form of felony for a chap like Demazis would be white-collar crime, fiddling the paperwork. Jumps to the eye in a business like that, there's lots of invoicing, export licences, juggle-juggle from one country to another. Typically Dutch; they buy carnations in Nice and flog them to the English, much to the fury of the French. Sounds piffling, but plainly there's a lot more money in flowers than you or I think.'

'Must be stronger than that. And what's the connection with this art boy?'

'How do you know there's any connection at all? Just because he has some potted plants in his living-room; doesn't mean a thing.'

'Look, he said to me, did you see one of my posters, and I thought posters he'd designed. There are these small ones for exhibitions, and of course they go round persuading shop-keepers to stick them in the window. Scotchtaped to the door of that flowershop, a print of the Rue de la Bain aux Plantes or whatever, one looks at these things idly without taking them in. I was at the door here almost before I remembered it.'

'Pretty loose connection. As you say, they ask shops to tack up notices for painters' shows.'

'But if you're a graphic artist, isn't there some technique in falsifying documents you might be good at?'

'Now I'm with you. Like washing cheques. Not laundering the funds, but literally, effacing the print with acid or some-thing to fox the computer.'

'Or just the ink. What is it removes ballpoint? And forging fresh figures.'

'And milking the business that way? And maybe he was on the verge of being caught and killed himself? It seems far-fetched. And what you say of this Taglang – he sounds an unlikely candidate for any complicity.'

'The thing that to my mind links these people together is that they've all so much money. This piffling boy, just out of art school. Place loaded with bottles of champagne. I wished I'd sneaked a look in that big fridge.'

'Got it cheap from some yobbo who knocked over a super-market.'

'Arthur you're not taking me seriously.'

'Not really, no. I think perhaps you're taking yourself too

174

much so.' He started quoting, in a special tone of voice. 'University type, forty-three, divorced, tender – no, gentle or perhaps sensitive – and joyous, sense of humour, romantic, loving life intensely – to the full might be better – not taking himself seriously . . . this is all plainly me.'

'What is it?' patiently, aware that Arthur was trying to sidetrack her.

'It's a phony advert a fella put in the heart-to-heart page of the Nouvel Observateur. "Wishes to encounter Young Woman, twenty-five to thirty-five."' He had hauled out one of his torn slips of paper. '"Intelligent and agreeable physique, to make of her a friend, a comrade, a lover, while awaiting better still if the atoms hook together. Bobonnes, emmerdeuses, timorées, contractées, aigries please stay away." The others are easy but how would you translate "bobonnes"?'

She gave it thought and then suggested 'Wifeys'.

'Not bad. As the fellow says, while awaiting better. Chap got ninety-eight replies and made a neat little book of them.'

'Are all those awful things me? Wifey, timid, uptight, hung-up, embittered, oh yes, and emmerdeuse, how does one translate that?'

'One doesn't even try. You are not in the least bobonne, nor these other things. Emmerdeuse? – yes, occasionally. As now. My advice is drop it. You've lots of more suitable business. What did you do with the lesbian woman by the way?'

'Told her it didn't interest me; I'm not a marriage bureau or a lonely hearts club. There's a woman who is, and she says nine phone calls out of ten are enquiries about group sex, and she finds it most discouraging. I'm not, by the way, about to get discouraged. I don't believe the fellow's distributing drugs, I mean it's too obvious, the artist's studio and dressed up like that. Far too much of a cliché. But how do they all get so rich?'

'The way we stay poor, by having nasty talents we haven't, which is why we find them nasty. Women are all the same,' said Arthur gloomily. 'They invite you out to lunch, ask your advice, don't take it: what I want to know is, do they pay for the lunch?'

175

'Dutch treat,' said Arlette nastily. 'Stick to what is it – Unreadable Heroines. Come across something interesting and all they say is Drop It, as though you were a dog.'

'I'm giving you good advice you know,' said Arthur mildly, 'but I might have known you wouldn't take it. Too obstinate. Where are you going now?'

'Home to be a housewife.' Men! A lot of use they were . . .

29. 'The Marginals'

'The ironing-board is the girls' computer'. The phrase was Arthur's, of course. Arthur being funny. Men being funny . . . No patience with men right now. Least of all with Arthur, excessively annoying, English, and sociological; roughly in that order.

It was at least slightly funny, since of course true. The ironing-board was a sounding board. Give it a note and it gave you back a note – not always the same note. Resonance added.

Once at home, car parked crossly and rather carelessly, Arlette flounced about a good deal. Her little lemon tree gave her pleasure: she took it to the workroom and stood it in a good light, turned it around several times to get the right angle – but it would need turning regularly for the light to be evenly distributed. She stormed about tapping her heels being bourgeoise. Cleaning women are always so happily lavish with materials they have not had to pay for. Always too much polish on the furniture. The tiles always smell of too much eau-de-javel slopped in the bucket. Three times as much Harpic as anyone needs is put down the lavatory. The paper bag of the vacuum-cleaner is never never emptied. Taxed with this they put on their most cretinous look and say they don't know how. And they always always stack empty cans with beautiful precision back in the cupboard without dreaming of a note asking for a full one.

Fulminating to herself did no good; irritated her further. She scrabbled in the deepfreeze and slapped things on the table hoping that they would give her an idea, eventually, about supper. The laundry basket was full, as it always was: she separated whites from coloureds spitefully and flung a great bundle in the machine. When its stomach started to rumble in that peaceful digestive pattern she felt better. Its antics drove Arthur – any man at all – utterly frantic. One ought to be able to make a limerick out of that.

There was nothing else to think about. Nothing on the telephone tape, nothing in the letterbox but the electricity bill, heavily padded as usual with bland estimations, fixed charges – and tax on both – added to the meter reading and tax smeared thickly overall like jam. She dragged the board out of the ironing cupboard. After falling down once and settling itself twice at the wrong height – the computer did this too – the camel consented to kneel and be burdened.

I don't like ironing but it does help me think.

Arthur, watching her ironing, with admiration for efficiency, remarked idly that the computer was just the same. Write a bad programme, give it silly instructions, and it would be recalcitrant. He had done this often, ending by kicking it and shouting phallocrat expressions while the wretched thing went on spewing paper into the bin. He had made one of his systematized fantasies, watching her pull rough-dried clothes (and being told to take two corners himself and pull) and fold them neatly. If the cards are not properly punched, in the wrong order or – no, stop it, said Arlette.

But if the computer 'thinks' (tenacious piece of nonsense) then so does the ironing board. If you start to think it will put disjointed scraps of idea into order, retrieve stuff stored in your memory and then lost, perform calculations. Give you, occasionally, the result in one piece that would otherwise have taken you months. The best way to achieve this is not to think at all. She was thinking too much. Ironing is not a mechanical

177

chore. It takes a special female intelligence, which men don't have.

My liberated sisters . . . oh dear, I've given up feeling sorry for them, poor bewildered things. Talk about throwing the baby away with the bathwater.

No earthly use bringing this to the police. Their male intelligence, stuffed with rubbish about rules-of-evidence, couldn't grasp it at all.

The artist, so-called, has a connection with the flowershop, since he has a poster on their door. The flowershop has a connection with Taglang Horticultural Whatnot, of whom they are good customers. Anybody can be someone's customer. As Arthur points out.

Now I see myself standing there, looking in. There's a tall, middle-aged, well-dressed sort of man, thinks himself wonderful. Hands in pockets. Proprietorial air. For a good reason; he is the proprietor. Had that special way of watching the girls. Almost certainly same man – I never saw him properly – at Taglang. Because of that machismo Maserati. Ugly stupid little thing but leave that.

Girls: one girl, giggling, is pinning orchid to stout bosom of German bonne-femme. Second girl is wrapping up pot of chrysanths for a biddy to take to the cemetery for All Saints. Stripy paper, apple-green, dark green, gold medallion; fancy.

She stood the iron with a thump and belted into the workroom, where in the wastepaper basket . . . Right: Mr Taglang had wrapped my tree in the same paper: that is why it looked familiar.

Idiot! The flowership is Taglang Enterprises. Or, much more likely, the other way round.

There can be a connection between Taglang and the artist. Stretching it very thin to extend that to Demazis. Anyhow, Arthur's thing about washing cheques . . .

When she went to the bank to pay cheques in she had commented idly on the new colour of her own. Yes, said nice Monsieur Bidule, always ready for a chat, new ones, something magnetic (she hadn't really listened); you can detect if

178

any comedian has made alterations. To be sure. Lots and lots of other papers you can forge though. Nicely engraved things with Republique Française – or Helvétique, or Bundesrepublik. But it's all too fancy, too tenuous, too ... 'There is just one doctor in the world that can save your baby, and he is in Vienna'. Too women's magazine. Demazis was killed, because of knowing too much or threatening to talk too much. I don't know this, but I do know it. He didn't want to talk and again he did. He told too many lies and not enough. He was too frightened and not frightened enough.

I wouldn't have paid any attention to the second Michel, if the first Michel hadn't been so unwilling to talk about him. He would just have been another phony, a ski-instructor from the New Hampshire backwoods who puts on a pretend Austrian accent.

So don't see him as something out of Freddy Forsyth who washes the Israeli visa off your passport and ... oh, stop it. He's simply a character that is making too much money and how? How does everyone make money, including me? As a go-between. Hardly anyone actually produces something, and they don't make a penny from it. But the world is cram-full, and this, basically, is what's wrong with the world, of people who juggle and make pots, simply by passing a thing from hand to hand.

Like what? Like drugs say. After all, what drew your attention to this jokeboy – could you find a bigger contrast than that between the two Michels? Marie-Line, and if she sees something in the one what can she possibly see in the other?

Go back to the beginning and suppose he handles dope. He says he doesn't and wouldn't because it's so obvious. Yes but that's a double bluff. Who uses dope? Anyone who's at odds with the world. The marginals. And who are they? It used to be supposed the hippies, the on-the-road gang. Nonsense; they don't have any money, and any sort of drug beyond a handful of shitty marijuana leaves is much too expensive. Drugs, of any sort, are sold for a great deal of money. The

179

users, the profitable users, are not children like Marie-Line who have no money. But the rich. The bourgeois, well insulated and protected by money. They are the real marginals, if the sociological gibber-jargon about alienation means anything at all. They are unsuspected, and if they were suspected can protect themselves with large bribes.

Doctors like Freddy Ulrich, dentists like Armand Siegel, might know a great deal more than they say. No sealed lips like a doctor's lips. Why do they say anything at all? Because they are genuinely upset at Marie-Line being used.

Girls like Marie-Line are used as 'contacts'. Where possible, to tie them down and have an efficient means of shutting their mouths, they are corrupted into a habit. A small habit, it need not take much to pay for. They are the ones who are caught, of course. The poor little wretches found in a coma in public lavatories. To pay for their habit, the girls prostitute themselves, the boys rob supermarkets. The police make a loud noisy fuss. How many are there? A few hundred. But in a very wealthy country like Holland, very respectable, how much quiet money goes to keep publicity away from the door? Going to join the other quiet money.

Arlette knew something about this but not much. Piet did not talk about it. A 'professional' secret. But every doctor in Europe knows of, and treats, rich drug-users.

Marie-Line is not a prostitute, and does not rob supermarkets. But she may do a bit of quiet pushing. For example, *Chez Mauricette*. Whereas an artist, with a bourgeois clientele . . .

You could pass drugs in a flowershop. But she knew this much: the ones that make money of it are never the ones who push it. If anybody gets caught, it's always somebody else. The obvious 'marginals'. Folklore figures: Corsicans in scruffy little bars in Marseille. Paid off with a couple of thousand franc notes to gamble on horses. The real marginals, both those who use and those who profit, live above suspicion in the Avenue Foch. Not on the shady side, either.

The computer had stopped spitting neatly folded paper in

180

the bin. The ironing was over. The camel was bidden rise, and shamble off back to its cupboard. She went to have a bath. She wiggled her toes, with a lot of *Air du Temps* in the water. When she dressed she put her gun on. While computing away about Michel and Albert and Marie-Line the ironing board had given her a sudden jolt. Concerning that funny little woman Norma.

30. 'Shrouded Hammer'

The gunbelt was broad, flat, of supple leather from some unlikely-sounding animal, and no worse than wearing stays, once you got used to it. It had two unobtrusive buckles and added little to a waistline that hadn't been exactly famous to begin with. Since she inclined to be heavy farther down – euphemism for a broad behind – it stayed reasonably in proportion. The holster was a much more tiresome business. Stiffer, heavier, a piece of saddlery, with a spring-clip mechanism, you could try it in front or behind of the hipbone, it remained hostile to the female pelvis. In the privacy of the bathroom, worn roughly where she kept her appendix, it was hysterically funny; combined with boots and a hat, simply the Playmate of the Month. Once outside the bathroom, a great deal less funny. At the back, quite impossible. It quarrelled with one's behind and stuck out like a shelf. Oh well.

'The Americans, I believe,' said Arthur straightfaced, 'call this a belly gun. Well named.' She was prudish about toting it around like one's diaphragm in the old days. The gun itself made a difference to weight but little to bulk: it had a short barrel. Totally inaccurate if not quite ineffective at anything over very short distances, said the police, but you aren't trying to shoot one out of the guy's hand. The purpose of it is to knock him flat in the last resort: this it will do, definitely.

It was not too ugly; it would even have been a fairly good-looking object were it not for a lumpish thing that stuck out at the back and spoiled the proportions, known as a shrouded hammer; a technicality, explained Corinne, designed to prevent one's long woolly scarf with bobbles sticking in the mechanism and fouling it.

'Don't have scarves with bobbles. Or long flowing locks. Or anything at all save maybe too much tit.' But she had to put up with it, and after experimenting with various sorts of loose jacket, slightly like being pregnant (luckily one was tall enough to wear them; poor Corinne, who was on the butty side) and 'my gunslinger's trousers' – very expensive but beautifully cut; no pockets, no earthly chance of wearing stays – she had cast most of her selfconsciousness.

But this was the first time she'd worn the thing in the line of business, and the selfconsciousness showed up.

She put on her apron before leaving. Cooking in a gunbelt was also a peculiar sensation she hadn't tried before. She had a turkey leg, and she had some stuffing; leastways she had some old bread, a chicken-liver and an onion. She took the bone out, shoved the stuffing in, and put it to braise with a few rather black mushroom stalks.

'Don't wait for me I might be late for supper,' she said into the cassette. 'It'll hot up with no trouble.'

In the car there was trouble with the gun. The seatback was too upright, and the holster stuck into one in a very naughty way, not only obscene but highly uncomfortable. She let the seatback down, and then there had to be a lot of wriggling and plunging, exactly like having one's knickers stuck in the crack, and she hoped nobody was watching. Both driving mirrors were now in the wrong position. It was six-thirty before she reached Hautepierre.

She knew nothing about Robert save that he was a long-distance lorry driver. Sure enough, outside the 'link' was a gigantic articulated truck. She didn't know whether it belonged to him; it looked unlikely. Gossamer International, it said in large letters. Girdles, Panties and Soutien-gorges – was there

182

that much gossamer in the world? This belonged to the Marx Brothers rather than to Robert.

She entered the block, in the usual strong smell of ham-hocks and cabbage, avoiding the elevator. The whole place was as before, neither clean nor really dirty, but seemed barer, sadder, more sordid. The time of day perhaps. Night falling, men and women coming home tired from work soured and unsatisfied. How many felt warmth and gaiety and happiness in their homecoming? Perhaps it was the knowledge that Norma was gone; with her talent for enjoying life, her children with their eager curiosity, their knowledge that the world was a bad place but that one can cock a snook at it. Sentimental? Yes: since Victor Hugo forced tears with the death of Gavroche. But there is a better scene; that in which Gavroche breaks the streetlamps in the quiet bourgeois street, immortalized in the police archives as 'Nocturnal attack by dangerous revolutionaries'. Norma's children would vandalize telephone boxes. Highly regrettable. But who do the poor telephone to? The doctor, the police, the mayor? 'Not on your Life!' as they were fond of saying. If children will go on breaking up a school, one starts asking what is wrong with the school.

She rang at the door. The bird was at home. The noise of the radio came distinctly. The world of the long-distance trucker is curiously populated, and the radio a lung through which it breathes. There was a shuffle and a bump. A woman would scrutinize the unexpected visitor through the 'judas' spyhole, but the last shadow of doubt was removed at once by that big sunny smile.

'Why hallo there.'

'Hallo Robert.' He grinned again at that, much amused.

'Come on in.' And she did.

A confusion of thought, of too many thoughts, and none of them properly thought out . . . There was indeed a voice that said, Oh Arlette . . . Idiot . . . but there was also the thought which said, What did you come for at all then? Vanities: you don't really think you can't cope with a clown like that. All right then; why did you think you needed a gun? As to that, well; wandering around a place like Hautepierre at night alone might not be very safe.

Snobberies: there's that vile old woman on the landing opposite, probably listening behind the door this minute. One has things to discuss; no business of the neighbours. Am I the kind of person one keeps in the doorway, like I was Jehovah's Witness?

Self-satisfaction: I'll wipe the grin off that Robert's face. He needn't suppose I'm his dupe or pigeon. Foolish inexperience, really. And the same streak of sentimentality that tripped me on Norma. One can afford to be sentimental about children. Victor Hugo, wandering about the outskirts of the old, fortified Paris, listening fascinated to the slang of one urchin, quite failed to see that a second had neatly slit his waistcoat with a razor and removed a handsome gold watch. He said first 'Well I'm damned' and then 'I got what I deserved' with no rancour at all.

But the physiologically adult hooligan . . . Arlette had had that sadly confused cliché of 'a dialogue' in her mind. And she had felt too, obscurely, that she had played Robert a dirty trick, somehow. As, plainly he had thought himself . . .

One could tell straight away, by the smell, that Norma was no longer there. Not that it was strictly speaking dirty. A man used to being alone, to looking after his truck, has rules that he keeps. It was no more than unaired stuffiness and the amiable negligence of a man who expects to find the screwdriver where he left it, which was in the sink. All the piggery– he'll have a purge one of these days, when it gets a bit excessive. No man has ever been able to see why the women fuss about the washing-up each time. One does it when there are no plates left.

The living-room, while full of dog-eared magazines and unemptied ashtrays, had a raffish comfort. A man who makes good money, who is confident in his ability to earn more. Expensive chairs and high-fidelity equipment, and odd clashing things, sometimes in good taste and as often very bad but who cares? The things of a man who took a look and said "I like that" without hesitating. He can afford it, so why worry?

'Have a drink,' said Robert.

'All right.'

'Sit down, then. Don't be frightened,' now enjoying himself vastly.

'Scared you, didn't I? All right, I don't bear no more grudges.'

'I didn't go to the police, you know. I thought perhaps I'd tell you why I decided not to.'

'How d'you know where to come?'

'How did you know where to come?'

'Ol' woman opposite. She saw you. Did a bit of peeking, bit of listening, same as always. Wormed the rest out the kids. So I thought you put your nose in my business, I'll see how you like it, for a change. Like it?'

'I understand it. But suppose I had gone to the police.' Robert snorted, amused.

'No proof. What, me? 'S nothing to me.'

'And the old woman then?'

'Knows better than to talk to any cop. Know she'd get a right slap around the chops if she did.'

'And Norma?'

'Gone, hasn't she? Gone back to England? Knows nothing about it, right? Wouldn't worry me for a moment. Cops come here and say what's this, what's that, and what do you know about it? Nothing. Not interested. Prove the contrary.' He sat in the big 'male' armchair, stretched, yawned, showing very good teeth, folded his arms across his chest, laughed again silently. 'Pow, right through the windscreen. Aimed careful not to hit you. Just shake you, like. Oohoo, the gangsters are here. Bundle of kids' fireworks, needn't think you could trace those, bought in Germany. Yoy, big bomb attack. Shook the neighbours up too, that one. Like a cigarette? Here,' tossing the packet at her.

She caught it, put it down, and said, 'No, thanks,' controlling her voice.

'Bit too casual, was it? Not nice manners? Bad, that. But I'm in my own place, see? I please myself.'

Arlette looked at him carefully. Yes, if he wanted to, he could easily appear attractive. Average build, nothing immense. The bulging biceps and Pop-eye forearms of the old truckers had gone out with power steering. Tough though, and wiry. A high, bumpy forehead freshened and tanned by the open air. Reddish-brown hair, wavy; yellowish-brown eyes, alert and intelligent and glinting with the entertainment. Handsome whiskers and a long sharp chin. The big scarred hands of the mechanic. Expensive trousers, stained, but nothing the cleaners wouldn't fix. Sharp shirt with a long pointed collar, suède waistcoat affair, astronaut wristwatch. It was at this moment that she began to feel fear. She took the cigarette packet up slowly. Davidoffs, fancy, bought in Switzerland. The gossamer underclothes trundle round everywhere. She picked up a matchbox and lit it.

'Your place needs cleaning up.'

'Perhaps you'd like to stay and do it,' merrily.

'Why be so mean to Norma? Why be so ungenerous? She'd have made you a good wife.'

'And you told her to piss off. Which she did. Real sly. How d'you like that?'

'What else could she do? Put yourself in her place. She loved you. You could so easily have made her happy.'

'What you mean, in her place?' genuinely puzzled. 'She's a woman. Ought to know her place. Got too cocky, thought she could run me. So I put her down, a crack. Didn't know French, didn't know German. Right, that'll keep her at home, stop any fancy adventuring about. Started wanting to go out 'n' work. None of that, Nellie,' he added suddenly in English. 'Saucy cow.'

Arlette had nothing to say. What could one say, that would be of any use?

'And you worked her up. Encouraging her. To attack me. As though I'd care. I don't go short of crumpet. Get plenty, climbs in the cab and volunteers. You don't have a clue. But

186

your crowd makes me sick. Go on strike you think, keep y'legs crossed, cut the men down. Know how to cope with that.'

'Yes, we know,' said Arlette tartly. 'Get the rifle, stand Norma up against the wall. With the children. I irritate you, put a bullet through the windscreen. All this violence. You don't need it. What does it gain you?'

'A lesson is what it gained you. Strikes me it wasn't enough. Maybe you need another.' He looked at her casually, head on one side, perfectly calm, selfconfident. Silly girls were always climbing into his truck too, knowing damn well what they'd get. 'Not all that bad at that. Many a good tune played on an old fiddle.'

'My dear Robert,' preposterously: she always wondered afterwards why she didn't think of the famous gun at this moment. She had forgotten it altogether. She cleared her throat. 'Don't be ridiculous. For one thing, I can let out the most colossal scream.'

'You would?' lazily, enjoying the idea, eyes glinting. 'Lovely. Nobody'd pay no heed, round here. Know how to mind our business, we do. Norma tried that, once. Not twice though.' With something like panic she thought of Arthur's horrible story, of the old woman who was beaten to death while half a mining village lounged about outside, uninterested.

She was taken completely by surprise. He had been sitting back there grinning, arms behind his head, relaxed the whole length of his body. He was on her like a cat. A trucker's reflexes. In one movement he pinned her wrists and held them and threw her backwards. He spoke softly in her ear, amused.

'But you won't scream, love. You'll enjoy it.'

Little things. But talk about the skin of one's teeth . . .

For one thing he was in too much of a hurry. For a second he wanted to show his strength, to paralyse and frighten her with one swift stroke of mastery. The third was that he used his right hand. Since this was on her left he didn't feel the holster, and did not understand the gunbelt.

He had hooked his hand into the waistband of her trousers

187

and given a massive rip. The buttons tore and so did fabric. But the gunbelt held and resisted, and it disconcerted him. Not the ordinary woman's elastic girdle – what is this? He changed his grip and tore the trousers down but the fumble relaxed his left hand for long enough that with a frantic twist she got her own right hand free, and the instinct to claw changed into an instinct to protect the holster, not let him find it out. His hard body was up against hers, but he was still tearing awkwardly at the solid buckles, expecting a simple hook clasp, disconcerted further, and she was able to force her hand down. His left hand twisted hers cruelly, mashing it against her mouth and nose. His right hand delved under the belt, gripped her tights and panties and tore them, but hers reached the holster, and the lovely spring clip delivered the gun just as it was supposed to, and as his body arched in the effort to hold her down she jerked the barrel up and felt it go hard into his stomach muscles.

The shrouded hammer did not catch in the wool of her pullover. Just as damn well. His own hammer was unshrouded, definitely.

She did not fire. She was eternally grateful for this. It would have killed him, certainly, and forever afterwards she would have thought 'I killed him'. An end to this career, and every other.

It would have been very easy to fire. As she had been trained, the gun was only loaded in five chambers; the safety off and the hammer down on the empty one.

He stopped moving; she could almost hear him think 'what's this hard thing, then?' She could not bite or even breathe: she jerked the gun painfully and felt him wince and the pressure on her mouth shifted.

'It's a gun you fool. It'll blow your whole back apart.'

He realized it was true, that she meant it. Oh yes, she meant it. Her larynx was bruised and her lip damaged by her own ring, and she had no breath, but she'd gasped it out in a voice that left no room for mistake. She would have fired because she could not breathe.

He let go of her altogether and jumped back. He knew about guns; he stayed still. Some are ittybitty little things and women don't know how to hold them, but this was held solidly slotted into her hipbone, and a shortbarrelled nine millimetre pointed at you close up looks like the Russian Army, and you stay quiet.

Arlette breathed pantingly, sucked her sore lip. There seemed nothing left but rags below her waist: she was in a right pickle. She bent herself forward, and jerked the gun. 'Go on back. Back. Back. Go backwards.' She felt for the entanglement round her knees, found bits of trouser, hitched them, stood, feeling a fool, looking a fool, but less of a fool when the other person looks a fool too. He said nothing, judging it better not to. He was not going to do anything. No ideas about being tough. No ideas about anything at all.

Never mind about her panties: she wasn't going to stay here redressing herself. Trying to control her breathing, with a horrible frightening wish to shoot and see the bullet squash him flat against the wall like a bug in a smear of blood and guts. She got air back in to her lungs, tucked the ripped trousers under the gunbelt, keeping the gun pointed at him the whole time.

She slammed the outside door. They were used to doors slamming here, and a gunshot would just have been another. She walked down the stairs slowly, for the sake of putting one foot in front of another and training those stupid legs not to lurch and land on her nose. Her thighs trembled. She held the gun, which she was still clutching mechanically, stiffly along her side. She met nobody. Down in the hallway she remembered to put the gun back in its holster. Her thighs felt novocained and she stopped to rub them. They ached and wobbled like an unaccustomed skier's.

189

31. 'Between Jerusalem and Jericho'

The air outside was so fresh and keen that she felt giddy.
Like going out on deck of a Channel ferry on a rough crossing.
It was mercifully dark. She got over to some bushes, thoughtfully planted for the purpose by the municipality, and was sick.
Like the young lady of Spain. Again and again and again. She
had nothing to be sick with. No hanky. She wiped spit with
her sleeve. She got up and wobbled off. People passed her but
she paid no attention to them; they didn't give her a glance.
She didn't know where she was nor where she had left the car,
but she had to walk.

It must have been the right direction more or less, because
she recognized the little shopping-centre of the Maille
Cathérine. One or two lights were still burning. Nobody to be
seen, though.

Yes. There was a girl sitting in the back of a shop, her dark
head down, doing accounts. Arlette banged on the glass with
her fist. The girl looked up, frowned, shook her head, made a
'We're closed' mouth, looked again more sharply, got up,
came over to peer better into the darkish passage outside. Her
eyebrows shot up. But blessings on her she did not hesitate.
She undid the bolt, turned the key of the top-and-bottom lock,
and opened.

'What's the matter? Are you ill?'

'I've been raped.'

'Seigneur! Come on in. I'll look after you. Lord yes, I can
see. Come in the back. There, sit down. One moment – I must
lock the door again . . .

'He'll have bunked, the bastard. We'll never catch him
round here. I'll phone for the lousy cops, but they'll take half
an hour.'

'I'm okay, I mean he didn't, I mean I managed to break
away.'

'You've blood on your mouth. Your clothes are all torn. I can drive you, I've the car outside. One can't let them get away with it. We must make a complaint at once, and go straight to the hospital then. If you don't, afterwards, they don't believe you. I'm sorry, I know it sounds horrible, but we want to get a vaginal smear done straight away.'

'No, I mean, he didn't get into me. I – put him to flight.' Unable to explain, she lifted her jacket. Eyes widened at the gun belt.

'You're wearing a gun! . . . well good for you . . . You're a cop . . . right. I understand. I'm not supposed to ask. Doesn't matter; you've had a battering. I've a first-aid diploma. You mustn't have alcohol. What you must have is tea, strong and lots of sugar. I'll put the kettle on.'

She was half Arab, or more, a tiny thing, thin like a sparrow. Masses of black hair in ringlets pinned back, huge eyes tremendously painted, a pink tender mouth, beautifully cut.

Comic in her shapeless loose woolly frock; tiny feet in big boots. Gentle, and very kind.

'I'm sorry to have made such a fuss. I kept thinking if it were me, and nobody wanted to know, and nobody helped. I'm strong. But one's never strong enough.' Corinne's very words.

'Here, for your face.' Cotton wool, and ninety-degree alcohol.

'It'll be all right. It was my own ring. He pushed my hand down over my face.'

'Damn lucky you had the gun. Tea won't be a sec.' Arab tea. Green and with mint, sticky with sugar, boiling hot in a big mug with 'Annick' written on it. The kind from souvenir shops in Brittany. She sipped steadily, feeling it go down through her, doing her good.

'If you like,' said Annick timidly. 'I mean, I can mend your trousers. I've everything one needs. In the shop I mean.' Arlette had not looked at the shop. Knitting-wool, sewing materials, embroidery. Jumble of decorative objects. Wicker birdcages with bright parrots of coloured felt, spinning wheels, tambour frames. 'I'm handy with my fingers,' humbly.

She was as good as her word. Arlette sat wrapped in a blanket, drinking tea, flooded with gratitude, watching the nimble professional hands fly. After a while she managed to get rid of the ruined tights. Annick gave her a needle and thread. With fingers still stiff she mended her panties and wriggled back into them. Annick kept her eyes down; the sewing-machine whirred, putting in a new zip.

'I'd have pissed in my pants,' was all she said. A pause.

'If you need to wash the lav's there behind you.'

'You're a Samaritan.'

'Wog Samaritan.'

'I seem to remember,' embarrassed, 'that the original Samaritans were wogs too. Fact handily forgotten.'

'You bet.'

'I can only say, not any more by me.' The girl said nothing, turned the trousers over, bit her thread and knotted it one-handed. Her needle seemed almost as fast as the machine's.

'Did you have a handbag, or did he pinch it?'

'No. Only my car keys.'

'You've transport, then? You able to drive? You going home?'

'No. My husband would make an awful fuss. I don't want him to know. He'd say it was my fault, and he'd be right. He'd be angry – because he was frightened, you know?'

'Yes. This is almost ready. I'd say, come back and eat with me. You need something in your stomach, and a good drink. Only I've nothing in the house.'

'Come and eat with me. We'll find somewhere.'

'You know mostly these evenings I work late I just go and have a pizza or something.'

'Do me fine.'

'I know a good place in Schiltigheim.'

'I'll follow you.'

'I'll drive slowly. Here. Good as new. Better, if Ɩ say so. They're good, though. Be a pity to lose them. And almost

192

new.' Arlette stood up and put them on. Annick's gazelle eyes rested on the gunbelt but she said nothing.

'I've got to tidy my book away.' She put the lights out, locked the door, rolled the shutter down. 'Where's your car?'

'Somewhere over here.' Hers was right next door, a Dyane emerald-green as a lizard. She was tickled at the contrast with the prim, pale Lancia.

'Can I drive it?'

'Of course. I'll follow you in the Dyane.'

'I'll go carefully.'

'Don't be daft.'

'Yippee,' like a small child.

The Dyane is a more powerful, more luxurious version of the 2 CV Citroën. It was exactly like the days before Arthur. So it was somehow symbolic. She wasn't going to run back to Arthur again, to say she'd made another hash-up, and have a cry, and be tucked into bed with a tisane after some bellowing and many Told-you-so's. She had to fight this one out on her own.

Her humiliation and her stupidity no longer were important. Norma was gone and free. Robert, seeing ways of being vengeful and funny at the same moment, had shot at the car, had put the bomb in the letterbox, had smeared blood and guts over the door. It had been perfectly obvious, but her stupid mind, all tangled up with Marie-Line's nonsense and her own wild fantasies of gangsters knocking off Albert Demazis, had got into a flounder. Dear old Arlette. My so-called brains got into a twist before my pants did, but oh boy, did they both get tangled!

Annick's quite right: what I need now is to get my teeth into a crude hearty meal, not that twee little turkey leg back home, have a lot to drink, and then go quietly home and to bed, rested and sorted out. And in the morning it will all make sense. And above all say nothing to Arthur.

Brightly lit main drag of Schiltigheim. Annick parked feather-light without scraping the tyres on the kerb. Arlette was clumsier. Italian eating-shop, just like all the others, with nets and glass floaters, lumps of cork and bottles in raffia.

'Don't worry. Looks phony. But the pizza's real. That one's nice,' leaning over and tapping the menu. 'Hey, Arturo. Finocchio! Big fiasco classico.' Arlette rapidly became hilarious, because Annick blossomed after two drinks. She could not speak Italian, but what she did speak was the old Levantine lingua franca, of Arab, Provençal and Spanish mixed together.

'Yes, it's handy. There were two cops one day and they started saying really filthy things, thinking I couldn't follow, and I came out with even dirtier, and their mouths fell open.'

The Pirate Genoese thought Arlette in the Davidson side of her mind – *Hell-raked them till they rolled, Blood, water, fruit and corpses up the hold* – 'Shall we have another pizza, a different one? Or a spaghetti split between us?' – *But now through patterned seas they softly run* – 'I can patter a bit Provençal.'

'I was born in Constantine. Father was a Pole out of Sidi Bel Abbes. Wog both ways, what. Could have had blue eyes and coalminers' shoulders, think about that.' Arlette laughed: the girl did not sentimentalize herself.

'Big soft silly blonde mare.' Like me, what.

'Men,' said Annick, 'would say that it made no odds with a sack over our heads. So fight the sack, Poppyhead.'

Yes. Efforts were made. It was the answer to the question why she was carting round Hautepierre at night wearing a gun, which the girl was so careful not to put.

'You know where to find me,' said Annick when they left. 'Needles, thread, all the things to keep the little woman busy and stop her from ever thinking. Ciao.'

'Indeed I won't forget. The other is effaced. This not.'

'Is the other effaced?' cocking the extravagantly painted eyebrow.

'The fellow who went to Jericho. He fell among thieves. Nobody remembers the thieves. One remembers the Samaritan.'

'Sure,' said Annick. 'It's a department store in Paris. Kind us, always seeking new services to offer the customers. Use your credit card.'

32. 'The Nasty Accident'

Even Arthur, who might have been fidgety, and could become downright nasty if she was out late without his knowing where, had been placid when she rang him when going for a pee after reaching the coffee stage.

'Sorry, things sort of evolved. Girls together, stuffing themselves with Italian grub in Schiltigheim. Figs you know, and grappa, and cassata icecream.'

'Pissed again I hear.'

'Yes, rather. Don't be surprised if I belch.'

'What does this mean exactly, things evolved?'

'Oh, you know, the talkative bald-headed seaman. He set the crew laughing and forgot his course.'

'Ah yes – *with great lies about his wooden horse.*'

'I'll tell you when I get home.'

'No no, you're much too jolly. Anyway I'll be falling asleep any moment. I went to bed with Jacques Ellul. Soporific, you know.' The austere and exacting Professor of Sociology from Bordeaux!

'Rather hedgehoggy, I should have thought, in bed. Or no, they curl up and have fleas. A lean and active porcupine, rushing fiercely about.'

'Good, then, enjoy yourself.'

She was driving home, sober, monumentally correct (showing that she was not quite sober), well under the speed limit, scrupulous about red lights.

One could draw a line under Robert. Margin to margin: she didn't suppose either of them wanted to hear any further from the other. Albert Demazis – an irritating bundle of loose ends, but best not fussed with any more. Marie-Line – that great silly, possibly with encouragement from the phony-artist brigade, had probably been trafficking in palfium and librium and similar nasty things doctors were much too casual about

195

prescribing. One would have to go a bit further into that. A discreet enquiry *Chez Mauricette*. That girl Françoise . . .

She reached the Saint-Maurice Church, swung off for her right turn. The Rue de l'Observatoire, short cut between half a dozen different university faculties, buzzes with student activity during the day but is not too uproarious at night. It was raining very softly, not even enough to turn the wipers on; just barely enough to marry with a gently alcoholic haze of well-being. It was her own slowness no doubt, the slight blur on visibility and attention, that made everything so abrupt and rapid and effortless.

She was rummaging about in the car as usual to see whether anything had been left behind that would attract the light-fingered, and she had her driving glasses still on, most incompetent because they promptly spotted up with rain. She scrabbled in her pocket for house keys. Damn. Oh there they were; in her hand. Stupid, she'd thought those were the car keys. Which, presumably, were still in the ignition lock. She was feeling along the dashboard, wondering why on earth she hadn't the sense to take her glasses off. If Arthur were here he'd be tapping his foot, definitely, and putting on that indulgent male face that means 'silly-women in-cars'. Somebody a great deal less indulgent took hold of her other wrist. Made sore by Robert, so that she squeaked. Her arm was turned and pulled up her back, very painfully indeed, but she squeaked no more because a hand came over her mouth, also made sore by Robert and a quiet decided voice said 'Don't scream'. For a second she thought it was Robert, and was swamped by total panic. There seemed to be several Roberts.

The one who held her opened the back of the car and propelled her in. She plunged and staggered and clutched the seat. Another turned the inside light out – or did that happen earlier? That was the one who had got very rapidly into the car from the other side and slammed the door. He gripped her like a parcel, set her abruptly upright and held her strongly with both arms.

'Do not struggle, do not yell. You're all right.' It was too

196

painful to struggle, and she was too astonished to yell. This wasn't anything like rape. It was a great deal more business-like. The one who had pushed her got into the driving-seat. The warm motor caught instantly, and in a smooth unfussed way they were at the crossing of the Boulevard de la Victoire with a green light and turning left into the Rue Vauban. The car gathered speed. The quiet voice said, 'No harm will come to you. Make no fuss.' There seemed to be three men, the one holding her in the back, and two in the front. Whoever had spoken had an educated voice. Neither Robert nor his friends. She had not been hurt: it was simply that both her wrist and her mouth were tender. The car did not go up the ramp to the Pont d'Anvers but turned left along the canal.

This, the initial shock and the nasty feeling of a film being rerun once over, was surely the moment to do something with the gun. What did one do? Couldn't hold up all three. Presumably one could have a go at the one nearest. Very near indeed; the back seat of a Lancia is an intimate affair, and he had his arms lovingly around her, not she was bound to admit in any horrid Robertish way.

'I told you not to wriggle,' he said. It occurred to him then to see what she was wriggling at, and his large hand patted the hard thickness of her holster.

'She has a gun,' indifferently.

'Has she now?' said the voice from the front, amused. 'Give it to me. Really, really. I'm putting this in the glove compart-ment; you'll have no occasion for it just awhile.'

They had swung round through the Conseil des Quinze quarter, crossed the bridge over the canal opposite the Orangery, and turned right down into the back streets of the Robertsau, streets lit only at intersections and which she did not know well. She could hardly see anything anyhow; her glasses were quite smeared. Two or three more corners lost her totally. Perhaps out at the end of the Rue Melanie, somewhere near the Château de Pourtales.

'This'll do,' said the front voice, which seemed to be in authority.

197

The car stopped, lurching and squelching as it left the road. She could see nothing save a vague impression of fields and trees. The driver flicked his lights twice and cut them; perhaps it was some sort of signal.

There was no need to repeat any instructions. The man holding her grunted as before, 'Don't struggle and you won't be hurt.' She didn't feel inclined to struggle. He was large and strong; one big hand sufficed to hold both her wrists and his body wedging her in the corner made any rearing or bucking impossible.

The man in the front was busy with something that made a ripping sound. Tearing a length of fabric? – she got the answer when her glasses were taken off, roughly but not brutally, and a piece of wide adhesive plaster was fitted over her eyes. It did not hurt. It would hurt when she got it off, she remembered thinking, because of the fine hair over her ears and temples, and she wondered whether she would be alive to worry about this.

The next piece was fitted more carefully: a light hand touched her cheeks and nostrils, closed her jaws, and when the gag was in place made sure that her nose was not obstructed. They didn't want her to asphyxiate, which was kind.

'Go mum-mum-mum,' said the front voice, pleasantly. She obeyed. 'Good. It's only to stop you screaming needlessly, which would have no point at all.'

With the ventilators no longer going the driver had opened his window to get some fresh air. She could feel it. And at this moment, ears sharpened by the blindfold, she heard a car, being driven quite slowly; a big car with a soft motor and broad wheels grating on the surface they had left. Dear man, kind good man, do be curious for once. It isn't a fornicating couple: that fear had now left her.

The three men were quiet. The car slowed further. Oh whoopee, he is curious. Some little way behind them, the car stopped. She could hear the motor idling softly. With a sickening lurch of disappointment she realized when no move

198

was made that this was their car. Come to pick them up. In answer no doubt to their signal.

Something new was being prepared, something that unwound with a squeaky sound. Electrician's tape, she thought, as her left hand was laid on her knee and the wrist rapidly taped to her thigh.

'Right,' said the light authoritative voice. 'A short explanation. Listen carefully.' Her right hand was still being held by the man next to her: she wondered why they didn't finish tying her. 'You are wondering about all this: you will now have time to think it over. Think, then, thoroughly. You are not being killed, or kidnapped. That would simply draw attention to you, something I have no use for. You will not even be here very long: you are lightly tied. If you do not manage to free yourself quite soon I shall be surprised. If not, you will be found before morning, though in your own interest I recommend you to try.

'You have been meddling in other people's business. Innocently – it is possible. But it was not a good idea. It never is. Now you are getting a warning to stop it. One warning – that is all there will be. You have understood? Nod your head.

'Very well. I waste the least time and trouble possible. You are putting me to trouble now and I don't intend to have any more. What follows will show you this. I am not a brute, nor a sadist. I have no enjoyment in inflicting pain. The injury will not be permanent. It will, indeed, hardly show. You will, though, remember it. Give me her hand.'

She struggled then, which was quite futile, and tried to scream, which just produced a mum-mum and hurt her ears and her sinus.

The one held her wrist and kept her hand steady. The other gripped her sharply by the tips of her fingers, bent her hand out flat on the back of the seat, and cut her twice across the palm in a cross. Her heart turned over and she made a whining sound like a whipped dog.

The man had prepared everything. He slapped a lump of cotton wool on her palm and covered that with a generous

199

piece of the elastic strapping. Her limp arm felt broken by the force she had tried to use to pull it back: they took it and taped it to her leg like the other. She lay doubled over with her head on her arms, a few hot tears behind the blindfold, a shadow of a last whimper behind the gag. To the blinding pain succeeded extreme misery.

'That is all,' said the voice, drilling through the numbness. 'You have been warned. Think about it now. Think thoroughly.'

The fresh air came in a gush, saving her from fainting. They had all three got out of the car. 'Watch your footsteps,' said the light voice quietly. The doors slammed. She was alone. On the other side of the thick red haze more doors slammed, a motor accelerated, changed gear, died out of hearing. She was alone with the tick of the cooling motor of the Lancia and the pump of her blood.

33. 'Suite of the nasty accident'

How long Arlette sat, bowed, limp, she had no idea. Very gradually, bit by bit, she came to herself.

The soft rain was still pattering on the roof. It was not cold, but she was cold and getting colder. With every moment that passed she was getting stiffer, more cramped. Soon she would be able to do nothing at all. She must move. Moving would start the blood flowing again. Her hand was just a sticky wet mess: she could not tell if blood were still flowing. She thought not. The palm. Surely there was no artery there. Or was there – how deep were the cuts? Small blood-vessels – with any luck the constriction of the tape on her wrist, and the rough bandage, had stopped the bleeding, and coagulation would begin.

God – suppose there are tendons cut. I may never again have my right hand to use.

You better not think about that. Just do something. Now your legs are not tied. With a fumble you ought to be able to unlock the car, get out on the road. Walk? No, not walk: walking with the wrists taped to your knees – ever try it? You could get across a room, but you're not getting far on a deserted country road, and there's nobody much around at three in the morning – how late is it? Had she been unconscious? Examining her body, and thinking about it – there seemed nothing much wrong there except – yes, she had wet her trousers. Too bad about those trousers. And Annick had done a lot of work there. But there were more important things in the world. Like her head, which was alarmingly swimmy, empty.

Get your head down. It needs to be lower than the rest of you. Wriggling slowly and timidly, because if she fell between the two sets of seats she wouldn't be able to get out again, she got herself lying laterally. Head down, legs up.

She could kick the window out. What good would that do? It might not be as easy as it sounds, with safety glass, and apart from a spoiled car will it be of any use? Somebody comes and sees feet waving out of the window?

Help yourself. Do not rely on others to help you.

One could get the head down on to the thighs. The electric insulating tape is smooth. But it has rough edges where it is stuck to the fabric of the unpleasantly sodden trousers. If you rub away at the edge with the other edge, the sticky edge under your ear, you might get this gag off. And that will be a start.

This worked. A good deal slower and more laborious than a dog scratching or a cat washing itself but by repeated efforts of the head and neck the plaster rolled itself back, millimetre by millimetre, very slow but it became less slow and at last, oh what bliss, she could breathe through the mouth, move it, yell, but she wasn't going to waste energy yelling. Her mouth was bruised, and messed up with sticky goo tasting unpleasant, but she now had teeth again, and teeth worrying at the tape around her left thigh would, with lots and lots of patience, eventually free her left hand. This was interminable, but this too gave results in the long run. Yes. Long run. A marathon. She was breathing heavily, sick and giddy and a horrible mess, but she got her left hand free, and that freed her eyes, and now it was only a matter of being patient and exceedingly relaxed.

Sometimes one was too relaxed, and sometimes not relaxed enough. The scales were too delicately balanced altogether.

Now she was altogether free, with an unusable right hand wound about with sticky sopping plaster. It wouldn't do any good but it might keep things cleaner: she used the plaster off her mouth and eyes to make further vague bandaging. It frightened her to think she had lost a lot of blood. She tried to use her common sense, and tell herself that all this immense mess of gore amounts probable to a cupful. Less than you'd give as a transfusion donor, woman. And you can now move. What is more, Arlette, you are going to drive this car.

God. They would have taken the keys and tossed them in the bushes.

No they hadn't. The keys were still in the lock. Kneeling on the driving seat, she got the parking brake off with her left hand.

Now what? You can drive with your left hand, but you shift gears with your right, and it's unusable. With some more manoeuvring she dragged the gearshift into second. Lovely, beautiful little Lancia, you are going to get me home in second gear.

There were lots more difficulties. Starting the car, putting on the wipers, putting on the lamps. Then she got halfway across the road and had to reverse. This was the worst yet. The gearbox moaned and screeched. Would she get picked up by the police for being drunk?

She weaved around a great deal, in roads that looked vaguely familiar and then turned out unfamiliar, and kept on coming back to the same crossroads, but she got the string untangled at last and yes this was now definitely the Rue Melanie.

Down at the bottom of the Rue Melanie, just before getting out on to the High Street of the Robertsau, is the Hospital Saint-François. She thought about this, knowing the hand must be looked to by a professional – ho ho. But blurrily – no. The priority was to get home. And they'd ask such a lot of questions. That much of the lesson had been learned. She did not want a lot of questions, and the more because none of the answers would be of any use.

It was only two-thirty – she'd thought it must be four at least. There were still belated revellers on the main road, but nobody who saw anything noteworthy in a small wet car travelling slowly. She crossed the big bridge past the Palais de l'Europe, turned to skirt the Orangery, came out on her familiar peaceful Boulevard de la Marne. Nobody was afoot in the Rue de l'Observatoire. As she walked tipsily up to her front door a car that had been parked drove away, but she wasn't bothered about it. They might be checking up on whether she had got home, and it might be pure coincidence, and she just did not care. All she needed now was Arthur. She had strength enough to get up the stairs: no more effort was needed. She switched on lights.

'Arthur. Arthur. Arthur!'

However absent-minded or uncoordinated these English may be in the small day-to-day affairs there is nothing found wanting when the going is tough. He was out of bed and standing upright at the mere tone of her voice, before he found his glasses, snapped them on, and took one look. He laid her down on the bed, put pillows behind her, made one brisk smack with the lower lip on his teeth at the sight of the hand, and was back in ten seconds with a bottle of alcohol. She waved her left hand feebly to say no no, bad for me, don't, but drank some, and felt the better for it.

'Tea,' she said.

'Of course.' An English remedy for anything short of death. Not Arab tea, Annick dear, though yours did me all the good in the world. Thick soupy milky English tea, Super-Ceylon

203

from Lipton, please. Instinctively, this was what he provided.
He took a look at the hand.

'This is a horrible mess, but seems to have stopped bleeding.
I don't want to frig at it now.'

'It'll stain the sheets. Get an old torn pillow case. No, help
me undress, first, I pissed my trousers. I want a shower. Or a
bath. Help me.'

The poor boy wanting to do ten things at once, and all
efficiently! She felt sorry for him, all white and shaky. In
common with most women, she knew that it didn't do to be
ill. Husbands will end up a great deal iller. One thing however
he could control was his tongue. Not a single question!

'Help me balance,' wobbling on the bathroom floor. 'Ow.'

'Is it too hot?'

'Yes it is rather. No, don't touch it, it's splendid . . . Ahhh,'
breathing strongly out.

'This has to be drunk very hot too.'

'Help me sit up. I'll sip. Have you noticed? – people in
Newsweek always sip, they never drink. Likewise they never
eat, they munch or they nibble.'

'Don't talk so much.'

'No, but let me. Travis McGee sits in hot baths and drinks
ice-cold gin.'

'What would you expect? – he has gin-coloured eyes. All
right let's look,' hitching the stool closer. He had put a pillow
on the edge of the bath. There was a lot of heavy breathing
during the peeling process. The wound gaped nastily. The heat
of the bath was doing things to her circulation and it oozed.

'Keep it well up. Is this a car windscreen or a metal edge or
what?'

'No the car's all right.'

'A fat lot I care about the car. Was there nobody to drive
you to the hospital?'

'I didn't want that.'

'But who bandaged this? Rough but luckily fairly efficient.
Who drove you home?' Now that he was no longer so worried
the floodgates were unloosed.

204

'Arthur, please. I'll tell you as soon as I can.'

'Sorry.' He poured a big slosh of whisky for himself, crossed his legs and studied her carefully.

'Your arms are bruised, and around your neck. Nothing seems broken and you've no internal injuries.'

'Darling, please. I'm just shaken up nervously, I promise. All I ask is that you don't let me fall asleep in the bath.'

'Good. Just tell me what it is you do want.'

'I want to move the hand, very slowly, just to see there are no tendons cut. I don't want any doctors. I've seen too many just recently. I want a clean nighty. I want to fall asleep in my own bed. First I want to tell you that there's nothing to worry about. No, first I want to tell you I love you.'

Hm, yes; that was all very well: there was a face there full of disquieting Britannic obstinacy. She was awfully sorry; she just didn't care. Total lethargy was now arriving in great galloping waves. She managed to get out and stand, and be dried, and hold arms out, and not burst the seams of the clean nighty. The hand was swathed up, and the arm put in a sling. She managed to say, 'One more thing, darling – no cops.' His lips were set in a horizontal line; he only nodded.

She slept till midday. She felt refreshed. Everything was fine. She got up to go to the lavatory and everything wasn't fine at all: she was extremely light-headed and tottery. Arthur appeared at once, all cool competence, sat her on the lavatory, helped her back. Her senses were oddly alert; the living-room door was open; there was a funny smell.

'Who's there?' as though it were a burglar.

'A doctor. Do not fuss. Discretion is assured.' The doctor appeared. A young girl. She had to laugh really – one of Arthur's little fiddles . . .

'I'm not a doctor at all, I'm only a student. So this is illegal practice. Show me. Oh well, that looks pretty awful but it's not really bad, I think,' touching with gentle fingers. 'It'll heal all right. Thing is, not being done properly, likely leave a scar. Oh well,' with some relish, quite enjoying this, 'if you'd taken it to surgery they'd have made a fuss. That hospital would kill

205

you quicker than this will. You've lost a lot of blood though. I fiddled some stuff from the pharmacy, haemoglobin and whatnot. Still – clean. Stay quiet and keep it quiet. Eat a big steak when you can. We'll have to watch it though, make sure you get all the movement back. When did you have an anti-tetanus last? Look, Arthur, I'll be in tonight, and I'll get a second opinion. No it won't leak out.'

He didn't say much when he came back. Only, 'Can you eat?'

'You bet.'

'It was a razor cut, wasn't it?'

'Yes.'

He brought scrambled eggs, tomatoes, coffee. It was delicious. She ate like a wolf, and promptly fell asleep again.

It was nearly twilight. The curtains were drawn but she looked. And Arthur was conspiring again, damn it. The doors were opened, to hear if she yelled or had nightmares. She could hear muttering, and smell cigar smoke.

'Arthur,' she bellowed.

He appeared at once, falsely genial.

'Ah, you're awake. Splendid. Like some coffee? I've a splendid steak when you want it, or liver if you prefer.'

'Look, are you taking more of your girlfriends into my confidence?'

'Ah. Caught me, have you? Just as well. Yes. I've a visitor for you. Do you feel up to it?'

Might have known, she supposed. He didn't breeze in with false geniality – not his style – but it was the commissaire of police just the same.

34. 'The Police Judiciaire'

'Don't mind my cigar do you? Look, set your mind at rest. Nobody knows I'm here. Nor will anybody know. My car's marked with an Aesculape. You know, the little insignia with the snakes. A doctor, okay? Just in case you're watched. But I have to know about this, you realize.'

She looked at Arthur. Arthur looked at the commissaire. You tell her.

'You've been marked on the hand with a razor. This is a variation on an old gag thought up in the gangster-film days. Known as the croix des vaches, and put on faces of people who had been too talkative to cops. Which tells us a good deal.'

'Which, together with the way you behaved, and the fact the car hasn't a mark on it, told me a good deal,' said Arthur apologetically.

'I'll get you a doctor, incidentally. Girlfriends who are medical students are fine, but we don't want to take any risks. I'll repeat that, if you didn't catch it. These are professionals. Not necessarily the cinema kind. Nor, necessarily, good professionals: what they did was only half smart. Perhaps they thought you a hopeless amateur and that throwing a big scare into you would settle the matter adequately. In that, I suspect, they may misjudge you.

'Put it this way. You have stumbled, perhaps accidentally, even amateurishly, upon some trace of a professional operation. Quite possibly you don't know what it is. They thought you knew more than you did. Two conclusions. This gets now turned over to professionals, which is why I'm here. Agreed? And two, we have to make a pretty thorough enquiry into what you know and what you don't. You're in no shape for interrogatories. But in a day or so. Oh, and another thing. We'll do this here at your house. And, incidentally, we'll assure your protection. Okay?'

'Yes.'

'There are one or two invasions of your privacy. Like we tap the phone.'

'No need. It has a recorder on it.'

'I put on the thing,' said Arthur, 'which says Miss Otis regrets she's unable to dine tonight.'

'Then when you can, you answer your phone normally but leave it on record. And you notify me at once of anything funny. We'll have somebody here, anyhow. A woman, I think. I'd like to do this throughout with women, if possible.

'So I'm not going to worry you today. I'd like to know whether any trace is likely to exist of your adventure last night. Incidentally, I learn you were carrying your gun. Were you expecting something?'

'Not really. I had it because of something different, and I was out late in a strange quarter. I didn't get the chance to get near it. I was just bundled into the car.' She told.

'I see. Is it likely there are any marks on the car?'

'I doubt it – the confident way they behaved.'

'Exactly. The occasions nowadays when one gets anything from prints are a rarity. We'll look, in case. Bring the car down, would you, Doctor Davidson? Or it might be stolen – coincidence-like. Now have you any idea where they took you?'

'Somewhere beyond the Robertsau, because I recognized the Rue Melanie both ways. But I don't think I could tell exactly, even with a good deal of trouble. And it was raining too. I don't even think there'd be footmarks – I remember them saying to take care.'

He nodded.

'A chance of your identifying voices?'

'Maybe,' with a dubious face.

'Yes, it's identity-parade evidence. A judge wouldn't place much faith in it. Well, we shall see. Now Doctor Davidson has been telling me about some of your notions. You had lunch in the town.'

'I keep thinking narcotics. Dismissed it all the time as

madly melodramatic. In light of what's happened, I'm just not able to say.' She told, hesitantly, about Marie-Line. 'But now that you know this – I got into a bad enough pickle already. The doctors. If you start they'll be furious. Treat it as breach of confidence.' The commissaire nodded, quite unsurprised.

'My dear girl,' he said in a fatherly manner, 'I have nothing to do with doctors if I can help it. I'm not speaking now of being threatened with all the diseases they themselves are most frightened of. I'm speaking of an over-privileged group that will go to extraordinary lengths of hypocrisy and perjury to defend those privileges.'

'There were stories about bent prescription forms – stolen and then falsified.'

'Hence the tight grip on your little friend Marie-Line.'

'I thought it all seemed very small-scale and amateurish.'

'So it is.'

'But that – I mean – if this were professional . . .'

'What's Rule One would you say? – I mean in regard to not getting caught. Not to distribute in the area where you yourself operate. There is not a great quantity of narcotics distributed in this area. Much more towards the south and over the Swiss border, and in Germany. Where the pickings are a great deal richer. Look at the geographical situation of Strasbourg. Where does most of the stuff come from? Notoriously, from Holland. That train that goes down from Holland to Italy – there used to be a lot of jokes about it. We've busted that train several times. The stuff's coming in by road. Leave it for now; you're getting tired. You kept thinking there were two different affairs and this confused you. So there are. Fiddling about at this little affair of selling pills to students you stumbled on something real, and didn't quite believe in it. Try and think it over – I'll be back tomorrow.'

'How do you feel?' asked Arthur coming back.

'Fine. The hand's painful, nothing more. I can tackle the steak. You'll have to cut it up for me.'

'Good. Take your pill.'

209

'Pills – take away one's appetite, leave one feeling sick, depressed and probably constipated. What I really want is a bottle of burgundy: that's the real specific for loss of blood.' Poor old Arthur – he was as bucked as though he'd drunk the bottle himself.

Poor old became startlingly good old. The steak was a sirloin and fillet together on the bone. There was marrow with it. There was watercress. There was a cup of bouillon. There was a bunch of flowers. The steak was too much for her, but he made no problem about disposing of the rest. There was not much conversation.

'The thing I find noteworthy,' said Arthur, 'is Demazis, a man probably involved in a criminal operation and feeling unhappy about it, seeking to confide in someone and choosing a woman. This makes the whole thing worthwhile.'

'Mm,' she said. 'I'm sorry darling; perhaps I've overeaten.' And the burgundy was soporific. He took himself and the débris off, tactfully, after very nicely suggesting he make her bed for her and get the crumbs out.

One is alone. One is and always will be. One is so more and more. She realized she was exceptionally lucky. A good marriage and a good man. Moreover, the second. She had not really wanted to remarry. Had done so, perhaps, for bad and selfish reasons.

Not altogether. Arthur had had a rotten time, and deserved something better. And was it a good idea to clutch widowhood like a comfortable old fur coat? Was that fair on the children? They had their lives, and she didn't want them coming on bright family visits, to cheer up old mum with a display of family solidarity, a chat about the old days, some sentimental memories dressed up with funny details and trotted out, well-worn and practised family-gathering pieces between the flowers for mum's birthday or the Toussaint, and the obligatory bottle of champagne. One boy was actively contemplating a marriage, the other hovering. Mum could come and stay, mum could babysit. All very merry. She got on well with real or putative daughters-in-law. The boys were nice boys; they acquired nice girls.

She had her pension: Dutch money, worth a lot in France. She had a job, her health. But if she lost these things, and the old bag became an old drag ... she had been frightened of being alone.

Arthur's patient kindness was as real as his generosity, his simplicity. Well, she'd had something to give. Without her, he would have retreated further and further into the eccentric professor act; crankiness and comedies to mask the steady desiccation of a fertile personality, embittered by the failures of his life.

Yes, a marvellous marriage. But as Arthur himself said 'On est tout seul, ma poule.' Always and inevitably.

Yes, it did some good. Norma, Demazis, little Marie-Line – how alone they were. Yes, even Demazis.

She hadn't agreed with Arthur. Poor Albert – strange that he should have the same initials as Arthur: it had hooked her, absurdly – hadn't confided in her. That was a sentimental notion. A man who went on complicating things, who realized perhaps in the end that there was no real way out, and whether he had been killed, or killed himself, or expected perhaps to be killed had planted an obscure clue. Confide in a woman?

She shrugged. Counted perhaps on female curiosity and tenacity – or vanity.

She looked at her hand. Hurting, in a lethargic way. Hadn't the kidnappers been rather stupid? No, they'd expected her to react in a male way, swallow the lesson and profit by it.

That is surely idiotic. If she'd been a man they'd have killed her.

Well, Arthur Davidson being what he was, it was police business now. And they wouldn't have any woman nonsense. They'd move her politely aside, and conduct the matter in their fashion.

A faint stirring of obstinacy moved inside Arlette. But she had better drag herself out and do her teeth before she fell down in a heap. She'd slept all day. And was quite ready to sleep all night.

Arthur Davidson, doing the washing-up and enjoying it, since for once he could arrange the job properly – no woman had any real idea of how to wash-up – tidied the kitchen, sat for some time in the living-room fiddling with a pipe without smoking it and gazing at the television screen without taking it in – whatever it was ... When it started to gabble too much he brought himself to turn it off, thought of something, hunted among records till he found Schubert's *Winter Journey* and put that on. It was right somehow.

An hour and a half later he got up and went to bed. His wife was fast asleep. Flushed, and a bit sweaty. Burgundy, or that stupid menopause, or the radiator she'd forgotten to turn out? Bit of each. Well rolled up anyhow in the complicated 'nest' she arranged for herself. Peculiar slight obstinate grin she had upon her face. Grin of thorough satisfaction. He opened the window. No other French person one knew liked fresh air at night. Must come from having lived in Holland. French women are a tougher proposition than French men. This was a truism, and like most such, suspect. All that Davidson was prepared to say on the subject was that he was happy with his. Absolute nonsense anyhow. Were she Dutch or English she would be just the same. Nowadays French women didn't even want to cook any more, the silly asses. Blasted pest of a woman, but I'm happy with mine I'm happy with mine. With this little song he fell asleep.

35. 'Interrogations'

She got up and dressed.

'Why not?' she said when Arthur tried to be disputatious. Well after all; why not? Washing and dressing was troublesome and laborious, but she wanted to be normal, to behave as though nothing had happened. Rendered gloomy by a long prospect stretching ahead of shopping, cooking, and having the washing-up all to himself – less attractive a notion somehow than it had been last night – he shooed her out of the kitchen altogether.

'If we're both here we'll only quarrel. My domain; let me handle it my way.' Since this was exactly what she would have said there was nothing but to withdraw, silently forecasting that everything would be unfindable. He'd be popping in cross: where the hell d'you keep lemons? Jacques Ellul would get covered in greaseprints, and all the food would taste of mustard.

Good, now she's gone off in a sulk, barricading herself in the office and going to have a soothing long chat with that tiresome lesbian woman.

A doctor appeared. A bit curt about amateurish treatments – nothing was said about Arthur's student girl. Her pills were looked at, snorted at, and thrown away: new and more sophisticated ones, which would have exactly the same effect, prescribed.

'Anti-inflammatory, get this thing healing, bring it to me in a couple of days to look at,' as though it were a urine specimen, and fled. This was not, unluckily, the end of the troubles, because Divisional-Inspector Papi arrived a quarter of an hour later.

Just like that damned commissaire to send a Corsican – must have been to pester her! He was tall, thin, dry, knotty; tuft of wiry hair like dunegrass in the middle of a bald brown

213

forehead, broken nose, strange small curly ears and mouth. Looked like the razor-carrying expert all right. With him, less expectedly, Corinne.

'I'm just here to carry spears,' she said. 'To make notes because nobody can read his shorthand. Woman's job. To look after him, carry his shopping bag or whatnot. Be his guardian gorilla a bit. Drive the car you know? All the women's jobs in brief. The boss wants you to lead a normal existence. Nothing reckless, but not so intimidated as to skulk all day in cellars.'

Monsieur Papi paid no attention to this. Sat, made himself comfortable, arranged the biggest ashtray handily and said, 'Let's have the whole thing from beginning to end.'

'This'll take all day.'

'I've got all day.' Cops are the same everywhere. It is always difficult to distinguish between the ones that are dense and the ones who pretend to be dense. France is no exception; neither is Strasbourg.

'From what I've been told,' he said slowly, 'you believe that you were seized by a group of professionals. I'd like to hear your definition of professional in this context.'

'People organizing and exploiting crime like any other business, purely for the purpose of making a large profit.'

'The profit motive by itself is criminal, some people would say.'

'What I believe or say isn't perhaps very relevant.'

'It might colour what you say.'

'I don't understand at all. Are you thinking that I might claim to have been kidnapped with an idea of embarrassing the administration?'

'No. I have to start by distinguishing between crapulous crime, which is what we call an act committed uniquely for money, and a crime or what appears to be, committed for publicity, which might turn out to be something political. The first might be my business: the second wouldn't. That's why I want to get it straight.'

'There's no doubt in my mind at all. The man who seemed

214

to be the principal said as much. He used these words: "we don't want to draw attention to ourselves".'

'So he goes and does so, by cutting your hand.'

'I've thought about this too. I'm hoping we'll find the answer.'

'I'm only pointing out to you, Madame, that it seems inconsistent. You did something to arouse the hostility of people. They try to intimidate you by various means. I'm told you had your car shot at, and a sort of little home-made bomb blew your letterbox out.'

'No, that was pure coincidence. I discovered only that day all this was due to somebody else altogether.'

'Yes? P'raps you'll let me be the judge of that?' Not very happily, she told about Norma. Corinne was there too, saying nothing, taking notes. This inevitably led to her explaining the narrow squeak from getting raped. Corinne only once glanced up and made a face: Arlette made a face too.

'I agree. I was very foolish.'

'All this violent attack, and you didn't make any complaint?' said Monsieur Papi.

'Well, first of all I wasn't raped. And if I tried to have him chased for assaulting and injuring me, I can't see that it would make him any the less aggressive. More so, if anything, towards women anyhow.'

'So this is the explanation of the bruising on your neck and arms which the doctor describes,' turning over a piece of paper.

She saw light. Had he really believed she had been beaten up while making love, and invented the kidnapping tale to make it look better?

'Funnier things have happened.'

'And that's true, I'm afraid,' added Corinne.

To be very suspicious indeed of anything a woman says in such circumstances is a professional police deformation. However many real rapes there are, there are still a lot of phony ones. There is also a strongly-held legend that women

215

rather enjoy being beaten up. Arlette supposed such women to exist somewhere, but hadn't ever met one.

'So you were all that evening out in Hautepierre?'

'There's a witness to it you know, and she can be found. I had a meal with her in Schiltigheim. I drew it out deliberately to give myself time to get well calmed down. Strangely enough, I didn't want it known. It would worry my husband.'

'Nobody's disbelieving this, Madame. Just that the coincidence is there. These people then were lying in wait outside your house. They must have waited a long time.'

'Yes, that has struck me too. I suppose it's conceivable that they went to a lot of trouble anyhow, and took the extra trouble of following me. I was in no state to notice. They bundled me into my own car and not theirs. It must have been prearranged. They had a car which picked them up, out there in the country. So there were four at least, and at least one car.'

He let her talk, nodding sometimes, making an occasional longhand note.

'We'll look out there, though it's not very likely we'll find anything.'

'I told the commissaire as much. I'm not even sure of recognizing the exact spot.'

'So we go over the day's movements. You were out in Geispolsheim. And you had lunch with your husband in town.'

'I'd been looking up these students. Boys the girl Marie-Line had been going with.'

'So there's a sequence in time, and perhaps you arranged it in your mind to make it consistent. No intention of misleading, I accept. But the story seems more satisfying this way?'

'You know I anticipated this. Some connection there is, though I admit slight. That flowershop has an advertisement for this boy's drawings, or whatever they are. Isn't it too much coincidence? Of course any artist sticks up posters wherever he can. But isn't it all too pat?'

'You realize that I have to be sceptical of things. This sort of auto-suggestion is a commonplace.'

216

'Of course I realize that, and that's why I try to answer patiently.'

'Right. What we have is this. A plainclothes type checked up a bit, discreet-like. This arty guy, and these cafés around the university quarter. It's obvious, and it's known about. All of them do a bit of trafficking in a small way. Stimulant or sedative pills – doctors hand this shit out, and people sell it. Likewise there's always smallish quantities of weeds and hash. The long-distance lorry drivers come across the border here, you're aware, and there's always stuff seeping in from Iran and Turkey. Not much, because the Germans and ourselves keep a close eye. Drivers making pocket money for themselves, mostly. Okay? Now there doesn't seem to be any evidence that any traffic is any less trivial than usual.'

'The commissaire remarked that any real distribution network wouldn't operate on its home territory.'

'That's right, and I only bring the point up to say you needn't worry about getting this kid Siegel involved. We know Doctor Siegel. Like we know him enough not really to want to know him any better if you take my meaning.'

'I do,' with a faint grin.

'Now I'll come to the big question. We don't know, so we agree to hypothesize, and see if any known fact tends to confirm that hypothesis. Okay we're talking about narcotics, real ones, not students popping pills. Good, there's what the movies call the French Connection and we've busted that, or supposed to, right? Thing like that isn't ever really busted but what we do is take the profit out of it, and put too much publicity into it. Find an illegal lab., seize a large amount of morphine-base and kick up a lot of newspaper comment, those boys don't enjoy that, stands to reason.

'So now we hear the morphine comes down from Holland. Maybe that's so and maybe it isn't, we'll leave that aside. Assume it. Good, here's a plant place in Geispolsheim gets a lot of merchandise out of Holland. I'll go this far. It just maybe could be so.

'Now we come to Demazis. Accountant, but he buzzed

217

around a good deal. He doesn't draw attention to himself, to pick up your phrase. No unusual signs of affluence, say. He owns this flat in the Rue de Labaroche, bit more property in the town, that's the wife's. Nothing inconsistent. Pursue the hypothesis. They do plenty of business in Switzerland, he could salt money away there, little at a time, nice flat in Zurich say; we'd know nothing about that. Done all the time, hundreds of examples. He's a nice little business. Now why should he suddenly upset the applecart by running to you with this ridiculous story he's getting threatening phone calls?'

'I have simply no idea. The fact is that he did. I can only think that he was trying to be clever. Build up some insurance, or create a pretext for getting out of a tangle that was beginning to worry him. If I started nosing around in his existence – maybe he could have used that as an excuse. He might have thought me very naïve and inexperienced – which heaven knows I am. He might have planned to say I was blackmailing him. But he got killed, so we'll never know.'

'We've no proof whatever he was killed,' reprovingly.

'Then perhaps he killed himself. He might have been showing signs of unease or instability for a long time. The wife won't say. Whatever happens he's not going to have any news for us. But suppose this. I went to see Madame Demazis. Say that fact is noted, and if she has any knowledge of anything, she could pass this further item along. And then – by sheer coincidence, this other interest – I went to the plant place, and then – look, I was in the street hanging about that flower shop. In fact I was gaining ten minutes, waiting for my husband. But if I were seen, and if it were noticed further that I'd been at that studio on the pretext of my interest in Marie-Line ... would that add up to a warning sign? Would they conclude that Demazis actually had said something to me that might lead to a giveaway?'

'But in fact he didn't?'

'I give you my word of honour, no, he didn't. I don't have any ambitions at all to be a detective. I went down to the PJ to ask whether there was anything funny about his death.'

'Yes, I know . . .'

'But I didn't know,' she said tartly.

'Mm hm,' said Monsieur Papi, and retreated into silence, turning papers over and making marks on them.

She took hold of what was rapidly becoming frenzied irritation, and sat on it firmly.

One had to realize that standard police procedure always does lead to frenzied irritation: they are like this. The air of never being quite human, and behaving as if you weren't either, is deliberate. It is part of a technique designed to shake you up thoroughly and then stand you on your head to drain. Keep you off balance, keep you guessing. The curt question-and-answer stuff, monosyllabic and bleak, is often followed by a talkative show of bonhomie, of pretended confidences. They will feign sympathy in one breath and hostility in the next, a blank stupidity and a sophisticated cunning, the back-slapping pally-pally and the frigidly indifferent. You end up by disbelieving everything, from your own identity to the accuracy of your own senses. You no longer trust the ground you walk on: at any moment a trapdoor will open under your feet.

How to avoid being tainted? Even the best and the brightest, who turn this sort of thing on and off like electric current, must surely be blunted and desensitized? Are they all no more than cynical timeservers from the ones with soft voices at the top to the coarse oafs at the bottom?

She knew that it was not so. The 'compassionate cop' is not quite fictional, not altogether a contradiction in terms. But it takes a strong character.

And the women . . . She looked at Corinne; sturdy, unimaginative, tough: staring off into space with a deliberately cowlike expression while fiddling with her pencil, not wanting to exchange any glance of secret sympathy or female complicity.

'All right,' said Papi suddenly. 'That's all for today. We'll keep in touch, Madame.'

'What about it all?' asked Arlette drearily, knowing the answer would be just like a doctor's: a bluff jolly air, but we've got to wait for the results of the tests, Missis.

219

He smiled though, brilliantly, eyes disappearing in crinkles. 'Priority is to get that hand healed up. Just lead a normal life. And don't have any worries – you're under police protection.'

'I'll be along to see you,' said Corinne.

36. 'Madame le Juge'

You sleep well. Slightly doped. You complain a good deal about nasty pills. Chemotherapy is like *Ten-Sixty-Six-And-All-That*, vaguely a 'good thing', combating inflations and inflammations and so forth. But leaves you so sick you'd really have preferred the original malady. Even that sensible and un-Anglo-Saxon invention the bomb in your behind, vulgarly known as a suppository, upsets your digestion much less but still leaves you listless and depressed.

You get up; you dress. It's only a wound. You are going to lead a normal existence. You have quite large hands. Arthur's hands, for a man, are small. You can borrow a soft leather glove. It doesn't look bad at all. You feel undeniably low and ill. It's reaction. Not much to be done about that. Arthur is suffering from it too. He has been so good, unwearyingly kind and patient. Today he is just barely keeping irritation in check.

Uncannily, the long settled spell of lovely weather, imperturbably still and sunny, was keeping up. But winter was advancing on stockinged feet. The heavy mist clung more obstinately each morning. Cold, wet, smelly, catching at your throat, like cottonwool drenched in ether. The sun struggled through at last, and shone then with surprising heat, so that you went to turn your thermostat down.

220

'Look,' said Arthur in an abrupt way, smoking a small cigar and stabbing with it at the shopping list, 'you leave all this to me, right? Housekeeping is a thing only one person can do efficiently at a time. I can do it, okay? I've told them straight I'm taking a few days off. I intend to see this through.'

'I've really made a complete distaster of all this, haven't I?'

'No. You haven't. It was my fault. Encouraging you with that silly game about Marlowe. Now we have to face the realities, as they are brought home to us. This is not a game for children.' She was saved from expressions of abjectness by the front doorbell.

'You take that,' said Arthur, who was wearing her apron.

A middle-aged woman, looking round her with an expression of interest at the panelling and spotlights of the little waiting-room. A customer? A youngish woman with her. Both burdened with luggage. A big briefcase, and what looked like a typewriter.

'Madame Davidson?' with a glance at her gloved hand. 'I'm Madame Flavien. The judge of instruction. This is Madame Sellier, my clerk.' Arlette, flustered, led the way into 'her office'.

'Do please sit down. I thought you summoned people to your presence,' foolishly.

'Oh no,' smiling. 'We pop about all over the place. Can she put her machine there on your table? Tuck yourself in at the end there, Denise.' She opened the briefcase at her feet and shuffled with papers.

'Arlette, wife Davidson, widow van der Valk, that's right? Born when and where?' The usual routine, what.

Fortyish. A blonde, fairly considerably faded, lined, wrinkled, not to say battered by years of her profession. Good, pretty, steady blue eyes, short-sighted behind strong lenses and pinkish shell frame. Earrings. An elaborate, bouffant hairdo, recently and professionally done, the hair skilfully touched up and freshened. Too much lipstick. Too much make-up. The clothes too feminine – no, just a bit too fussy: the pleated navy blue skirt was fine and so was the open-collared blouse, but the silk scarf was too brightly coloured, too casually knotted, too fussily displayed and drew attention to the throat. Square competent hands with colourless varnish, a trace of suntan. Very good voice, professionally pitched and paced just right, a clear soprano that carried without penetrating. Nothing in the least legal; she could have been a journalist, an editor – a business executive in pretty nearly anything.

Arlette knew she must repeat everything, whether she had told it ten times or not. And must not tell lies: this woman was intelligent, experienced, and had done her homework thoroughly. And she was thorough now: very.

The girl Denise was what you would expect, good at her job. This judge would be a taskmaster, and peppery upon occasion. Well trained, she sat still and unfidgety, her forearms relaxed. When she had to type she did so rapidly and accurately. Occasionally with a tangled bit she would ask, 'How am I to word that?' At which moment one saw the judge as editor, dictating in spare brief sentences, saying, 'Semicolon . . . stop. Paragraph.'

'Good. That will do. See that that's neat, Denise. That was well told, and lucidly. To make it brief, the Prosecutor has laid charges against X for this affair of yours. Kidnapping, physical violence, blows and wounds; that'll do to go on with. You are well enough acquainted with legal procedure to realize that I have been designated as instructing judge, that I am putting a dossier together – good now, let's leave that. I issue a rogatory commission to the Police Judiciaire, tra la, we leave aside for the moment this presumption of narcotics traffic and all the rest; that need not concern you. We'll stick to this, as contained in the deposition which you'll sign when Denise has it ready for you. May I smoke?' with abrupt politeness. 'Stupid things,' apologetically, holding out the packet. Arlette took one. Madame le Juge took her glasses off, stared unseeingly at the light from the window put them back on and came back to business.

'Let's understand one another, Madame Davidson. You're a witness, the principal witness. No more. I don't want you playing any role, active or otherwise. To wit the private detective. Clear?'

'I have the clearest understanding that I know where police business begins.'

'Yes, I know, Monsieur le Commissaire told me. I've no reproach to make you.' She looked around at the office. 'You can do useful work, I have no doubt of that. I've no hostility towards these activities, quite the contrary. I'm a woman. As long as you keep the definitions sharp in your mind.'

'I'm capable of that, you know.'

'Yes, from what I've seen of you I think you are. You got badly hurt, I'm afraid. I hope it's not giving you pain.'

'It's nothing much. It's clean – I think it will heal quickly.'

'And the psychological shock – make no mistake, that can be severe. Even when you think you're over it. I don't wish to be personal. It can go on, creating unforeseen ripples.'

'I think you're right. I have to learn to cope with it.'

'I'm not sure that it's a good idea to work at home. One has to keep one's private life from getting contaminated by – call it professional preoccupation. You've children?'

'They're grown up. I don't think I agree, you know, about keeping things separate. I don't want only comprehension and support from my husband. I want him very closely involved I think, every minute.'

'You do? Well, it's a viewpoint. There are others. Come on Denise, hurry up.'

'Ready. Can I have your signature, Madame? Fine, thanks.'

Madame le Juge stabbed out her cigarette, rose swiftly, held out her hand, realized that didn't work, grinned.

'I'll want you in the office eventually. When they catch these birds. I'm fairly confident. You may be able to make identifications. You find me insensitive? This job,' with a small shrug.

'I find you professional . . . which is as it should be.'

'Good luck with the hand . . . And thank you; that was useful.'

It was? One couldn't help wondering how.

Arthur brought her a cup of coffee which she didn't really

want. And he had absent-mindedly put sugar in it, so that it was disgusting. She did so wish he wouldn't be helpful. It would be infinitely easier if he had gone off to work as usual and eaten in the canteen. But one would never dare suggest that: according to him the place was infested with every bacteriological hazard known to the human race. Bilharzia, he would mutter darkly. Nothing would stop him hanging about protecting her, simply because he felt guilty. She would be perfectly capable of scrambling an egg or something one-handed by ingenious means. Would rather enjoy it. But it was 'not allowed'.

She threw the coffee surreptitiously down the washbasin and brought the cup back, about to say, 'There are lots of things I can do,' but was quelled by the air of patience tightly held in.

'The worst thing you can possibly do is roam around like this, working yourself up and not even giving it a chance to heal. Why on earth can't you lie down quietly and read a book? Everything's under control.' Yes, that was just the trouble.

She retreated to the living-room, which was tidied and hoovered and God knew what so that she didn't dare move for fear of getting ash in a clean ashtray. Arthur indulging his passion for being meticulous. In this mood he was capable of every folly; washing the kitchen curtains or something. She was supposed to stay quiet and listen to soothing Schubert, whereas what she needed was something as horrible as possible gyrating and writhing in sweaty black satin under a purple spot. She uncorked a bottle with her teeth: the cork squeaked and she looked round guiltily lest Arthur catch her and deliver a lecture about how bad alcohol was for you when you'd been cut with a razor.

The worst had occurred and he'd decided to have a good turn out in the kitchen to help poor disorganized Arlette. She was of course the classic dirty housewife. Rubbish collected on shelves and attracted greasy dust. Rinds of cheese turned up in unexpected places. There were innumerable half-empty packets; one-eyed and one-legged veterans everywhere, stragglers from campaigns in Russia or the Peninsula, three

224

kinds of stale curry powder and horrible sticky bottles which had lost their labels. Arthur was having a simply glorious time and she would never find anything again. To go and say, 'Look – I've been a housewife for thirty years; I know my job,' would be fatal. She knew he had reached the stage of talking to himself.

'How long have we been here – a couple of months. How is it conceivable that anyone could create a bordel like that in that space' forgetting the lorryload of junk brought from the Krutenau, which she had promised herself to look at and never had. 'Would you believe it; jam three years old, pickled pears left behind by Frankenstein, the thyroid and the thalamus.' Had he but known – stuff made by Ruth during an adolescent passion for vinegar, five years ago out in the country . . . 'The Little Grey Home in the West' as Piet called it sarcastically. And I wish I were there now, thought Arlette oozing tears of self-pity, forgetting much coarse Dutch humour about pea soup heavily laced with penicillin.

Now she was going to start as well, muttering to herself.

It brewed steadily for a couple of hours, before exploding. One uses a razor too to lance an abscess.

The row when it came was something frightful.

'Like a fucking old maid there in the apron. Sociologist – what's that? It doesn't exist. English Amateur.'

'Ah yes, now we're going to hear some more about Piet The Professional.'

'Fiddling at people. Going on about the French. The most barbaric and backward women in Europe, we heard it all. The great lazy useless mare. All her brains between her legs and even that gone desiccated.'

'Wasting your entire existence, the moment their biological function ceases to be the centre they sit idly back and wait to be granny. Knit and make pickles and quarrel with their daughters about child upbringing.'

'I didn't want in the least to get remarried. You pushed and pushed, to conceal your own utter sterility, insisting on this idiotic activity, crapping about meddling with things that

225

should be left to proper cops, and the second it gets a bit tough, oh, the hullabaloo about the little woman. Me! Me who had a man shot dead in the street, a man who'd gone on for years with a hip smashed up by a huge rifle bullet that dotty Belgian cow fired at him. Do you think I know nothing about violence? I lived with it twenty years, day by day. While you were snivelling in your pram worrying about your anal satisfactions.' This simply glorious picture of Arthur aged eighteen months in a romper suit reading Freud and viewing Mum with the darkest suspicion brought on howls, hiccups, hysterical laughter. Finally she hit her hand on the table and rocked to and fro silently, corkscrewing pain in and out. Arthur poured out two socking glasses of whisky.

'What's this business of loving people?' she asked rhetorically.

'Laurens van der Post somewhere talks about loving Africa. Pretty well. Harshness and pain, cruelty and heat. Bushman paintings and tin shacks. The incredible wealth and beauty, and you can't move without stumbling over bleached bones. You can't see out of the Land-Rover because the flies are so thick on the windscreen. It's not a marshmallow affair, love.'

'It's holding on, come what may.'

'He gets a bit mad. You'll get on terribly well with old so-and-so because you both so love Africa. Toasted marshmallows.'

'So may I go out?'

'You may go anywhere you please and do anything you please. May I come with you?'

'And even if you can't?'

'Then let's go to the movies. Woody Allen for preference.'

'What about the police?'

'Look, I know nothing about the police, and care less. No, I know a good deal about them. They'll tell us nothing. No good expecting your pal the Commissaire to drop in and smoke a pipe and tell you all about it: they won't.

'I'm allowed to do my little circus, right? That's fine as long as they're left completely tranquil, as long as I don't go screaming for help, yelping I've been mugged, as long as I say and do nothing that could conceivably embarrass or annoy them. This I know about; lived with it twenty years.

'Right, I stumble upon something that unwittingly I followed when it was their business. Demazis was accident or suicide and does it really matter? I can get hunches about homicide but that's not their way of thinking: they're interested, slightly: it might prove something. They go all soothing and tut-tut: poor you, don't worry, we'll watch over you. All bread-and-butter and soft-boiled egg: they just want me immobilized and not kicking up any further dust.'

'You think they're not watching the place at all?'

'Christ knows: they could be there and we don't know it. They don't have a little man up there in the Observatory with binoculars, you know. They could pretend to ignore the whole affair, or they could hang about ostentatiously hoping to provoke something. Whatever they tell us you can be sure it's lies.'

'So if you go out . . .'

'I'm frightened to. But I have to. Lead a normal life, they say. What is, I wonder, a normal life?'

'What does Madame le Juge say?'

'She doesn't say. I annoy her. I'm a sort of hermaphrodite, not competent enough to do a male job in a male way, nor with the sense to do a female one. Just as well she didn't see you cleaning up my kitchen.'

'She wouldn't be impressed by me either.'

'She can get stuffed. Madame le Juge,' said Arlette, sounding like Louis Quatorze, 'is me.'

37. 'A foggy evening on the autoroute'

'So we go to the pictures?'

'Why not? I can't think of anything more normal. And I'm in the mood for a bit of artificial life for a change.'

They took the bus on the Boulevard de la Victoire. Strasbourg seemed quite depressingly normal. Nobody seemed to be hanging about. Nobody followed them or shadowed them.

Arthur liked to walk when he came out of a cinema. It disintoxicated, he said. All that wirra-wirra in front of his eyes, he said. And why did they turn the soundtrack up so loud? It's for the people who go to pop concerts, Arlette said: they're all as deaf as posts. He supposed this must be so; he could think of no adequate reason but force of habit. Was she not too tired?

Not a bit. Felt in fine form. Loved walking anyhow. And it's a lovely evening. She loved autumn evenings just a bit foggy, when the lights were on in shops.

'Being protected by police anyhow is quite meaningless. Schleyer had how many – four·was it – just gunned down.'

'Aldo Moro had five. But that was a highly professional gang.'

'So is this,' said Arlette. 'Or is it? Nobody knows really. They behaved in a professional way, cutting me like that, and there is something strangely amateurish too.'

'This is one of the things that's bothered me,' said Arthur delighted that she felt able at last to talk about it.

'Madame le Juge is foxed by it too. "Curious" she kept saying, as though she didn't believe a word of it. But it is curious. The cops of course don't say what they think.'

'And what do you think?'

'I'm not sure that the idea isn't deliberately left vague. J

228

mean look at the point of view of the man who cut me. It's a warning, and at the same time a punishment.'

'Explain yourself,' said Arthur.

'Suppose I did something illegal, committed even something criminal, like suppressing evidence – the private eyes are always doing that. You'd get pretty hostile handling from the cops. Not necessarily slapped about, but various brutalities more or less subtle. The tribunal would take away any licence you happened to have, likely a month or two in jail, a fine or both. It wouldn't be just a telling off. A real punishment; that's professional. Isn't this more or less the same? I am kidnapped, like an arrest; badly frightened, severely hurt. I can't do anything much physically for a few weeks. Unless I take a lot of pills, which also diminish me and make me sick and muzzy, it's really painful. Pretty adequate I'd have thought.'

'And next time, goes the warning, it'll be your throat.'

'That's right,' said Arlette quite coolly. 'I thought for one minute he was going to kill me.'

'Were you frightened then?'

'Of dying, no. One dies, whatever happens. Of pain yes. Then he said he didn't want to draw attention to himself. Well, I thought, you do. And then perhaps no, perhaps it's cleverer than it looks. It might be senseless, like that imbecile Robert with his guns and his bombs. Or a personal vengeance. If I did something that really got to Freddy Ulrich deep down – let's say – would he do a thing like that?'

'Of course not. A bourgeois vengeance, you saw, is giving you bad publicity, hitting you in the pocket, having you slammed by the tax collector. Nothing to do with blood.'

'I'm none too sure. Hurt a bourgeois in his blood, which is his profit and his reputation, and he might well turn back at you with a thing like a razor.'

'But you don't think you were kidnapped by Freddy Ulrich.'

'No, of course not.'

Arthur bought some mushrooms, nice big ones, and a bunch of chives.

'Leave the supper to me,' he said. You could see his mind

229

going 'egg and breadcrumb? No, too much trouble. But perhaps a nice kind of batter with chopped chives in, and fry them? Sort of beignets?'

Arlette, who had switched her phone back to 'record' found the little light on and stopped to listen to the message. Then she made a phone call, which went on a long time.

'Supper's ready. What was all that?'

'Well, that was rather pathetic. And in a way what this business is all about. And it comes a bit close to the bone. There's nothing I can do really to help her. Console a bit, possibly. Reassure, explain – I don't know. I say, these are good.'

'There was sort of a tiny dirty leftover, bit of ham. Chopped it all up and flung it in the batter. Tell.'

'Well,' between bites, 'two teenage girls out of Duttlenheim, that's that village in the valley of the Bruche where the autoroute ends, hitch-hiked into town to go to a dance or something and never arrived. Disappeared on the autoroute. So they find out at home, quite early as it happens. Somebody rings – where are the girls? But aren't they with you? No? Then where are they? Gendarmerie, hospitals, police. No sign of girls. This was last night. So she's waited all day. And the police won't tell her anything. And she fears the worst. And she's naturally utterly distraught. Don't blame her. She's sure they've found the worst and won't tell her.'

'And what does she think you can do?'

'Heaven knows,' tranquilly, 'but the least I can do is go out and try to inject a bit of comfort and commonsense. She's surrounded by neighbours whose imaginings are each more hideous than the last. I'm trying to tell her that not hearing by now is as likely good as bad. At its most brutal, that if they were killed or raped they'd probably be found by now. Better that they flipped, thought it was going to be a heavenly invention, got taken somewhere, got made very drunk, and are still sleeping it off in some pad, the results not too terrible apart from ghastly hangover and feeling fearfully sick.'

230

'Mmm,' said Arthur. 'You mean you want to go there? I'll have to drive you.'

'It's only a quarter of an hour.'

'It'll be foggy. Always is out that way.'

'So you drive carefully. I have to, you see.'

The 'northern autoroute' which goes all the way to Paris, and links with the German autobahn at Saarbrucken, is very modern, quite luxurious, and madly expensive. The 'southern autoroute' is a perfect fraud, announcing boldly in huge letters that it will whisk you down to Colmar and Mulhouse, and various vaguely hinted destinations in south-eastern France. Once out of Strasbourg, you can indeed switch onto this road; for the most part an ordinary main road, which is to say good in bits. Stay on the autoroute and it will lead you bravely out towards the Vosges and the town of Obernai, for exactly thirteen kilometres, when it stops dead and chucklingly decants you into country byways. It is to be presumed that the highway authority of Ponts et Chaussées did once have a project for crossing the Vosges over to Epinal and Burgundy. Thought better of it after ten minutes. Someone probably made a lot of money in the process.

Duttlenheim is the second village out from the end. Notorious for a road surface straight out of the *Wages of Fear* – remember the truck loaded with nitroglycerine? This is where you'll meet it.

Arthur, after fussing with the Lancia's driving seat, took the direct way to the autoroute junction, Place de Haguenau. He was not, save over long distances when he found a rhythm, a good driver: far too slow in traffic and too fast once it thinned.

Fortunately around eight at night traffic is thinning. The suburbanites are already at home, eating indigestible food and looking at the news, which won't help. More of a mixed blessing is that the valley of the Bruche, a small river joining the Ill at Strasbourg, is a notorious foggy corner. Visibility on an autumn night fifty metres at best, thirty more often, and sudden patches really thick.

Good, it's an autoroute. Thus well marked with broad

231

stripes of paint. Smooth surface, regular curves. No oncoming traffic. Arthur clicked into top past the bright lights of the Colmar junction and adopted a steady gait around a hundred.

'Too fast,' said Arlette. He slowed to ninety, reluctantly. 'Still too fast.' He paid no heed, hit a thick bit, and slowed abruptly to eighty.

'Perfectly safe,' crossly. He was in the slow lane. Belated homegoers who knew it all by heart were whisking by on the fast lane.

'It's our skin, not theirs,' said Arlette primly.

You get oddly isolated in the fog. The cars in front of and behind you lose their identity, loom up suddenly as blurred lights. You don't see the car at all.

'Stupe,' said Arthur cross, pulling out abruptly to pass a cautious-Clara kerbcrawling, and forgetting to signal.

'Idiot,' a moment later. Sticking to his back end, and much too close were the glaring lights of a large truck. Too high, not properly adjusted to 'dip' and blinding white – a German probably. Very annoying; neither passing nor falling back. Arthur accelerated smartly to shake him off. He kept pace. People do this in fog and very annoying it is, as well as dangerous. What happens if you have to brake suddenly? 'Cunt' muttered Arthur viperish. He was up to a hundred and ten and still the big truck kept pace. He slowed again progressively.

Suddenly a frightening thing happened, which happens too in fog, where people become sillier than usual. The truck came up fast, swung abruptly out into the fast lane, bored no doubt with Arthur's manoeuvres, and thundered past at a hundred and thirty. Huge articulated thing.

'God DAMN it.' The thing was barely past, right under his nose, and cut in back on top of him. The brake lights flared up brilliant red; the whole enormous mass slowed as though it had run into a wall. Probably the driver had suddenly seen two more crawlers blocking both lanes. Going himself far too fast, he had had to take off speed in a great hurry. Too bad for the little fellow behind.

Arthur braked too hard, skidded a little towards the left, corrected a little oversharp, skidded to the right, lurched over the line on to the emergency track, slammed down into second with a howl from the motor, dragged to a stop more or less in line, found his nose two feet from the yellow metal post with the emergency telephone, sat there trembling and shaking. He had switched the motor out instinctively. The lights pointed down over the soft shoulder into field. Ploughed, looking soft down there two or three metres below. But not soft to fall into at sixty kilometres an hour. Like water. At that speed it's concrete. He undid his belt, got shakily out, leaned on the roof, took big breaths of night air.

'Great leaping Jesus,' he said. Arlette got slowly out on the right. She had the torch from the glove compartment. She looked down into the ravine.

'Things keep happening to me in this car,' she said softly.

38. 'A Masterly Throw of the Net'

'You don't imagine that was on purpose,' said Arthur at last in an over-casual way.

'No. Of course not. You can't organize a thing like that. Nor plan – well, maybe you can. I don't know. Nobody knew we were coming here.'

'But we're ready to believe anything,' said Arthur taking the torch to look. 'Now if I'd been going just a little faster . . .'

It is one of the things one says. Life went on as before, tranquilly. Cars went singing past. The truck driver had doubtless already forgotten what was not even an episode.

'My dear mother,' said Arlette, 'used to say always make sure your underclothes are clean in case of a road accident.'

'Very sensible of her. What else is there to be afraid of?'

'Losing you.'

Arthur looked at her, and said, 'No, don't let's lose one another.'

'Are you all right?' He was a lot more shaken than she was, she realized. Surprised.

'Foot in the stirrup. One must remount at once after a fall. I haven't a scratch. Good car that. Stable.'

The German police had found the two girls, in the company of two Canadian airforcemen in, of all places, Ludwigshafen. They'd been looking for a pale blue Audi reported stolen an hour before in Mainz, so naturally their eye had lighted on a pale grey Ford. There were at the present no further explanations: plainly the story would be a confused one. Arlette came in handy to persuade the farmer's wife that she was not disgraced throughout eternity, and in soothing the farmer, who had already taken his belt off and was swinging it about in ominous fashion. Arthur, who'd had one beer in a café and time to imagine sinister machinations, drove home through villages. He'd had enough, he said, of autoroutes for the time being.

The Rue de l'Observatoire was amazingly quiet and undramatic. Nobody was hanging about in shadowy corners. Life was normal. It was quite inconceivable, they both decided, that any sinister machination should have taken place. Things like that happened – they quite agreed – when one was a little over-nervous and perhaps a little clumsy. The Lancia was a sensitive car, and reacted at once to any heaviness of foot or hand. Really Arthur preferred bicycles. Arlette's hand was throbbing a little, so they both had some linden tea.

Lead a normal life. What is normal life? Podsnappery, as Dickens called it: getting up at eight o'clock and shaving clean at a quarter past.

'Go to work,' said Arlette. 'I'll manage.' If it hadn't been for the daily paper . . . With all its antique euphemisms on parade.

There was a big headline. "A Masterly Throw of the Net". Provincial newspapers are always like this. Their French, like detective stories, got enshrined about the time of the Stavisky scandal. A naughty man is always an individual little to be recommended, whose habits society reproves. He goes to houses of ill-fame, where he shows somewhat special tastes.

Briefly, our active and resourceful Police Judiciaire had been hard at work. It has Dismantled a Veritable Network. And the Commissaire had not abstained himself from commentary. Unusual. As Arthur said, nobody knew better ordinarily how to keep his trap shut.

There was nearly a whole page of the stuff, causing the more belated obituaries to get held over. Profiting by a recently tightened spirit of cooperation with the German and Swiss police, dating from the time when the whole corner had been full of real or imagined terrorists – that Swiss frontier was a piece of Gruyère cheese – but shorn of all the verbiage, plants in pots had been used as a cover for distributing narcotics. The honourably known horticultural commerce – oh, yes, Mr Taglang – didn't know a damn thing about it, was thrown into total consternation, but the Judge of Instruction wasn't having any of this. There was a naughty man in Munich – ramifications – and a naughty man in Lucerne. It was not yet altogether clear, said the Commissaire, who was the moving spirit in all this. One laid hands upon small fry. There was, further, a person who had met his end in dubious circumstances – that had attracted the attention of the ever-watchful – upon a railway line. Enquiry would determine whether or not he had been a cat's paw. People who dealt in drugs were very cunning. They employed 'straw men'.

'It's all a lot of nothing,' said Arlette. It was a funny sensation to realize that one knew a lot more, without knowing anything worth knowing. She couldn't imagine Demazis as a master mind. Nor Mr Taglang either. Nor to be sure the artistically talented Monsieur Michel; pegged, that one, for possession, and not released on bail: Madame le Juge had signed a committal order. 'Do you make anything of it?'

'Not much,' said Arthur. 'Cops like narcotics cases because of the publicity. A thing like this pleases the Prefect. Can't do

235

one any harm, point of view of promotion. Otherwise I'd think it a clumsy affair, clumsily leaked, and that's not like our friend the Commissaire. I suppose there might be grains of truth somewhere. This bit about the fruitful side-effects of the terrorist hunt is rather sweet. The Germans were complaining like hell about the Swiss and the French both. All the frontiers, naturally, are cheese.'

'Go to work,' said Arlette again. She wanted to be by herself.

A sense of anti-climax, she supposed. She'd done the work on Demazis and they'd pinched the credit. As for her getting kidnapped, which did or didn't have anything to do with the matter, they plainly didn't give a damn. She was little use, as a witness. If confronted with Mr Taglang, she couldn't say positively that he had cut her hand, and she couldn't really say he hadn't. Squashed into the back of a car, with sticking plaster all over your face, you aren't very good at recognizing people.

It was possible, she supposed. About twenty-five people worked for that nursery. He'd have a couple of acolytes. No – more likely nobody there was involved. If you had a network you'd want as few people to know about it as might be. It only took one man to unpot a plant here and there, tuck in a little plastic sachet, and repot. You left, one supposed, a special mark on the pot. She had known nothing about any of this but she could understand: if Demazis had known, and presumably he did, he could have told her.

Were the acolytes the men in Munich or Lucerne, who knew which pot to look for, which flowershop to go to?

Well, she'd save something out of it all anyhow. She didn't know whether her phone was tapped or not, but decided she didn't care.

'Doctor Ulrich, please ... Arlette van der Valk. You've seen this morning's local paper?'

'Yes, indeed. I am grateful. I'll mention no names.'

'No, don't.'

'A young lady I know was plainly – probably without

realizing it – on the fringes of that, wouldn't you say? Quite unwittingly.'

'Quite possibly. I thought it in any event unsuitable companionship and I decided to say a word where I thought it might do good. I think that did do some good.'

'I appreciate it, Madame, you may believe me. My uh, relative is much relieved. I think we can regard the matter as closed. Er – you may be assured: there'll be no further doubt cast upon your uh, activities. Quite the contrary. Should it come within my capacities to make a recommendation ... That is purely hypothetical but could eventually arise. You see? I would in fact do so. I don't puff myself up, but such a recommendation could be of value to you.'

'You are very kind.' And a recommendation costs you nothing, Mister, which is always a consideration. 'For my part, should I be asked in matters of this kind for a reference, with of course total discretion – you wouldn't mind my giving your name?' He thought about that.

'Er – in confidence, it would have to be in complete confidence – I'll be glad to.'

Marie-Line won't be around any more. She won't want to think about any of this. Never mind, I got a doctor out of it. And a lawyer, and that's a thing I'll need. Something to set against the cut hand.

And poor old Robert ... Living all by himself with his fantasies in Hautepierre. Pinning paper women to the wall and shooting them.

It took her the whole morning to make an eatable meal. The weather had changed too, probably for good now. Arthur returned complaining about a chilly drizzle. He couldn't complain about the food, which was a bit Germanic in character. Eintopf; everything in one pot: she made a bit of comedy showing how she'd got the pot out of the oven with one hand and one wrist.

237

39. 'The Beginnings of Execution'

She had to do some shopping in the Boulevard de la Marne. And with an idea of a breath of fresh air, as much as anything else, she pottered up the Rue Goethe, into the Botanic Garden, out very quiet and leisurely across the Rue de l'Université, over into the Boulevard de la Victoire. She could swear, following this manoeuvre, that absolutely no one was dogging her footsteps.

She wondered who, if anybody, would take trouble to dog her footsteps. The indiscretions of the Commissaire were calculated all right, but to what end? This emphasis on straw men and stalking-horses: more to the story than Taglang Enterprises. Nor was Mr Taglang a man who cut people; his razorblade was kept for delicate operations on small plants. A likelier candidate was perhaps the gentleman with the elegant red car, but the paper had made no mention of any such.

The likeliest stalking-horse hereabouts is me, surely!

Because – this loquacity of the police: what had been the commissaire's sources of information? The eagle eye? – that might do for the local paper but not for her. Nor the razor-artist. Been a lot of soothing talk about protection: what protection?

Apart from naughty men in Lucerne, suppose there are still a couple of acolytes loose? There is nobody in the garden, over-casually raking dead leaves, save gardeners. A henchman dressed up as a gardener is quite ludicrous, as much so as Papi with a wheelbarrow, or Corinne as a botanizing Miss Marple. She decided that even if the police were using her as a decoy of sorts she didn't care. I want to get my hand healed, please. It's a nuisance when I want to try to write things down. And Arthur, frankly, is equally bored by now with the kitchen. She dropped in *Chez Mauricette* for a cup of coffee. This as she expected was funny because of the topic of conversation,

238

which was plainly unchanged since that morning and was making them some money as well as something to roll on the tongue. The voices were loud.

'Imagine the blasted cheek – this Corsican bastard coming in here and insinuating that we were handing out dope to students – I ask you!'

'Place a hotbed of vice, what.'

'These kids do a bit of trafficking in pills – well, that's nothing to do with me, is it? That I should go ringing him up – no Inspector, I said, I deal in what my licence says I deal in, and don't you go making no insinuations,' Plainly a word she enjoyed.

'They take all sorts of speed and stuff before their examinations.'

'And smoke joints – but they don't do that in here. Botanic Garden's full to the brim of cannabis, I'm telling you!'

'What's this stuff look like?'

'How should I know? Grow it onna windersill they tell me. Go smoking geranium leaves fr'all I care.'

'What's this thing here all hanging down?'

'My asparagus you silly bugger and keep your great paws off.' Arlette paid and went.

Arthur came back from work in good fettle.

'Did you go out?'

'Oh, I walked around the block before doing my shopping.'

'Did anything happen?'

'What on earth should happen?'

'I suppose not. A faint shadow of disquiet.'

'I don't see what there is to be uneasy about. Even if there were, what are we supposed to do about it? Stay cowering in the cellar?'

'Well good. That's fine then. We've an invitation for drinks.'

'Parties!' said Arlette, no great party-lover. 'I'm fairly tired.'

'I thought it might do you good. We've lived rather in one another's hair. It's only Philippe.' A young assistant lecturer in Psychology, with anarchist leanings, whom she rather liked.

239

'Be full of students.' Having brought up three children, Arlette said occasionally that she'd had enough of students. 'Oh all right then.'

'We needn't stay late.'

'Shall we take the car?' asked Arthur after supper, helping to zip his wife into a gay frock 'suitable for students'; one should never try to dress like them, she said, and least of all in blankets.

'No, why? It's stopped raining and it's only the Rue de Palerme.'

'All right by me. Bound to be terribly stuffy anyhow. And noisy. As well as full of marijuana smoke. Bit of fresh air on the way back will do us good. What do we contribute?' rummaging in the drinks cupboard, 'perhaps as it's getting colder, gluh-wein?' coming up with a couple of bottles.

'As long as it's not spiked too heavily: the last one had vodka or something in it and I got a bit pissed.' They set out, Arthur with a shopping bag – 'I like to eat the peel; is this a biological lemon?' – and Arlette with her gloved hand in her pocket. Explanations were so boring. 'I got into a fight with a tin of cannelonis.'

A pleasant five-minute walk, just what one needed on the way back to get rid of fumes. No fog. A fairly mild atmosphere with a bit of scotch mist, not enough to make one wet. Tiny beads of moisture on one's coat and hair.

The Esplanade is the most campussy part of Strasbourg University: a big space that had never been built on, having been jealously held onto by the Army ever since the town had been fortified by Vauban. When the Army finally decided that the war of 1870 was over, roughly ninety years after that traumatizing event, one had this huge area. The building promoters fell upon about half of it with the usual expensive results, draughty outside and rickety within. The University made a better job of the other half and planted a lot of trees. All they had to do was cross the Boulevard de la Victoire and take an alleyway running straight across, dignified with the suitably academic name of Rue Blaise Pascal, but it is nice,

240

because there are no cars and there are four rows of lindens. In the evenings this is fairly deserted, but you don't run much risk of getting mugged. There is plenty of light from fairly high street lamps with quite pleasant white mushrooms on them.

You pass by the Library, and the big boring administrative building, with the tall tower of the Chemistry Institute on your left: an ellipse with its ends clipped like a cigar: quite a good-looking building. You pass a variety of shapeless things devoted to Biology and Molecular Something or other, and come out on a big oval space half enclosed by the wings of the Law Faculty, with a decorative pavement and such shrubs as survive the gale-like draughts. It would be quite good for skateboarding if it wasn't so flat.

The other side of this is Human Sciences, where Arthur had a little niche appropriate to a visitor, not all that distinguished a one. It is a series of drearily rectangular blocks joined by glassed-in catwalks, looking extremely like a jail and covered in slogans of unimaginative rancour about FASCHISTS. Nobody in a Human Sciences faculty ever knows how to spell.

Cross a parking lot and you step down on the Rue de Rome, where students buy books and supermarket food, and occasionally send their clothes to the cleaners. Philippe lived just the far side.

The party was what she had expected, but Arlette enjoyed herself. Students were better-mannered than those of her generation, or even her sons. Much more ignorant, while about as incurious. But kinder surely, gentler, less aggressive. Or was it just that Philippe, being nice, had nice friends? Ruth's friends, only two or three years ago, had seemed so much shriller and less washed, and much more brutally egoist. Was it that she herself was becoming just a bit nicer?

There was the usual conversation.

'It's always said to be a cliché to say that history helps one understand the present, but is it?'

'What is a cliché is to put it the other way round and say the present is the only way of understanding the past.'

'There isn't any present. There's an immediate future. And

241

a past which immediately becomes very far away and small because of no perspective – talking about the present at all is a cliché.'

Arlette came under fire.

'Now Arlette, what's all this do-good lark?'

'I try to overcome solitude.'

'Exactly like the people who hold talk sessions all about their innermost it sounds like.'

'Except they don't have to bawl it all out in public. I don't make them take their clothes off either.'

'She steps in where all the priests are now scared to. A modern confessional. Do you talk to them about Jesus?'

'No, but if you'll shut up a moment, I'll tell you what I do do. Then you can come tomorrow.'

'What do you charge them?'

'I don't charge them anything at all unless they feel that I've done something valuable. What word would you use? – Positive? Tangible? Since I'm not a shrink, nor a lawyer, nor a detective. Nor an introduction bureau. I find out what I'm not, bit by bit.'

There were the usual drinks too; things you give somebody else to drink.

'What's wrong with your hand?'

'I caught it in the door. It's rather swollen and sore, that's all.'

Arthur rescued her before she got too silly.

'You had a nice time: surrounded by girls.'

'Well you seemed to have virile young men in sufficient number. Let's take the other way, it's prettier.' He meant simply the next alleyway down, the other side of the Law Faculty. It has no name. It is narrower and has older trees. 'Take my arm. You're not scared are you?'

'With you, of course not. A little chilled. They always turn their central heating too high.'

'If anything this is even better lit.' The lamp standards were the same here as in a street; high ones given a graceful curve, like tulips.

242

The plane trees, clinging to the last of their leaves, cast a pretty shadow. This was the edge of the campus; the tall residential blocks of the Avenue de l'Esplanade gazed blindly down. They passed the children's playground: Arlette liked the sandpit with its big irregular blocks of the soft red local stone. The Place d'Athènes in front of the Law Faculty, boasting an unseemly piece of sculpture, nominally Athena: she'd never win any golden apples. They were at the level of the Chemistry School, only two minutes from home, stepping out now, no longer chilled.

A man came out of the bushes three metres away. Low down by his side the blade of a knife, looking very large, shone in the light. He was tall and wore a hat. His face was a blur; there might be a stocking over it.

40. 'White Fang'

There was a second's stillness in which Arlette's intake of breath made a trembly sound.

Arthur wished he had a stick. He had a collection of sticks, and generally walked with one. Not only in the country; they were useful in crossing the road and helped, he believed, to deter unpleasant youths. It hadn't seemed worth the trouble, to go only as far as Philippe's.

Without a stick, there seemed very little one could do. He was fairly light on his feet and took exercise. But his reactions would be slow, far too slow. He concluded drearily that this was the end of him. He hoped it wouldn't hurt too much. Knives, he rather thought, did hurt, badly.

Arlette had a frock, and high-heeled shoes. Not very suitable garments these. She was trying to think of things Corinne had taught her about nasty youths with knives. She

243

knew they all involved her right hand, and she didn't have any right hand, only a limp thing in a limp glove.

She did have her pistol, rather guiltily brought along. The Lord knew what good it was supposed to be. She couldn't fire it with her left hand. One could squib it off perhaps, but that all needed lots of time. It was in her handbag, and that was tucked under her left armpit, and she was all out of time.

If they had made the mistake of clinging together... Antique instinct of mutual protection, or safety in numbers, or perhaps, most pitiful of all, the male putting himself in front of the little woman.

They had obeyed an instinct much older and separated, moving sideways away from one another. Wolves, contrary to a shocking amount of myth, virtually never attack men. If a man seems to behave aggressively, and the male is with his mate, and she on heat, they will both attack. They will do so in coordination: one going for the arm, the other for the leg. A man who knew a lot about wolves once forgot this. He got badly bitten. He said, 'That was entirely my fault.'

The man with the knife hesitated a second. He wanted the woman. He wanted the man too. His only mistake was in being greedy, and wondering for just too long which he wanted first.

Arthur didn't know anything at all about combat, or men with knives. His military days were long behind him and had been a great bore, with occasional intervals of being alarmed and wondering why one was not much more alarmed. But he had once been to an English school. He had made up his mind in the second of hesitation. There was nothing for this but an effort at a rugby tackle. If you went at somebody head first, that surely decreased the target. And wasn't it barely possible that if you plunged at someone the knife might miss you?

He didn't have a scrumhalf build, unhappily. He lurched forward clumsily at the same time as the man made a horrible low pass with the knife. A short right hook, very nasty indeed, at his genital apparatus, which he valued. He tried to swerve to his own right, which spoilt his aim. He got hold of one leg.

He felt the knife sting him like a nettle. He fell on his face on the hard ground, and let the leg go again. It wasn't in any way a nice leg. He had a sad feeling of failure. He always did seem to fail things and this would be one time too many.

The man had been taken off his balance, and his knife had got mixed up with Arthur's raincoat. At this moment Arlette hit him with her handbag with the gun inside it, with all her force, and launched as ferocious a kick as her skirt would allow at his crutch.

Neither effort was really good. She'd wanted the gun to catch him on the temple and it didn't: it hit him on the ear and only made him madder. The silk skirt tore with the kick, which didn't have enough force in it. Even quite a small kick in the crutch with a high-heeled shoe will put paid to your evil-minded inclinations for a long time but it hadn't been accurate enough: it only jarred his hipbone. Arlette fell on the hard ground, hurting her knee which she didn't notice, and her sore hand which she did: she uttered a howl of consternation and pain, and couldn't get up.

The man went staggering. He wasn't in the least hurt. He was bumped, and banged, and unbalanced, and anger exploded inside him, making him powerless for a moment. He reeled back three or four paces, his legs wide apart and one of them not quite answering properly. He still had his knife, though he'd missed with it twice. Now they were on the ground, and that would be the end of them. Two sitting ducks, who had flapped their wings and spoilt his aim, but he'd clipped them and they were swimming feebly on the water and now would put paid to both, these two silly, struggling objects. He caught his breath back and got his feet together. Arlette, on the floor, watched and waited to die. The knife was a big one, with a curve to it. A Catalan knife. A thing more evil than any gun.

As she watched the man's legs were taken out from under him as though by a jerked lasso. The four pistol shots came very close together, so that she heard only one enormous noise. Unable to move at all with a stunned leg and a stunned arm

245

and waves of pain making her sick she sat and gawked. The man's head hit the floor with a bump and the knife fell out of his hand. She wasn't going to die on the street. Like Piet.

A man was running, fast and furiously, in an apish kind of way, with speedy tough legs and long arms that hung by his sides. Stupidly, she recognized Divisional Inspector Papi. He went for the man on the floor with controlled concentration: he caught the man's head by the hair and jerked it up, but it was limp. Very fast, he dropped the gun he was holding, snapped the man's hands behind his back and handcuffed them. He came running over to Arthur, who was lying on his front getting his breath back from a kick in the chest he hadn't even known about.

Simultaneously Arlette felt hands under her armpits. Something warm and female put her face against her own and Corinne's voice said, 'Are you all right, oh are you all right,' breathless and panting.

Papi was lifting Arthur, and then let him go again. Arlette wondered why. What was he doing? He let Arthur go and fumbled at his gunbelt. His shirt came out. He ripped at it with big apey hands. It tore away in a strip. While tearing more strips he raised his head and bawled, 'Samu' at someone unseen. He said, 'Keep still,' and heaved Arthur's raincoat up out of the way. He wound strips round Arthur's thigh and twisted at them

Arlette was on her feet, heaved up, limping, running, she was down again on her knees by Arthur. Corinne's arms took her gently by the body and the warm jerky voice, like blood flowing from a cut artery, said, 'All right, all right, don't touch, he's doing the right thing.'

'All right,' said Papi in his Corsican accent. 'It's not the big artery, he'll be all right.' They kept saying all right; it was maddening. Say something else.

She took his head between her hands. His mouth was open and she suddenly saw his teeth, in a rather expensive couturier colour-scheme under the bright street-lamp. From dark brown to an elegant pale ivory, with contrasting bits of navy blue and discreet gold trappings. Arthur was grinning at her. 'I'm fine,' he was saying. 'Did it touch you?'

'No, I hurt my stupid knee. I'm fine, I'm fine and so are you.' They were hauling her up on her feet again. 'They got him,' she said.

'As nearly as possible didn't,' said Papi bitterly. 'I couldn't get a clear shot: you were in my light all the time.'

'I had to run sideways,' said Corinne, 'My hand was shaking; I had to brace to be sure of getting him.'

'You got him all right girl. Knee and calf. He won't be running away anywhere.'

Corinne holding Arlette up bent and felt her knee. 'That's just a bit of skin. And your tights bust. And your skirt bust. You gave him a good one. You know, that was what gave me time.'

'He'd have had you both,' said Papi. 'I couldn't shoot for fear of hitting you, and then I fell over in the fucking bushes. Your man did exactly the right thing. In the thigh can be bad but it glanced along the inside. If he hadn't dived he'd have had it in the belly. Samu'll be here any sec.' It is a nice acronym. Service ambulance medical urgency.

What with the shooting and the shouting a good few windows and shutters had opened along the big white wall of flats. It was like being in a theatre. Arlette felt she ought to be Maria Callas.

'White Fang,' said Papi picking up the knife. 'Catalan, that,' examining the S-shaped horn handle and the simple locking mechanism. 'Far worse wound than a gun shot. Stick you with that it's for real. If he'd got you the boss would have had my balls.'

'I don't have any,' said Arlette, 'but I know just what you mean.'

The fast van took all three of them to emergency-out-patients, Corinne and Papi following in the police car.

'My,' said the nurse, 'you've been in the wars,' looking at her hand, 'but it's nothing; just lie quiet a bit.'

'My husband – his thigh was cut.'

247

'Haemostatic – no I won't be technical. We had to put clamps, and it'll have to be sutured but it's nothing at all to worry about. The inspector did a good job with the first aid. Of course, if a cop can't do that what bloody use is he? Your man's in surgery but he'll be out in half an hour and you'll be over the shock by then. Just lie quiet and rest.'

'And the other?'

'His knee joint's in a horrible mess and cops are hanging over him like vultures. We had to clear them all away. One doesn't have to feel very sorry for him, I gather. Just that they were in the way. Now don't talk; I've given you a sedative.'

She went to sleep a little, she thought. She woke up as one does at a quiet movement, when one would sleep through the professional banging and shouting of nurses. A slim, grey, middle-aged man had come into her cubicle and was smiling at her. He had an academic look like a sociology professor. Oh well, not far out. She knew him very slightly by sight. He was the second-in-command of the Police Judiciaire, the sous-chef as he was called. He had beautiful manners. He said, 'May I sit down?' and then, 'I felt some explanations were due to you. If you feel up to that already.'

'Please.'

'Your man is out of all danger and will be up and about in a couple of weeks. A small cut, say five centimetres and not too deep, along the inner surface tissue of his left thigh. It'll knit up nicely and leave a barely perceptible scar. The genital area is untouched. He will walk perfectly normally; there's no real muscle or tendon injury. I've seen worse with flying glass. Would you like me to light a cigarette for you? Can I get you anything to drink? You fell on your hand, and opened up that nasty cut, but it sets you back a day or two at most; otherwise you're untouched. You're a bit sleepy from shock and a librium or something – want me to go on? Or wait till you're quite recovered?'

'No, now. I'd like some black coffee.' He went and got it.

'Paper cup was the best I could do. Let me help you sit up. I'll try to make it short. We couldn't get anything much on

248

that man: he was well covered up. You guessed it. He owns that flower shop. Right, a man with a red Maserati, who has a nice house in Switzerland and much too much money. We had to smoke him out. Your evidence about the razor cut was insufficient: no identity and he had twenty alibis. We brought him in, the boss questioned him. Leaked him a lot of what you'd told us, but the truth, and he knew it, was that we couldn't touch him. Goes off back to Switzerland. We had to hope he would come back. He's a vengeful beast. We had, or rather the Germans had, a totally unexplained razor attack on a man in Munich. That helped tie it in: there was a small coincidence in the pattern. The Swiss of course wouldn't have extradited him. We could only hope to tempt him back here.

'That done, we had to keep right out of sight, or of course he wouldn't have approached you. This is why Papi and the girl were rather far away. And we had to wait for what is legally termed the beginnings of execution. Not enough to have him hanging about with a knife in his pocket. That's just a misdemeanour. We had absolutely to have something really to throw at him. On the narcotics there's nothing whatsoever – they're very sly, these people, never go near it. So blows and wounds with intent to cause death. We would not, I beg you to believe, have placed your life at risk in this way if there had been any other chance: I shouldn't be telling you this. We had three men, all excellent shots. Your going back by the other path threw us out of gear a little. However . . .'

'All is well that ends well remains our favourite cliché,' sipping hot and not-too-weak Nescafé. Arlette accepted this offering with gratitude.

'You are both greatly to be congratulated for the courage with which you tackled him. A thing like a bayonet – would give anyone pause. We are most grateful. That girl Corinne wouldn't have forgiven herself. She didn't lose her head; she was unsighted by you, and she had to run, and worried this would spoil her aim; she took him low down and made a good job, but were it not for your tackling him, it might have ended much worse. There is small consolation in killing a killer. I could have expressed that better,' giving her his palm to use as an ashtray, blowing it off as dust.

'You got yourself into a scrape we were too late to pull you out of in the first place. After that, you were in too far. We don't use people as bait when it's not what they're paid for.'

'Man – do stop excusing yourself.'

'You did choose this job yourself, the boss tells me,' smiling. 'It does carry risks you don't foresee, from time to time. Not all just good advice to little girls who've run away from home.'

'Oh yes, I realized that. The risk was mine.'

'Well,' jovially, 'I imagine the lesson has not been lost upon you.'

'No,' said Arlette slowly.

'You won't perhaps be in a hurry to start again?' jovial.

'Oh yes,' said Arlette. 'I'd start again.'

He took her cigarette end and crushed it carefully out on his heel.